Tangled Webs

Maria McDonald

First published in 2023 by Bloodhound Books.

www.bloodhoundbooks.com

Print ISBN: 978-1-5040-8765-0

Oh, what a tangled web we weave,
when first we practice to deceive!
—Marmion, Sir Walter Scott. 1808.

Act 1

Chapter 1

Riverdale House, Belfast, August 1922

Mrs Jane Best paused in front of the portrait of her late husband Charles and took a deep breath. She smoothed her skirt over her slim figure and pinched her cheeks to add colour to her pale complexion. Her black widows' garb was softened by the addition of a ruffle of white lace over the high neckline and at her wrists. Pulling back her shoulders, she held her head high. Now that she was well past sixty, she had no wish to turn into one of those wizened old women with hunched shoulders and faltering steps. With an affectionate nod to Charles, she turned, opened the dining-room door and summoned her new lodger with her index finger. Iris's terrified expression strengthened Mrs Best's resolve as the two women made their way to the formal parlour.

The room was in the shade of the afternoon sun. A faint breeze fluttered through the open windows bringing the hum of bees and the sweet scent of roses in their last flush of summer.

"Good afternoon, Mr Jones." Mrs Best greeted her visitor as he rose from his seat, his cap in hand. A flash of recognition momentarily unsettled Mrs Best, and she felt a thud in her chest at the snapshot in her head of a younger Drake Jones. He hadn't changed much. The older version's face was drawn and weather-beaten, his hair scarce and his skin pulled tight over his skeletal frame. Iris followed behind Mrs Best and stood partially hidden as she nodded her greeting, her hands clasped in front of her as if to contain their shaking. Glancing upwards for a second, she dropped her gaze and fixed her eyes on a spot on the floor. Mrs Best fixed her public smile in place.

"I am very pleased to meet you, Mr Jones. Please, sit. May I offer you some tea?"

"No, thank you," he replied, his face screwed up as he studied her face. "I would prefer to get on with the business in hand."

With a puzzled expression and his back ramrod straight, he perched on the edge of the chair. Mrs Best took the sofa opposite him beckoning Iris to sit beside her. Silence filled the room, and she began to feel uncomfortable under his steady gaze.

"I beg your pardon, ma'am, but you seem familiar to me. Have we met before?"

"I don't think so, Mr Jones. I am sure I would remember you."

"Odd. I have the strongest impression we have met before."

"I don't believe so, Mr Jones. Now, if I may, can I ask what brings you here?"

"Why Iris, of course. While I must thank you for providing her with such fine lodgings, my granddaughter's place is at home, with her brother and me."

Mrs Best watched those beady eyes flick towards Iris. The latter remained silent, tension oozing out of every muscle in her tiny frame. Her hands shook where they lay clasped in her lap. Mrs Best took a breath and went over the speech rehearsed in her head. Then, keeping a firm but pleasant smile on her face, she looked at Mr Jones.

"Iris is happy here. She has made friends and works nearby. Surely it is more convenient for her to remain at Riverdale House?"

"Convenient for whom?" Puzzlement creased his already wizened features.

"Iris, of course."

"I want Iris to come home. She is my granddaughter, my responsibility and I want her to come home… with me… now, and that is an end to it."

"I see." Mrs Best gave a tight smile.

"This is a family matter," he said. "I don't mean to be rude, but it is none of your business."

"Mr Jones, as I said, Iris has no wish to return to your home. Her desire is to remain in Riverdale House, and we are delighted to have her here. I can assure you we will take great care of your granddaughter. Now, if you will excuse me? I have menus to prepare."

As Mr Jones stood, he pulled his shoulders back and jutted out his chin. His puny chest poked forward, and his eyes glittered with an ingrained malice that Mrs Best remembered.

"My granddaughter is leaving with me."

Ignoring the chill that ran through her, Mrs Best raised herself slowly to her full height and glared down at Mr Jones.

"Iris is staying here. She is of an age where she can decide where she wants to live, and Iris wants to live in Riverdale House. Good day, sir."

Her icy tone silenced him.

Mr Jones remained standing with his mouth opening and closing like a fish squirming on a hook. Flashing a look of pure hatred at Mrs Best, he shook his closed fist at Iris and roared at her, "You will regret this, my girl," saliva spitting out and onto the floor.

Mrs Best strode to the parlour door, opened it and gestured to the hall.

"Good day, sir."

Mr Jones stared at her, defiance snorting out of each nostril.

"You haven't heard the last of this," he snarled as he pushed past her. She stood still until she heard the bang of the ornate front door closing after his departure. The peace of Riverdale House settled again, as Mrs Best gave a sigh of relief and a reassuring smile at her young boarder.

"He is gone, Iris." Mrs Best resumed her place beside Iris on the couch and took her hand. "I doubt he will be back, but we will send him on his way if he does. We will not allow him to hurt you again."

She removed a delicate lace handkerchief from her pocket. Taking Iris's chin, she turned her face towards her and dabbed away her tears. Her reward was a grateful smile.

"Thank you, Mrs Best, I am so grateful to you and to Mrs Williams."

Once Iris had safely retired upstairs, Mrs Best stood in the hall and took a moment to compose herself. She would never have agreed to meet the man if she had known he was the former Private Drake Jones. Later that evening, she would discuss it with Mrs Williams in the privacy of their parlour, but it could wait until their day's work was over. She caught sight of her reflection in the mirror and started as James's grey eyes stared back at her. The creak of a door opening into the hallway shook her out of her reverie.

"Tommy, will you oil the hinges on the dining-room door, please. The creak grates on my nerves, and we don't want our young ladies annoyed by something so mundane."

Tommy nodded. "Yes, ma'am, I will get to it straight away. Mrs Williams asked me to let you know dinner will be served slightly later this evening."

"Thank you, Tommy."

Mrs Best gave an involuntary shudder. "Someone's walking

over my grave" she thought and heard an echo of another era and her grandmother using the same expression in her head. She pulled her shoulders back. "Stuff and nonsense," she told herself. Then she made her way to the dining room to set the table for the evening meal, her head held high and her public persona back on view.

Chapter 2

The Kitchen

LATER THAT AFTERNOON, MRS BEST SAT AT THE SCRUBBED OAK kitchen table with Mrs Williams. Both were tall women but there the similarity ended. Mrs Williams had the classic English rose complexion. The slim build of her youth had rounded with age while her former chestnut dark hair was now pure steel grey. A perfect foil for Mrs Best's silver-streaked auburn curls, pulled smoothly into a chignon, above her ramrod straight posture with not an ounce of excess weight. They always had afternoon tea with their housekeeper, Mary, before she went home for the day. It was that quiet hour when the house was cleaned, the laundry finished but before the dinner preparations began.

Riverdale House was a well-oiled machine ran with military precision by Mrs Williams and Mrs Best. Over the previous forty years they had built up a reputation for providing top quality boarding for the young women who flocked to Belfast for work. Together they were a formidable force for good in the lives of their young female boarders. Most of their young women were originally from rural areas and had moved to the city for work. For women who worked in the big houses, accommodation was usually part of the package. But, for those who came to work in the mills and the industries that sprung up around them, women needed a safe place to live. And Riverdale House provided the home away from home the girls needed, and their parents insisted on.

Mrs Best interviewed all her potential boarders, choosing only those she felt were a good fit for her existing clientele. Riverdale House offered spotless accommodation and excellent food of a standard that wouldn't be amiss in a top hotel. Every evening at seven o'clock, she presided over the dining-room table. She facilitated conversation, ensuring each of their boarders felt comfortable and at home. Mrs Best believed each point of view should be considered and appreciated. Something quite difficult after the massive upheavals in Ireland over the previous few years. The division of Ireland had a significant impact on Mrs Best, although her young women would never have guessed it. She had been raised in Louth, a county that, conveniently for her, lay on the Southern side of the border. With her birthplace in a different jurisdiction, Jane Best was hopeful her secret would stay hidden forever, leaving her free to continue her work in Riverdale House.

"Well, that's me done," Mary said, finishing her tea. "If I don't get a move on, that husband of mine will be home before me, wanting his dinner."

Mary was more friend than employee. After an early start and a hard day's work she went home to look after her own family, a husband who drank more than he worked and two young boys. When Mrs Williams learned of her circumstances at home, there was always a basket of "leftovers" waiting for Mary to bring home with her.

"Your basket is ready for you in the pantry, Mary," Mrs Williams said.

"Thanks, Mrs Williams. I'll see you in the morning."

Riverdale House was a happy house. Mrs Best and Mrs Williams had built up quite a little family around them. Besides Mary, the housekeeper, there was young Tommy for the garden and the hard grafting plus two young girls for the daily cleaning, all live-in. Between them, they looked after a dozen young women lodgers, single women, alone in the city, but at home in Riverdale House. Mrs Best looked after their lodgers while Mrs Williams looked after the kitchen and the staff. It was a happy household, upstairs and down, despite the ongoing turmoil in the outside world.

Occasionally those events were discussed around the dining-room table. Mrs Best would never identify as a suffragette, but she believed in education, formal or otherwise. She encouraged debate around the table during and after their evening meal.

Tonight, with the newspapers full of the funeral of General Michael Collins, her young women had much to distract them.

"Such a tragedy, Mrs Best, such a loss." One of her young women wiped a tear with a lacy handkerchief.

"He was a murderer. How can you shed tears after what that man did? Michael Collins has been responsible for the deaths of hundreds of people."

"He was a hero. His death is a great loss to everyone," a quiet yet decidedly firm voice cut across the table.

"And such a handsome man. He wasn't married, you know, such a loss."

"He may not have been married, but he was betrothed."

"Ach, the poor girl, how sad."

"No loss to any of us," said a dark-haired young woman whose father was a prominent member of the Orange Order. "The man was a terrorist."

"Ladies, whatever our opinion of Mr Collins, he was a man cut down in his prime. Who knows what he could have achieved in the future? He managed to put an end to that dreadful war against England. There are encouraging signs that the violence in our small corner of the country is abating." Mrs Best's calm tones silenced the murmuring around the table. "Compromise, ladies. Never be afraid to voice your opinion but always respect the opinion of others. Remember that, and you will get far in life."

As the debate continued around the formal dining table, preparations were underway for the evening meal in the kitchen.

"What are we having today, Mrs Williams?" Tommy sniffed the air trying to guess as he washed his hands in the scullery.

"A nice mutton stew, Tommy, and plenty of it," Mrs Williams said.

Tommy was always hungry. Tall and lean, he looked like he hadn't eaten a decent meal in months, yet he sat at her table every night and devoured a dinner for two men. She tried to fatten him up with extra dumplings in his stew and lots of bread but to no avail.

"Sure, you can't fatten a thoroughbred," he told her, and she had to agree with him.

Tommy tucked into the colossal steaming bowl in front of him.

Mrs Williams took her seat at the table and bowed her head.

"Tommy, will you say grace please?"

Tommy dropped his fork, murmuring apologies in the general direction of Mrs Williams, his face colouring. She patted his hand, and Tommy relaxed, eyes closed as he said "amen" before tucking in again.

"A long day in the garden can give a growing lad quite an appetite." Mrs Williams smiled at him. Tommy worked hard all year round, and they were eating the fruits of his labour. The carrots, onions and potatoes in the stew and an apple and blackcurrant crumble for dessert. Mrs Williams could often be found in the kitchen gardens. It was her second favourite place, after her private parlour, where she retired every evening with her dearest companion, Mrs Best. It was there they could put away their public persona, relax in each other's company and be true to themselves.

Chapter 3

The Parlour

"TEA?" AGNES WILLIAMS ASKED JANE.

"Please." Jane teased the pins from her hair and shook it free, stretching the tired muscles in her neck. Her armchair was positioned to the left of the small fire. Its once emerald-green upholstery was faded to the shade of a gull's egg. But it was her favourite, her mother's chair, the one piece of furniture she had taken from her father's house. On the right side of the fire sat Agnes's rocking chair. Its sturdy hardwood was polished and covered with chintzy cushions, the product of Agnes's handiwork. Between them, a coffee table held their books and their teacups. At the side of each chair sat their baskets containing their supplies of wool and thread.

Their private parlour was to the front of the house, across the hall from the drawing room and dining room but out of bounds to all their staff and boarders. Its décor wasn't as formal as the other rooms in the house, each woman bringing their personal touch to the room they retired to every evening. On the right of the room was the entrance to a long corridor with a door at the end into the back hallway. Off the hall were two bedrooms and a bathroom, their private rooms.

Agnes brought the tea tray from the kitchen and placed it on the sideboard. She poured the strong hot tea through a tiny sieve to catch the tea leaves, added a drop of milk and placed the Royal Albert bone china cup and saucer in Jane's outstretched hand. Jane sipped it delicately as her mind whirred, retracing the day's events. Iris Seoin had only been with them for a few weeks. She had started in the linen mills earlier in the year and had become friendly with Sarah, one of their young women lodgers, who had implored them to allow Iris board in Riverdale House.

Agnes's touch on her shoulder shook her from her reverie.

"You're very tense, Jane."

Jane reached up, lifted Agnes's hand and kissed it.

"Sit, Agnes. I have something to tell you."

"Whatever is the matter, my love."

"I met Iris's grandfather before... before today, I mean."

Jane waited for Agnes to sit before continuing.

"We met him in South Africa."

Jane watched as Agnes's full lips formed a perfect O.

"He is an ex-ranger. He knew Charles… was a subordinate of Charles…"

Jane dropped her eyes to her cup, still extended in front of her. Her mouth felt like it was full of sawdust, and she couldn't say any more. She took a hesitant sip of the hot, sweet tea.

"He said I was familiar to him. I told him he was mistaken but still…"

Agnes rose and knelt in front of Jane. She cupped her hands on each side of Jane's face.

"Look at me, Jane. It was over forty years ago. He couldn't possibly recognise you."

Jane's cup rattled against the saucer until Agnes took it from her and placed it on the side table. She put her arms around Jane, who melted into her embrace.

"I hope you are right, Agnes. I got such a fright. I would

never have allowed Iris to stay with us if I had known who her grandfather was, and I certainly would never have agreed to meet with him."

"Jones is such a common name. How could you have known?"

"I suppose it is, but the meeting has left me anxious, scared even," Jane said.

"As you say yourself, stuff and nonsense. Jones couldn't possibly know, not now after all these years. So put it behind you. Mr Jones was dispatched today, and we will never see him again."

Jane felt a wave of relief. Agnes could always put things into perspective. Sometimes she wished she could be more like her. Agnes was so practical. A straight thinker who didn't allow emotion to colour her judgement. She smiled at Agnes who settled herself back into her favourite chair and picked up her latest knitting project, her fingers clicking furiously within seconds.

"Have you ever regretted coming to Belfast with me, Agnes? Leaving London, your career, your family?" Jane asked.

The frantic clicking stopped and Agnes's eyebrows rose in surprise.

"Why, of course not. Why would you even ask me such a question?"

Jane shook her head and bit her inner cheek as she struggled to find the right words.

"I don't know. I just know that Mr Jones's remarks about feeling like he had met me years ago shook something in me. It's been over forty years. Sometimes I wonder what would have happened to me if I had taken a different path. What would have happened to both of us? Did we do the right thing?" Her voice trembled, and she cleared her throat.

"Of course we did. Look at what we have achieved here."

Agnes dropped her knitting and placed her hand on her friend's arm.

Jane smiled gratefully and patted Agnes's hand.

"One thing I am sure of is that you are the most important part of my life. I don't know what I would have done without you."

Agnes held up her hand to Jane. "Stop, stop right now. We have a good life here. We have built a fine reputation in this house. I am thankful every day, but I also know we work hard, both of us. So, do not get maudlin on me. I couldn't bear it."

Jane laughed. "Agnes Williams, always the pragmatist."

The two women retired to their bedrooms with their private thoughts. Ten minutes later, Jane gave a perfunctory knock on Agnes's door before entering the room and slipping into bed beside her. After the upset of the day, she needed Agnes to hold her, to feel her reassurance. Her husband Charles may have been her first love, but Agnes was the love of her life.

Chapter 4

Mr Jones, October 1922

"Good day."

Mrs Best masked her surprise at finding Mr Jones standing at the end of the driveway.

"I know who you are," he said. "Did you really think you could get away with it?"

Fear crept through Mrs Best's veins, snaking closer to her heart which threatened to jump right out of her chest. She drew herself up to her full height and stared at her accuser, quickly covering her fear with a smile.

"Whatever do you mean, Mr Jones? Of course you know me. Your granddaughter lodges in my home." She smiled and tried to sidestep him, but he moved directly into her path.

"Don't worry." His tobacco-stained snarl struck fear in her heart. "I'll keep your secret, but it'll cost you."

Mr Jones stepped back off the pavement, swept off his cap and gave an exaggerated bow in her direction. Grinning, he turned and marched out of the cul-de-sac, whistling as he swung his stick like a baton. Mrs Best stared after him, trying desperately to maintain her composure. She hurried to the house and directly to her private parlour before any of the staff caught sight of her in her distressed state. She crept to the end of the corridor and signalled to Agnes in the kitchen. Her panic grew as Agnes followed her into their parlour.

"What is it, Jane? What's wrong?"

Jane told Agnes what had transpired, wringing her hands together.

"Whatever shall I do?"

"Nothing, you will do nothing, Jane. You don't know what he knows. It could be something and nothing. Sure, how would he know anything? It was forty years ago."

Jane looked at her friend. "But he says he knows who I am. What else could he mean, for goodness' sake? He knows."

"Think about it logically. It was so long ago. What could he possibly know?"

Strands of hope started to wind their way through Jane's terror.

"We have a house to run. Get yourself ready. Dinner will be served in the dining room in ten minutes. Our young ladies await you."

Jane smiled. A weak smile but a smile, nonetheless.

"You're right, Agnes, of course you are."

Agnes left Jane to tidy her appearance before joining her young ladies for their evening meal. Sedate and smiling, she entered the dining room with no outward sign of her earlier distress.

Several weeks passed before Mr Jones made a second appearance. Jane had put his threats to the back of her mind, convincing herself that Agnes was right, and he could not possibly know their secret.

Autumn was her favourite season. The tree-lined avenue was magnificent in shades of russet and gold. They had experienced something of an Indian summer, but the days had started to turn colder. A strong breeze wreaked havoc on the trees, forcing them to shed their leaves in sudden forceful gusts that whooshed down the road.

Mrs Best was strolling up the avenue on her way back to Riverdale House when Mr Jones waylaid her. She was carrying a full basket of wool and thread in preparation for a new layette she had planned to start later in the evening. Preoccupied with her plans, Mr Jones startled her by stepping suddenly out from behind a tree. Mrs Best stepped back and dropped her basket in fright. Balls of wool tumbled onto the pavement, scattering in three different directions.

"Mr Jones, you startled me."

Dismay clouded her features as she watched her purchases tumbling along the avenue, chased by the autumn breeze and getting tangled in the russet and gold blanket which crackled underfoot.

"I'm here to do a deal. I want twenty pounds on the last Friday of every month if you want me to keep my mouth shut. That gives you two weeks to get it organised."

"Why on earth would I give you anything?"

Spots of anger sprang to Mrs Best's cheeks, her usual public composure shaken by this sudden intrusion.

"You know why." His guttural growl, a concealed threat. "Mrs Best and Mrs Williams. Ha!"

He spat on the pavement in front of her and gave a derisory snort.

"Last Friday of the month, 0800 hours."

Mr Jones turned and sauntered down the avenue, swinging his walking stick and whistling an old war tune. Jane watched his retreating figure in horror. Her fear turned to anger as she watched his jaunty swagger disappear around the corner of the avenue and on to the main road into the city.

Indoors she went in search of Agnes. She found her in the garden never far from the kitchen, harvesting herbs for inclusion in the evening meal. Tommy was at her heels, ears cocked while pretending to be engrossed in his chores. Jane's public demeanour never gave a clue to the inner turmoil she was experiencing.

"May I have a word?"

Agnes glanced up from her position behind the thyme bush and caught the fear in Jane's eyes. Leaving instructions with Tommy, she followed her into their private parlour.

"What is it, Jane? What has happened?"

"He waylaid me on the avenue again. He wants money."

Jane paced around the room, her hands shaking, her normal composure consigned to the compost heap.

Agnes sat and exhaled. "What exactly did he say?"

"He said he knew me... knew us. He said he knew who I really was..." Jane stopped her pacing as her voice cracked. Raising her hand to her chest, she took a sharp intake of breath then exhaled before continuing.

"He said he wants twenty pounds on the last Friday of the month, or he will talk." Jane continued to pace while Agnes sat, her face closed.

"Well, he is not getting anything from us." Agnes pulled her friend down to the couch beside her. "Do you hear me, Jane, nothing, not a farthing. Pay him once, and there will be no end to it."

"But, Agnes, we must pay him, we must. This could ruin us. Everything we have worked for, destroyed. Our reputation..." She stopped as the realisation dawned on her. "Our income. Without this house, we have nothing."

"Hush, hush, we will think of something. We have been through so much worse." Agnes hugged her friend, and Jane relaxed into her for a moment feeling the support and love she had come to depend on. But as Jane's fear subsided, Agnes's anger grew.

"How dare he threaten us? He was an odious individual

forty years ago, and I doubt he has changed. Look what he did to his granddaughter."

"I know, Agnes. That man is evil, pure evil, always was and always will be."

Her clipped tones were dripping with ice; the only visible signs of her anger were the two red dots on her cheeks. She clenched her fists and clipped them to her side. Her entire body was rigid with compressed outrage, like the red nutcracker doll they kept in the dining room – a present from the Wolff family.

"I must go back to the kitchen. Stay here for a while, compose yourself." Agnes laid her hand on Jane's arm.

Jane patted Agnes's hand. "Thank you. I don't know what I would do without you."

"I swear, Jane, we will not let that odious individual blackmail us."

Each day that passed brought a fresh stubbornness to the women. Both became even more determined they would not accede to Drake Jones's demands. Jane and Agnes sat each evening in their private parlour, and between them, they devised their plan.

On the morning of the last Friday of the month, Mrs Jane Best stood back from the drawing-room window watching the front driveway. The house was ominously quiet. They had sent the girls into the city with lists of cleaning materials and hardware. Mrs Williams estimated their shopping would keep them out of the house for at least another three hours. She had dispatched Tommy by horse and cart to Annalong to collect stone for the new flower-bed she was planning for the side of the house. They didn't expect him to return until nightfall. Their young women boarders had left for work and the days' chores were well in hand.

Jane wondered if Mr Drake Jones would be bold enough to knock on the front door or if he would go to the staff entrance at the rear of the house. Movement at the end of the driveway caught her eye, and she followed Mr Jones's progress. He put her in mind of a weasel. Scrawny jerky movements displayed his anxiety, watery eyes darting left and right as he crept along and around to the back door. She smiled, a triumphant grin; he had done exactly what they expected of him.

Her thoughts turned to Tommy and the load of stone he would return with. The planned flower-bed would shield the side entrance from the avenue, something she had intended to do for many years. The thoughts of the blooms that would brighten the corner brought a sigh of contentment to Jane's lips as she made her way to the cavernous hall which led onwards to the back quarters.

Several loud bangs coincided with the grandfather clock chiming out the hour. Mrs Jane Best hesitated when she heard the first bang and then stopped in front of the hall mirror. On the third bang, she adjusted her hair, on the fourth her collar, spreading out the lace to cover her neck. On the fifth bang, she pinched her pale cheeks; on the sixth, she smoothed her skirt. Finally, on the eighth bang, she made her way to the hallway of the rear entrance.

Mrs Agnes Williams stood over Drake Jones's body, panting. Wearing only her petticoat and in her bare feet, in her right hand she held the marble rolling pin, stained crimson, blobs of dark blood and brain matter dripping onto the floor. Strands of her hair had broken free from its restraints, and her cheeks were flushed with exertion. The heavy iron lay on its side outside the door, the strands of string it had been suspended from still attached.

Jane surveyed the scene. "Give it to me," she said, gesturing to the rolling pin.

Agnes handed it over without uttering a word.

Jane walked into the kitchen and plunged the weapon into the scalding pot of water bubbling away on the range while

Agnes followed with the iron. They hurried back to the door. Between them, they hauled the body into the wheelbarrow, which Agnes had earlier instructed Tommy to place directly outside the door.

"Wash your face, arms and hands. Change your clothes; put the soiled ones in the cold water pot. Quickly, we don't have much time." Jane issued her instructions with military precision.

Agnes moved like lightning. Her clean clothes were on the kitchen chair, and within seconds the blood-stained clothing was steeping in cold water in the scullery. Jane lifted the jute sacks which covered the back-hall floor, taking care not to spill any blood. She threw them over the wheelbarrow shielding the battered corpse from view. She lifted the handles, straining under the dead weight, but managed to push off around the corner. Agnes followed in her wake, checking the ground behind them for any sign of bodily fluids which could give them away.

At the corner of the house, the flower-bed lay empty with piles of black clay on either side. Earlier that week, Agnes had instructed Tommy to dig it over several days, telling him that there was a leak in the corner of the garden. She instructed him to dig down nearly six feet to uncover the pipework. Tommy protested saying there couldn't be any water pipes buried so deep, but Agnes insisted.

At Jane's signal, Agnes went to the front of the house and checked the driveway and beyond to the avenue. All was quiet. The avenue was empty, devoid of any visitors or neighbours who chose to stay indoors on such a chilly day with signs of rain gathering in the darkening sky. The two women upended the wheelbarrow, depositing its contents into the rectangular-shaped hole. Mr Jones's lifeless body landed with a dull oomph, face down in the clay.

"Good riddance." Jane threw a jute bag on top of his

bloodied body. She vigorously rubbed her hands together above the unconsecrated grave as if shaking off every trace of him. They threw the other jute bags over the body covering it from sight. The two women lifted the shovels and started shovelling soil, just enough to hide the jute bags and what lay underneath. Working in silent harmony, they were both conscious of the time constraints. They rinsed out the wheelbarrow and returned it to its original position by the back door. Agnes got to work on the hallway walls. Jane scrubbed the kitchen and washed the blood-stained clothing. Both women's blistered hands stung as they scrubbed away the evidence of their crime. They managed to wash and change only minutes before hearing sounds from the front driveway. The girls returned, giggling and laughing about some young man who had helped them carry their purchases the whole way from the city to the house.

Later that evening, safely ensconced in their private parlour, they lifted a sherry glass to each other with shaking hands. Agnes's clothing hung on the clothesline, pristine and snowy white. The rolling pin was restored to its place in the cold room, boiled, scrubbed and shining. Their mud-stained clothing was steeping in the bath in their private bathroom, ready for washing the next day.

The next morning, under Agnes's watchful eye, Tommy was set to work filling in the hole with the remainder of the soil. By the next day they were ready to implement her design of an elaborate flower-bed surrounded by stone. In the middle, she placed her newly acquired fountain, in the shape of a granite fairy spewing water skywards over its head then cascading into a stone basin underneath. A week later, they surveyed the completed project. Both women thought it appropriate the granite fairy was named Drake.

Act 2

Chapter 5

Charles Best, 1871

Charles Best wandered around his stately home, alone, bored and looking for something to occupy himself in the last few days before he went away. His father, the Colonel, was away on business. Lady Best was recovering from a cold and hadn't ventured downstairs in a few days, so Charles was left to his own devices. The library was his favourite room in the house. At the ripe old age of eleven and ready to start boarding school, he regarded his nursery as childish. The library was lined on two walls by books stacked on walnut bookshelves and framed by two tall oval windows with views over the estate. Today, heavy rain, pounding from a forbidding sky, obscured that verdant view. The storm had been raging unabated for several days. Even the family retriever, Aria, was refusing to venture outside. Charles felt stifled.

He peered through the window, rivulets of water distorting the view of Spence's Mountain. As he turned back to the room, his eyes landed on his mother's writing bureau. It sat to the side of the windows, close to the ornate marble fireplace. After spending her formative years in India, she had never grown accustomed to the damp and cold of Ireland, so the fire was lit winter and summer alike. The oaky scent of the freshly hewn logs permeated the room and mingled with the warm sweet aroma of beeswax polish. The top drawer was opened slightly, offering a faint peek of ribbon and the top right edge of her scrapbook.

Charles glanced furtively around him even though the room was empty, the books his father had recommended sprawled in front of him. He had read most of them, some twice over. Now he needed something to distract him. He didn't know how his mother would react if she saw him with her scrapbook. She kept it in her private writing desk, away from prying eyes. He was curious about it, but when he had asked her what it was, she had closed it and put it away, telling him it was of no interest to him. Her drawer was open, and the brightly coloured cover enticed him.

Gingerly he lifted it out of its hiding place. Pushing his schoolbooks to one side, he laid it down on the polished table as if he was placing a baby in its cradle. He glanced behind him again. The door was firmly closed, the house peacefully quiet, other than the groans of its walls withstanding the exterior gale. Charles took a deep breath and carefully opened the scrapbook.

The parchment crackled as the first page opened, and he gasped. They were exquisite, a collection of calling cards from various army officers and their wives, beautifully decorated, in vibrant colours evoking the imagery of India. He traced the intricate designs with the tip of his finger, admiring their colour and their beauty.

The next page held an exotic pressed flower, not Irish, he thought, or at least not like any flower he had ever seen around the estate or further afield. He continued to turn the pages on his mother's scrapbook.

There was an image of his parents on their wedding day; his father in full dress uniform, his mother seated, regal and unsmiling. Hiding behind that was a ribbon, presumably from her wedding dress and telegrams wishing them every happiness on their wedding day.

He was intrigued by the baby picture of his older brother and the picture of him in uniform, a duller, quieter version of the portrait in the hall. Then his own baby picture.

Birth Notice
Born, April 10, 1860, at Glassdrumman Hall, County Down, to Lady Best, the wife of Colonel Randall Best,
a son, Charles Randall Best.

With a gentle touch, he turned the page to view his brother's death notice, cut out from the same paper the month after his birth notice. The death notice was pasted on one page, protected by tissue paper, so fine the print could be read through it.

Death Notice
May 10, 1860
Best, George, Randall died in India while serving for king and country.
The son of Colonel and Lady Best of Glassdrumman Hall, County Down.

Charles wondered how different his life would have been if his brother had lived. Twenty years his senior, his portrait hung in the hall. Tall and handsome, resplendent in his dress uniform. He wondered if the portrait was a true likeness or did it skim over the imperfections, showing only the good side like his parents' memories of him. Charles became so engrossed in his musings he didn't hear the library door open behind him.

"Charles, what are you up to?"

Charles jerked upright, his nerve ends jangling, then hurriedly slid the scrapbook under his schoolbooks.

"Just my books, Mother. Father said I must be prepared for my new school," Charles said, praying his reddening cheeks wouldn't give him away.

"Such a good boy. I will leave you to it but don't spend too long on them. I look forward to hearing all about it at dinner this evening. I have had enough of dining in my room alone and will relish your company."

His mother left the room without further comment. When the door closed behind her, and he heard her footsteps cross the hall to the drawing room, Charles rose and replaced the scrapbook in its home in the drawer of her writing bureau with a relieved sigh. Wiping the sweat off his brow, he returned to his books on the centre table. He resumed his studies, thankful his mother was on the mend and guilty he had somehow intruded on his mother's personal effects.

Chapter 6

Charles

Charles was looking forward to boarding school. Mr Allen, his tutor, had prepared him well. He had a good grounding in the basic subjects and a smattering of the classics. Lessons were held in the library on Tuesdays and Thursdays. Charles spent the rest of his time roaming the grounds of his home, usually accompanied by his dog Aria, supervised by a staff member. As he grew older, his presence was required at events hosted by his parents. The hunt was his father's favourite. They had visitors from all over the country who stayed for several days and sometimes nearly a week or more, joining the hunt during the day and in the evening, enjoying the hospitality of the Best family around their formal dinner table.

Charles was an accomplished horseman and an excellent shot. Against his mother's wishes, his father, the Colonel, taught him at an early age how to handle a rifle. He started his training with a .22 telling her that all young gentlemen should be proficient in the use of firearms, particularly if they intended to join the military. His mother, an accomplished horse woman herself, encouraged him to ride. She first instructed him when he was barely five, on a quiet pony who plodded along with Charles on his back around the front lawns. As he grew older, Charles became bored and begged her for his own horse, but his mother reminded him that he would be away at school for most of the year, unable to give a horse the attention it would need.

Every year in August, his parents sponsored the annual cricket match, held in the village grounds, and hosted an after-party with games and refreshments on the lawns of their home. Thanks to his tutor, Charles now understood how impressive Glassdrumman Hall was, for to him, it had always just been home. Built in the Palladian style by his great grandfather, Glassdrumman had been carefully preserved and maintained by each generation. Charles looked back at the house from his viewing point on the front lawn. The late-afternoon sunshine glinted off the granite façade and bathed the house in light. They had been lucky with the weather. A damp morning with misty rain had been replaced by hazy sunshine by lunchtime.

Villagers and visitors packed the lawns, all eager to enjoy the renowned Glassdrumman Hall hospitality. And they were not disappointed. White tents were laid out in symmetrical lines over trestle tables, covered with fine linen and laden with an assortment of food to satisfy the pickiest of eaters. Jugs of fruit punch and lemonade stood between platters of cress and egg sandwiches, jellied eel, dulse and plates of warm soda bread. Bowls of fruit were interspersed with dishes of cook's famous caramel fudge and yellowman. Charles loved the crunchy sweetness and honeycomb texture of yellowman. It was his favourite, made even more tempting as the cook only made it once a year. He was scoffing his third piece when his mother apprehended him.

"Charles, that is quite enough. You will make yourself ill," she scolded. "You're needed at the tennis court. The boys' tournament is about to begin."

Charles hurried to the side of the house where the tennis courts and croquet lawn jostled side by side. Charles played both but didn't often get to play tennis. One of the disadvantages of being an only child, he thought to himself as he watched the Quigley brothers play against each other, each evenly matched in skill and determination. His game was against Vincent Fraser, the son of the local magistrate. They had played against each other before, and Charles was quietly confident; however, his confidence took a severe battering when Vincent won the first set in minutes. He started the next set well, winning the first serve, but Vincent deftly put paid to his small victory by winning every serve after that. When the match ended in a crushing defeat, Charles, with his racket propped under his arm, shook his opponent's hand.

"Well done, Vincent, good game. I think I may get lessons before the return bout next year."

Vincent had to play the winner of the Quigley brothers' game. Charles shouted his support from the sidelines, delighted when Vincent soundly trounced his opponent. He noticed a young girl standing beside him, dressed in a yellow organza gown with matching ribbons in her dark hair. She quietly applauded every point like a gentler echo to his raucous shouting. When the game was over, and Vincent had been presented with his trophy, Charles once again offered his hand in congratulations.

"Thank you, Charles. Have you met my cousin? She's staying with us for a few weeks, visiting from Belfast. Charles, meet Amanda."

"I am very pleased to meet you."

Amanda nodded and smiled. "Hello."

"And what do you think of our lives, down here in the country. Quite different from the city, I would imagine."

"It is, and I am having great fun."

Charles smiled, suddenly feeling awkward and unsure how to act around a girl. Vincent broke the ice.

"Did you try the yellowman? It is delicious. Let's go and see if there is any left."

The three made their way back to the front lawns searching for their favourite candy. Charles found a bowl at the back of one of the tables, partially hidden behind a jug of punch and slipped it under his jacket. Calling the others, he found a sheltered spot near an old oak tree, and the three sat on the grass, laughing and giggling while they shared the sweet treat. Charles discovered Vincent was also being despatched to a boarding school although he was going to Belfast.

"It is so unfair," Amanda said. "Boys get to attend boarding school. Girls don't. My older brother goes to boarding school and plans to go to Trinity College in Dublin. My mother says a woman marries and has children and has no need for formal education. She says that if I can read and write and do simple arithmetic, those skills are sufficient to run a household."

"But what if you don't marry? What then?" Charles asked.

"An unmarried woman can become a governess, I suppose," Amanda said, a morose expression on her young face. Vincent and Charles both started to laugh.

"What's so funny?"

"I'm sorry. I did not mean to offend you. You just looked so sad at the idea of becoming a governess, as if to do so would be the end of the world. But a governess is a good position. Look at Miss Smithers, my old governess; I was very fond of her," Vincent said.

"Yes, you were. But where is she now? You are going to boarding school and what has become of Miss Smithers?"

Vincent was silent, and Charles realised Vincent did not know what had happened to his old governess. Then it suddenly struck him, Mr Allen, his tutor. Now that he was no longer required to teach Charles on Tuesdays and Thursdays, what would he do with those days? Had he been engaged to instruct other boys? Charles resolved to track him down and ask him. He had seen him earlier at the cricket match, and he was sure he had returned to Glassdrumman Hall.

There was no sign of Mr Allen anywhere. He checked each tent and strolled across the lawns eavesdropping on snippets of conversation as he went. The White Star Line's new ocean liner, the *Oceanic*, was the main topic of discussion in one group.

"She is something to behold. I must say, the cabins were so comfortable. It made the crossing so pleasant."

"Built in Belfast, of course. Harland & Wolff know how to build ships."

Around the corner, several women discussed a recent trip to Dublin, but it was when they mentioned the Dublin Horse Show, Charles's interest was piqued. However, when they went on to discuss in detail their attire and made no comment on the horses, Charles moved on. He paused and surveyed the myriad groups of people around him, all chatting and laughing in the late-afternoon sunshine. Charles felt a surge of pride warm his stomach and a sense of his place in this world. Then, out of the corner of his eye, he spotted what looked like Mr Allen at the far side of the lawns, which reminded him of the reason for his original search. Charles wanted to determine if Mr Allen had other pupils to replace him when he went to boarding school. He rounded the corner and opened the gate to the tennis courts. They were empty now, the tournaments over, the rackets and balls put away by the staff, and the courts swept ready for use another day. Charles was taken aback when he saw Mr Allen strolling along the side of the court, deep in conversation with a woman who looked remarkably like Miss Smithers. He backed out the way he came without saying a word and raced back to his friends.

Later that evening, when Mr Allen sought him out and

wished him good luck, Charles wasn't surprised when Mr Allen introduced him to his fiancée, Miss Caroline Smithers, a retired governess. Charles congratulated Mr Allen and bowed to Miss Smithers. He was delighted to see his tutor so happy, especially when he volunteered the information that he had received an appointment in a school in Belfast. After their marriage, they intended to settle in the city.

The festivities over, Charles said goodbye to his friends and neighbours and found himself still restless. He helped with the horses, grooming them and settling them down for the night. Charles loved working in the stables. He knew when he went to boarding school, he would miss his horse and his dog more than anything else. Only slightly more than he would miss Glassdrumman Hall, the view of the Mourne mountains and the sound of the sea, but he was looking forward to boarding school and making friends with boys his age.

Chapter 7

Charles, First Term

The school looked impressive. It was a solid grey structure with the midsection set back to form a courtyard with the imposing double doors in the centre. Above the solid oak doors, the school motto, "Sapere Aude" was engraved into the glass. The lawns swept down to the main road, a velvet emerald carpet sparkling with the remnants of the morning's autumnal rain and scattered with russet leaves from the sentinel trees bordering the site. Charles inhaled the earthy scent as he walked his father back to his carriage after his meeting with the headmaster, the Rev. John Turner. Charles felt a sense of pride in his family as he noted the respect with which the headmaster had treated them. Then again, as a member of the Board of Management, Colonel Best held some sway. He was surprised when he found out his father was involved with the Incorporated Society. There wasn't much discussion about religion at home. They never missed Sunday services in their local Church of Ireland and attended church fêtes; the local vicar was a regular at his mother's dinner parties. Still, he would never have perceived his father as an evangelist promoting Protestant beliefs. He said as much to his mother who had laughed out loud, her dismissive false laugh which sounded like a glass breaking on the polished floors.

"Darling, it is only right one should give something back to your community. The Incorporated Society gives foundation scholarships to poorer boys, boys whose parents could never afford a good education. The only payment they ask for is that those boys are educated as Protestants."

Charles was still surprised. With his father's military background, he would have understood him getting involved in charities for ex-soldiers. He would never have associated his father with the promotion of religion.

"Well, good luck, son. Not that you will need it. This is a good school. Your brother excelled here. I expect you will too." Colonel Best shook his son's hand. "Your mother and I look forward to hearing all about it at Christmas."

Charles watched the carriage travel down the gravel road and out towards the north. He felt a bit overwhelmed and incredibly small in front of this colossal grey building. Around him, boys of various ages and sizes made their way to the rear of the school. Charles became aware of a boy standing quite close to him, weighed down by large carrying cases. Still growing into his body, he appeared to be all limbs and no muscle topped by a full head of unruly auburn curls. He stood with his mouth open as if in awe of the building in front of him. Charles couldn't help but wonder if he were displaying the same apprehension of his surroundings. He put out his hand.

"Hello, I'm Charles. This is my first day."

The boy was startled out of his reverie, dropped his cases, shook Charles's outstretched hand and matched his smile. The autumn sunlight reflected off his auburn locks. His apprehensive expression changed to inquisitive friendliness.

"I'm James. It's my first day too." He gestured towards the school. "Impressive, isn't it?"

They stood looking towards the building, equally matched in height, but Charles's larger frame dwarfed James. The leanness of the latter gave the impression of a gangly calf beside his beefy and muscular new acquaintance.

"Here, let me give you a hand with that." Charles helped James with his cases. Charles's bags had already been despatched to his bunk by two prefects on the instruction of the headmaster. Charles led the way, and the two boys followed the crowds into the cavernous building, friends before they even got to know each other.

Charles found a kindred spirit in James. They both discovered that the hardest thing to acclimatise to was the constant noise of sharing with other boys. It was so different from their homes. Charles had rattled around Glassdrumman Hall on his own, with only his parents and the servants for company. His only interaction with the outside world had been with his tutor. He was surprised to learn that James had led much the same life. A largely solitary existence, although James had a sister, but his family home was in a remote location. His only interaction with the outside world was with his private tutor twice a week.

Charles loved boarding school. He embraced the male companionship and admired the tutors, but most of all, he made his closest friend, despite their vastly different upbringing or maybe because of their similarities.

"I've never been to the Cooley Peninsula."

"Why would you want to?" James said. "It's a wild place. Our house faces out over the lough on an elevated site battered by the wind."

"And your family?"

"Father is a country doctor. He took over his practice from his father just as I will take over the family practice when my time comes."

"I'm expected to join the army. Follow in my father's footsteps," Charles said.

Charles and James were inseparable from their first day at Dundalk Educational Institute. They were assigned to the same dormitory and were equally matched academically. They both enthusiastically joined the cricket team where Charles was the rising star while James spent most of his time on the subs' benches. They signed up for the athletics team when James discovered a previously unrealised passion for running, leaving Charles in his wake, along with the rest of his classmates. The days blended into weeks and into months, and before long, the Christmas break was imminent.

"I'm looking forward to getting home for Christmas. I never thought I would say this, but I miss the mountains. I even miss the peace and quiet." Charles laughed. James was silent and reluctant to talk about his home life when Charles pushed him on it. From snippets of information James had let slip, Charles got the impression that James was unhappy at home. His father was a hard man, who drank too much and showed little affection to his son.

"Why don't you come to Glassdrumman Hall for the Christmas holidays?"

James looked at him as if he had lost his mind.

"Seriously. You would be more than welcome," Charles said. "Oh, we could have so much fun."

Charles's enthusiasm was infectious, and he could sense James considering it but then he shook his head.

"I can't, Charles. My father is expecting me home. Grandmama is joining us. Plus, I haven't seen my sister Jane in months," James said. "Maybe some other time. Come on, we're going to be late for assembly."

Disappointed, Charles followed James out of their dormitory. Both boys enjoyed the structure of the school day. It started with the bell's clang at six am to rouse the sixty-five boys from their slumber. Next, they were expected to wash, dress and tidy their bunks, ready for inspection by the school prefects by six forty-five. The boys then assembled in the main hall for prayers and scripture reading by Rev. John Turner, the headmaster.

With the Christmas break only days away, Rev. Turner had much to say on the sacredness of the family, meaning prayers overran their usual thirty minutes by at least another ten. Charles was sure the growl emanating from his stomach was audible to every boy around him. An assumption confirmed by the smirk on James's face when he stole a glance in his direction. There was a collective sigh of relief when Rev. Turner finished with the Lord's Prayer. Footsteps rumbled on the oak flooring. The low murmur of conversation echoed through the corridors as the assembled boys made their way to the dining room.

"Good thing I like stirabout," Charles said over his shoulder to James as they joined the line of hungry boys with their bowls ready. "I'm starving."

"You have to like it. It's the only breakfast they serve here. But then again, hunger is a great sauce, as Ellen our housekeeper always says."

Charles could feel his mouth salivating as the familiar smell of hot oats and milk assailed them. He grinned his thanks at the red-faced cook who doled out steaming ladles of stirabout to each boy, her hair tied back under a white hat and her oatmeal-stained apron straining to cover her ample frame. They sat at long benches, the wood scrubbed white and set with water glasses and spoons. Muted conversation hummed around the dining room as the boys devoured their breakfast. They were more interested in filling their rumbling tummies than holding discussions about the day ahead.

The day started with a short exercise break before classes.

The school taught Arithmetic, Writing, Grammar, Algebra, History, Geography, Navigation, Geology, Chemistry, and Drawing spread out over the week. Every day before dinner, they had Scripture classes. James loved Sundays and Wednesdays when they had beef and potatoes, while Charles's favourite days were Monday and Thursday when they tucked into bread and broth. After dinner, they had a break for two hours before classes began again. Herr Crenn taught them languages, and Charles loved Latin and French, while James excelled in drawing class with Master Chapman. Sports rounded off the day before supper, served at seven thirty and usually consisted of bread or potatoes with milk. The boys were encouraged to finish off the day with some form of exercise before attending the Assembly Hall again for Scripture and Prayers with the headmaster. They retired at nine o'clock with lights out ten minutes later. Prefects patrolled the hallways and enforced the lights out policy.

One school prefect named Mulligan had a penchant for violence and took pleasure in meting out punishment with a cane that made Charles wonder about his sanity. Charles and James fell afoul of his temperament the week before the Christmas break. As the holidays rapidly approached James became more withdrawn. Charles was worried about him and tried to talk to his friend under cover of darkness when he thought the other occupants of their room were asleep. He crept out of bed and felt his way through the blackness to James's bed three feet to his right on his hands and knees.

"James," he whispered into the darkness.

James jumped with fright, knocking the book he had been reading before lights out onto the floor beside him. The clatter echoed in the silence like a giant beating a drum. Charles raced back to his bed but, in the blackness, knocked his shin against the metal frame, causing him to yelp, diving back under the covers. He pulled the blanket over his head and listened, but his heartbeat in his throat drowned out all other sounds. Minutes later, he heard Mulligan.

"Langton, what's going on?"

Charles peered out from under the blankets to see the shadowy figure of Mulligan standing over James, the candle in his left hand giving his sharp features a macabre twist. His right hand whipped the cane down across James's legs. Charles heard the swish of the cane as Mulligan raised it above his head for another lash, and he leapt out of bed.

"Stop it."

Mulligan stopped, his cane in mid-air.

"What did you say?" His voice squeaked, high-pitched and incredulous.

"I said stop. James didn't do anything. I knocked my book to the floor then hit my knee against the bedstead when I got out of bed to pick it up."

Mulligan leaned over James's bed, holding the candle higher to get a better look at Charles, standing on the other side, poised to fight. The light caught the malice in Mulligan's eyes as he grinned at Charles.

"You expect me to believe you, Best, do you?"

Metal beds creaked, and blankets rustled as the other boys woke and watched with bated breath. In October, Mulligan had put a boy in the infirmary when he had dared to argue with him over alleged infringement of the lights out rule. The boy was a foundation scholar, and his parents were not informed. Within a few days, he was back in the dormitory, but the bruises took longer to heal. Charles knew instinctively Mulligan wouldn't dare inflict that type of damage to the son of a board member, but James was a different story. Up until that moment it had never occurred to Charles to think James might be a foundation scholar. Charles decided on a conciliatory approach.

"I had no intentions of breaking curfew, Mulligan. I got

such a fright when the book hit the floor. I apologise. I will be more careful in future."

Charles held up his hands in a gesture of apology. Mulligan scowled.

"Well, see that you are." He threw a look of pure disdain at James before turning on his heel and sauntering out of the room.

"Go to sleep, the lot of you."

An audible sigh of relief raced around the room as the boys settled back down.

"James," Charles whispered.

"Go to sleep, Charles."

Charles sighed and curled up into his blankets. He would have to get James alone the next day and talk to him. He couldn't risk the wrath of Mulligan again. The next day he didn't get the opportunity to talk to James. It was as if James went out of his way to make sure they were always in the company of other boys. They parted company on the last day of term. Charles watched as James boarded a carriage driven by a stern hulk of a man and wondered just how hard life was on the Cooley Peninsula.

Chapter 8

Charles, Second Term

Charles looked out as the carriage pulled into the driveway of the Institute. The light scattering of snow had transformed the landscape into a sparkly wonderland. Boys were on the far lawns firing snowballs at each other. It wouldn't last long, so they would make the most of it. Charles jumped down from the carriage and raced to join in the fun, leaving his father to arrange for his case to be brought upstairs to the dormitory. The Christmas break had been great, and he had enjoyed spending time with his parents. Still, Charles was glad to get back to school and into the testosterone-fuelled school days' activities. James was already there, ganglier than ever, his cheeks red with exertion and cold as he took a snowball, full force straight into the face. He got back into the fight with a yelp, shouting at Charles to join him.

By suppertime, the boys were exhausted. They ate with vigour and then forfeited exercise for library time. The fire in the library was roaring, and many dozed before they were hauled to the Assembly Hall for prayers. Principal Rev. John Turner gave a speech welcoming them all back to the school and said extra prayers for the year ahead.

As they filed out of the Assembly Hall, the hum of conversation billowed before them.

"So, did you have a good Christmas?" Charles asked. "Did your grandmother celebrate with you?"

"Yes, she did, thank God." James glanced around him. "Listen, I don't want to talk about it now. Maybe we could talk tomorrow at break time?"

Puzzled by his friend's grim expression, Charles was anxious to press James further but thought better of it.

"Of course. No problem."

The next day during their afternoon break, the boys walked through the woods. It was a bright frosty day, and they wrapped up warmly. James's morose expression intimidated Charles and he wondered how to break down the walls James had put up around himself.

"New hat and gloves?"

"Yes, present from my grandmother," James said.

Charles nodded. Instead of trying to get James to talk he decided to entertain James with stories about the New Year's Eve ball his parents had thrown.

"It's an annual event at this stage. I think my grandfather started it one year and now it is just expected. Maybe next year you could stay with us. It's great fun."

"Sounds good," James said. "Better than my New Year's Eve anyway."

James hung his head as a tear wound its way down one cheek.

Alarmed, Charles stopped walking.

"What is it? You can talk to me."

"My mother died on New Year's Eve… in childbirth with my sister Jane and me. My father never got over it. He sits in the parlour with his whiskey and broods… he drinks and scowls and drinks and cries until eventually, he passes out."

"Oh, James, I am so sorry." Charles put his arm around

James's shoulders. He could feel his friend collapse against him, his tears moistening his collar where he laid his head. They stood that way for some time until James's tears subsided. Charles was unprepared for the tenderness he felt for his friend. With a start, Charles moved away, coughing and straightening his gloves and scarf. James followed his lead, and they continued walking but now two feet apart.

Over the next few months, James confided in Charles. For the first time, Charles realised how fortunate he was for the life he led with his parents.

"He can't stand the sight of my sister or me. If it wasn't for Jane, I'd never go back there."

"How does your sister cope with him?"

"She... she's Jane. She lives in her own little world."

Charles nodded. "I don't have much experience with females. I told you about Amanda, the girl I met at the annual fête last summer. She was actually quite vocal about how difficult it is to be a female. It never occurred to me before then that women don't get the same education as men."

James shook his head. "It's not like that. Jane is different. She has never spoken. Never uttered a word. I talk to her, read to her all the time. She listens and sometimes I swear she understands. But most of the time her eyes are lifeless. Like a doll."

"Oh, James, I'm so sorry." Charles put an arm around his friend's shoulder.

"There was this one time... we were about eight, I think. Grandmama bought me tin soldiers, a full regiment. They were delightful, absolutely splendid looking, dressed in their ceremonial uniforms. Some held their rifles upright; some had their rifles poised as if ready to fire at me if I dared to lift them from their stance. I was fascinated by them. Their bright red jackets and their tiny features. They made the most delightful clang when they hit off each other."

James's voice was almost trancelike.

"My grandmama handed Jane a beautiful doll. She didn't react, just held it in her arms. I touched her cheek to get her attention. I told her how pretty the doll was, how her eyes were the colour of the bluebells which covered the pathway to the woods last spring. The doll had lifelike golden tresses and an exquisite gown of blue and gold, its porcelain features perfect yet devoid of life, much the same as its owner. Jane looked down at her doll and back up at me, her grey eyes mirroring my own. We can have tea parties with her, I said, with the little tea set Grandmama brought you last year. We will pick a name for her, a pretty name, like… Violet."

"Such a lovely name," Charles said. "Did Jane like it?"

"Who knows? She just looked at me with the same vacant expression. I felt so lost, so disappointed I couldn't reach her. Grandmama said she understands what we say to her, says Jane listens intently. Who knows how much she understands? She told me it was my job to look out for her, to be her eyes and ears, and even her voice. Grandmama said I was Jane's protector, her best friend, two sides of the same coin."

"You must love her very much," Charles said.

"I do. When Grandmama said she was sending me away to boarding school, I said I couldn't go, that I couldn't leave Jane. Grandmama promised me she would visit more often to keep an eye on Jane."

"Your grandmama sent you here. I presumed you were a foundation student?"

"No. The Institute was Grandmama's idea. She's quite wealthy. Grandmama presented my enrolment as a fait accompli to my father. He was quite happy to let her. He doesn't want me around the place. I remind him of everything he lost when mother died."

Charles listened, heartbroken for his friend. He wanted so much to cheer James up, to support him. So, with mid-term break rapidly approaching, he invited James to accompany him to Glassdrumman Hall.

"You can't say no, James," Charles said. "You are not expected home. Why would you want to stay in school when you could come with me to Glassdrumman Hall? It's only for a few days, and I'm dying to show you the view of the Mournes from our library."

After several days of persuasion, James gave in and accepted Charles's invitation. When the Best carriage arrived at the Institute to collect them, the two boys were packed and ready for the short trip to County Down. Charles took pleasure in showing James around Glassdrumman Hall. The weather was cold and wet, so trips to the mountains were curtailed; even the view from the windows was obscured most days. The boys lost themselves in the library and played catch in the ballroom with Aria, the retriever. Charles felt as if the huge house had finally come alive. Their presence certainly brought a smile to his mother's face.

Every evening they sat to dinner with her and the Colonel. The cook adapted the menus to include Charles's favourites. Dinner in Glassdrumman Hall was a formal affair. Colonel Best presided over the dinner table in full dress uniform, served by an array of servants and their butler Mr Giles. The Bests were landed gentry who could trace their roots in Ireland to before the Plantation of Ulster in the 1600s. Colonel Best met his wife in India while serving with his regiment, the 88th Regiment of Foot. Her father had gladly given permission for his only daughter to marry a fellow officer, particularly one who owned an estate like Glassdrumman.

"I knew your mother," Lady Best told James during the main course on the first evening they sat in the formal dining room. Charles looked up in surprise.

"You knew James's mother?"

Lady Best nodded, sipped her wine and looked across the table at James.

"Your mother's family and I moved in the same social circles, so to speak. I met her several times at events and parties. She was a lovely woman, totally devoted to your father. You look very like her."

James stared at Lady Best, his hands resting on his lap.

He swallowed, stared down at his plate and in the tiniest voice imaginable, asked: "What was she like?"

"Like I said, you look very like her. Same hair colour. She had beautiful hair, the colour of autumn leaves. She was so vibrant, a truly good person. Your grandmother was so proud of her. She must have told you about her?"

"Yes, she has. She says she still misses her. I know it must be difficult for her. Mother's portrait hangs in the parlour at home. She was a striking-looking woman, but I never knew how accurate that portrait was."

"She was a beautiful woman inside and out. Smart and funny and quite the catch. She had quite a few suitors and very wealthy ones at that, but she chose David Langton. It was a bit of a surprise, I must say. A Dublin debutante marrying a country doctor, but David Langton was quite dashing back then. Next time you see your grandmother, give her my regards, and James, you are very welcome to stay with us in Glassdrumman Hall at any time."

"Yes, young man. I second that. It's good to have you," Colonel Best said.

"Thank you, Lady Best, Colonel Best. I appreciate your hospitality."

Charles beamed at James. It gave him immense satisfaction to see his friend so at home in Glassdrumman Hall.

Chapter 9

James, Last Term, 1872

Before they knew it, Easter was upon them. James wrote to his father informing him of his intention to travel to Glassdrumman Hall with Charles for the Easter break. His father's reply was short and succinct.

Dear James,

I had not expected you home until the summer, in any case. I am acquainted with Colonel and Lady Best. Making their acquaintance may be of advantage to you in the future.

Yours sincerely

David Langton.

"What did I tell you? The man couldn't care less if he never saw me again."

"That's not true, James. You know it's not. But..." Charles tackled James and rolled him on the ground. "The important thing is that you are coming home with me for Easter. We will have so much fun."

When the Best family coach arrived to collect the boys on the last day of lessons before Easter, they were packed and ready to go. The pleasures of the Glassdrumman estate beckoned. The weather was still cold but bright, so the boys practised their cricket skills on the lawns by day and their musical talents in the parlour by night, much to the amusement of the Colonel and Lady Best. Charles coached James in cricket, and James repaid the favour on the piano. Charles had played cricket with the local club since he was a small boy and was an accomplished player. James had never been involved in any team sports, but his skills had improved immensely under Charles's instruction. Lady Best strolled out to watch them on several occasions, shouting her support when either of them had an excellent swing. As far as James was concerned, the only sour note was his guilt over Jane. She was his first thought on awakening each morning and his last thought at night. James's conscience niggled at him, accusing him of abandoning his sister in favour of frolics at the hall. Even though his Grandmama had written to tell him she would be in Greenore over the holidays to spend time with Jane. He said as much to Charles.

"From what you have told me, old boy, Jane doesn't know whether you are there or not. And if you weren't here in Glassdrumman, you would be spending Easter at school, so you wouldn't have seen Jane anyway."

James had to agree that Charles was correct, but it didn't stop Jane from creeping into his thoughts. The holidays flew by, and before they knew it, it was the commencement of the summer term at the Institute. Longer evenings and brighter weather meant they could stay outside until bedtime. The boys made the most of the fine weather, practising their cricket skills every evening. The annual cricket match against their nearest rival was taking place in June, and both boys wanted to be on the team.

The Lord Limerick Grammar School was quite close to them in Dundalk. It only accepted the sons of the aristocracy, charged exorbitant fees, taught the classics and impressed on its pupils their superiority. However, the Dundalk Educational

Institute could hold its own against them, not only academically but in the sporting field. The annual cricket match had become something of a local derby and a day the boys looked forward to months in advance.

On the day of the match, muffled whispers rippled around the dormitory well before the six o'clock bell sounded. The boys leapt out of bed, chattering and jostling each other, eager to start the day. The school sports day heralded the end of the school year. Parents were invited to attend. The regular meal in the dining hall was cancelled in favour of a picnic on the lawns. Best of all though, the seven o'clock Scripture readings and prayers led by the Rev. John Turner would be the last of the school year.

James grinned at Charles as they dressed in their sports attire. James had made the cricket team. He was also on the athletics team. James knew Charles envied his speed on the track. It was his speed that had earned him his place on the cricket team; well, that plus the extra coaching Charles gave him every evening. James packed away the last of his belongings and stripped his bed, folding the bedding and leaving it at the base of the bed as instructed. He looked across at Charles's equally neat bedding.

"Good training for the military."

It was a perfect day for sports, woolly clouds floating overhead, occasionally parting to reveal tantalising glimpses of cornflower-blue sky and sunshine. A slight breeze brought salty sea air across the playing fields, teasing the ladies' hats and playing with the tents erected to protect them from the sun or rain.

"Failing to plan is planning to fail," Rev. Turner was fond of saying. "Always best to plan for any type of weather on the east coast of Ireland."

And plan they did. The track and field events were first. Charles stood at the finish line to cheer on James, who won gold in his events, the hundred-yard sprint and the relay. James was the final runner in the relay team and came from behind to win gold for the team. When James raised the baton as he crossed the line, every student jumped up and down, shouting and applauding. The four team members hugged, patting each other on the back, and James looked around for Charles. Their eyes met, and Charles rushed over, cuffing him on the shoulder and roaring his congratulations.

"Well done, James, well done."

James didn't get a chance to reply. Another team member hoisted him on his shoulders as the students milled around singing and applauding, jostling Charles out of their way. James looked back at Charles, grinning triumphantly. The celebrations died down as the bell rang for dinner, and the students, all hungry after an active morning, raced to the food tent. Under the direction of the masters, the students formed an orderly line, mouths watering at the display of food in front of them. Cold cuts, bread, cheese and fruit, the young men tucked in with gusto and washed down their picnic with lemonade.

Charles fell into line behind James, and they carried their food to a sheltered spot under the shade of a giant oak tree.

"My father is here," James said. "He's talking to your mother." He nodded in the direction of a tented area only feet away. David Langton stood out from the other parents. He was a tall man in a tweed suit, tufts of snow-white hair standing straight up, as he held his hat in his hand. He was broad built turning to fat, with the buttons of his waistcoat strained as if ready to pop at the slightest pressure. His complexion was red and mottled, his face dominated by a bulbous nose and a scowl. James and Charles averted their gaze as he glanced their way, both suddenly aware they had been staring and hoping fervently Mr Langton had not seen them. James felt his approach rather than saw it and jumped to his feet when he heard his greeting.

"James. Are you going to introduce me?"

"Of course, father. This is Charles Best."

Mr Langton extended his hand to Charles.

"Pleased to meet you, sir." Charles shook his hand and smiled. Mr Langton said nothing, shook his hand and turned his attention to James.

"Lady Best tells me you are the perfect house guest. See to it that you stay that way. It is exceedingly kind of her to welcome you into her home," Mr Langton said. "I saw your race. Keep it up."

David Langton shook his son's hand and then turned on his heel and walked off in the direction of the headmaster. James gave a sigh of relief, and the two boys flopped down on the grass again.

"Quite the conversationalist, your father," Charles said as he bit into his sandwich. "I can see where you got it from."

James said nothing as he followed his father's progress across the lawns and watched as he appeared to interrogate the headmaster. He felt Charles's gaze on him and glanced sideways at his friend. Charles lifted his arm and placed it across James's shoulder, but James shrugged him off and got to his feet.

"Come on. Let's have a word with your mother before the cricket game starts."

The game was a resounding success for Dundalk Educational Institute, winning by five wickets. Charles was the star and was carried off the field on the shoulders of the other players, including James. Colonel Best was charged with presenting the annual cup to the winning team captain. James cheered along with the other boys. He wondered if they recognised the pride in the colonel's eyes as he handed Charles the cup. James knew there was no way his father would ever look at him like that.

His first year at the Institute had been great, and he looked forward to the next one. The only downside was he had to go back to the Cooley Peninsula with his father after the prize-giving. The summer stretched out in front of him, and while he was looking forward to seeing his sister and his grandmother, he knew he would miss Charles.

A slap on the back shook him out of his reverie.

"My mother has arranged for you to visit us in August for two weeks."

James was ecstatic. Charles gave a whoop of delight as they hugged then jumped apart, feeling slightly awkward. They beamed at each other while the young men milled around them, dragging cases and shouting goodbyes which echoed along the corridors.

"It's going to be a great summer," Charles said, and he linked James's arm as they made their way to the dormitory to collect their bags.

Chapter 10

James

James enjoyed his first year as a boarder in the Dundalk Educational Institute. He was grateful for Charles's friendship and remained thankful they had met on their first day. James thought spending time in Glassdrumman Hall made him realise how bad his personal family situation was. The summer in Greenore had been difficult with his father, but at least he had spent time with his sister and with Ellen their housekeeper, and the closest he had to a mother. He had missed them both and delighted in telling them tales of their adventures. Jane had listened with her usual vacant stare. Sometimes he stopped talking mid-sentence, just to see if she would react. She never did, but James always remembered his grandmama's words. His sister was part of him. He brought her home a gift.

"Look, Jane, do you see this?" He opened the clasp on the green velvet case to reveal a polished farthing, split in two, each half attached to a gold chain. "This is me and you, see, part of the same coin."

James hung the necklace around Jane's elegant neck. She lifted her fingers to it and rubbed its surface. James swore he could see the shadow of a smile on her alabaster face.

"I will always be part of you, Jane, and you will always be part of me."

He tucked a blanket in around her legs and left her sitting in front of the fire while he went in search of Ellen and a snack to keep him going until mealtime.

"I am so glad you have made a friend, James," Ellen said. "Come on, tell me more about Charles. Imagine, his mother and your mother moved in the same social circles. Small world, eh? Never a truer saying."

James chatted about Charles and boarding school, but he noticed the anxious looks Ellen gave him when she thought he couldn't see her. She corrected him when he sat with his ankles crossed and told him to sit up straight, his feet firmly on the floor. Ellen corrected him when he walked, telling him to walk with his head high and his arms swinging by his side. When he was younger, he always helped her in the kitchen but now she shooed him away, telling him cooking was women's work, and he had no place in the kitchen. Ellen quizzed him about Charles and the other boys in the dormitories. She praised his sporting achievements and instructed Mick to construct a makeshift practice ground in the back field so he could continue to practise his cricket swing in the long evenings.

David Langton informed him on his first evening home that he expected James to accompany him on his rounds several days per week. The prospect of spending time with his father both frightened James and delighted him. Eager as he was to know more about the practice he would eventually take over, he worried about how he would get on shadowing his formidable father. He reasoned it was time to show his father how eager he was to learn from him.

On the first morning, James was standing outside with the horses saddled and ready before his father got out of bed. His enthusiasm was put to the test. David Langton accepted the reins from his son without comment, mounted his horse and rode out the gate and onto the roadway. James followed behind him until they got to their first call, a large house on the outskirts of Greenore, the home of Mr Fraser, the local magistrate. David Langton dismounted his horse, handed the reins to the groom who was waiting for them and entered the house without a word or a backward glance. James, still mounted, hesitated, unsure what to do. James felt as he always did, like some sort of ghost, in the background, of no use to anyone. As he dithered, the groom approached him.

"Can I take your horse, sir?"

"Yes, yes, of course," James said and dismounted and handed over the reins. The groom wasn't much older than James and a head smaller. He led the horses away, James presumed, to give them water and brush them down. Looking around him, James considered following his father into the house and then dismissed it. The front door was closed, and he took it as an omen. Turning to look towards the town, he spotted a grassy bank opposite and sat on it and studied the house. It was red brick and quite substantial, nothing like Glassdrumman Hall, of course, but still a fine house. The stables were to the rear at the right of the house, and James could see the groom watering the horses. A second groom was polishing a black carriage, and the low murmur of their chatter drifted across to James. He couldn't decipher the words, but the tone was casual and relaxed.

Not for the first time, James realised how lonely he was and how little he engaged with other people, particularly boys his own age. Over dinner in the evenings, he talked to Ellen about inconsequential things. Her son Mick joined them from time to time, but Mick was older and busy with the odd jobs around the house, a morose man with little to say. James thought about the friends he had made in the local school, but there was no one close to him, no one he could bring back to the house.

How could James allow anyone to witness his sister's quiet resilience or his father's rage? How would he explain it? No, it was safer to have no friends.

The clip-clop of the horses shook him from his reverie, and he walked back across the road to meet the groom. Bruno was watered, brushed and happy to see him. He fed him the apple he kept in his pocket for these occasions, which he munched on happily while James stroked his mane. He felt a shadow cross over and looked up and into the flint grey eyes of his father.

"When you are quite ready, shall we proceed?" His steely tone a command rather than a request. James nodded and followed his father's retreating back through the village. For the rest of the day, David Langton rarely spoke to his son, and when he did, it was to bark out an order, usually to feed or water the horses. The doctor never introduced his son to any of his patients, leaving him outside tending the horses. On his return, he never spoke to James about any of the patients, their ailments, or their treatment. That evening James thought long and hard on their journey home, and when they dismounted at their stable beside the house, James turned to his father.

"Father, why did you ask me to accompany you today?"

James gulped as David Langton looked down at him, his eyebrows raised into his unruly hairline and his mouth open as if shocked his son had dared open his mouth to ask a question.

"Why. Why not? Do you think you should sit around this house, making a nuisance of yourself, while you wait for the new term to start?"

"No, Father, of course not. But I thought you would bring me with you to meet your patients, to start to learn…"

James gasped as his father's hand slapped his cheek so hard his head swung to the right, his neck muscles squealed, and the pain shot from his cheek into his left eye. His hand reached up to the stinging pain, and he stumbled back, out of reach of his father's hands, who stood towering over him, his face red and blotchy, fists clenched. James felt his rage. It poured out of him. He saw his father take a deep breath, and then through clenched teeth, he spoke.

"You little upstart. I will teach you when I am ready; until then, you will accompany me. You will speak when you are spoken to, and when I feel the time is right. Then, and only then, will I teach you anything."

David Langton strode away, leaving James looking after him, deflated, scared and confused. His cheek was smarting, and he could feel the lump in his throat that heralded tears, but he refused to allow himself to cry. *My father is a bully,* James thought, and counted the days until he could escape.

By the time James was preparing to go to Glassdrumman Hall, he had resigned himself to the fact that his father hated him. David Langton spoke to his dog with more affection than he gave to his son. James packed his trunk and brought it down to the carriage. David Langton had told him to be ready to leave immediately after breakfast. James had learned to obey his father's instructions. Being late or failing to react to his father's order led to a beating and a berating he could no longer bear. As the carriage pulled away, he waved at Ellen, standing in the driveway, and wished he could leave forever.

The journey to Glassdrumman Hall in the middle of a hot August was completely silent. As they approached the house, James was surprised at the realisation his father appeared quite nervous and ill at ease. It was an imposing building. James had been in awe when he had seen it first at midterm. A long driveway wound around the extensive lawns and swept towards the front entrance. The granite façade sparkled in the early afternoon sunshine. The ornate flowerpots on either side of the front door were overrun with colour. As the coach came to a stop, Aria dashed around the corner, her tail wagging a furious welcome. James laughed as he jumped from the carriage and was practically knocked sideways by her. The door was flung open, and Charles ran out and joined in the mayhem, much to the enjoyment of his mother, who stood watching the tableau. Lady Best stepped forward as David Langton descended the coach, a scowl on his face.

"Welcome, David." She offered her hand for his kiss.

David Langton swapped his scowl for a reluctant smile.

"Lady Best. Glassdrumman is still as impressive as I remembered it."

"Why, thank you, David."

Lady Best led the way inside, giving instructions to Giles to organise the feeding of the horses and the retrieval of James's bag. James and Charles followed them inside to the drawing room where Colonel Best was waiting with refreshments for their guests. James was relieved to be excused by Lady Best. He followed Charles upstairs to his bedroom, where he unpacked his bag in between chatting and listening to Charles's plans for the next two weeks.

Lunch was served in the dining room. Despite her best efforts to engage in conversation with David Langton, he remained uncommunicative, responding to Lady Best's direct questions with a yes or no answer. The awkwardness was relieved by Charles who talked non-stop about Glassdrumman Hall, about the Mourne Mountains and about the plans he had made for James. When David Langton bade his goodbyes, the boys were itching to start their adventures.

They soon fell into a routine. The mornings were reserved for riding the horses, and in the afternoons, they trekked the mountains. Some days they rode to the beach and galloped along the sand, the horses enjoying the freedom from their usual constraints. They collected wild flowers and rocks and spent every evening after dinner in the library cataloguing their finds. Lady Best supervised them loosely, allowing them the freedom to do as they pleased. Colonel Best joined them for dinner every evening and told them stories about his travels as a young officer in India and the Balkan states during the Crimean War.

James had never enjoyed such freedom. He discovered a love of riding he never knew he had. In the Cooley Peninsula, the horses were work animals, used solely as a means of transport. For the first time, he discovered the joy of riding out for the sheer pleasure of it. Charles had assigned a horse to him, a chestnut mare named Georgia, and he adored her. Within two days, James felt as if he were an extension of Georgia as they galloped along the sands spraying water ten feet into the air like meteor showers. After every excursion, he rubbed Georgia down and fed her, giving her an apple as a treat. In the afternoons, James followed Charles along mountain tracks and listened to his stories. He inhaled the scent of bark and the damp undergrowth; the salty breeze was a constant reminder that the sea was close by. The family dog, Aria, accompanied them on their hikes. She galloped ahead, stopping abruptly every few feet, her nose quivering with the scents of the forest. James finally understood why Charles constantly talked about the mountains and the sea and teased his friend, telling him he would be homesick too if he had been raised in such a beautiful place.

At the end of the two weeks, both boys were refreshed and ready to return to boarding school. They were travelling together in the Best family carriage accompanied by the Colonel as prearranged with Mr Langton at the start of the summer. James stood in the driveway staring back at Glassdrumman Hall and at the mountains behind it. It had been a wonderful two weeks that he knew he would never forget. Colonel and Lady Best had treated him like their own son, making him happier than he had ever been in his short life. He smiled as Aria raced over and practically knocked him down. James nuzzled her soft coat saying his goodbyes. He joined Charles in the carriage, and they hung out the window waving goodbye to Lady Best until Glassdrumman Hall disappeared behind the trees.

Chapter 11

James, Second Year in the Institute

Their second year at Dundalk Educational Institute started along predictable lines. James and Charles were assigned bunks beside each other and settled in quickly. They were no longer the new boys and felt relatively superior as they watched the new arrivals, bug-eyed and shaking, anxious to fit in. Of course, Mulligan was back and ready to take on the prefect role again, but Charles had a plan.

"James, you should put yourself forward. That Mulligan is a spiteful brat, and no one likes him. You would make a great prefect."

"Do you think so?" James was surprised and touched by Charles's faith in him.

"Without a doubt. I will be your campaign manager. What do you say?"

The campaign was short and pointless. James was disappointed but not surprised.

"I don't understand it, James. They all say they hate Mulligan. They all complain about his mean spirit, yet they vote him in again."

James shrugged. "He is obviously more popular than we

gave him credit for. With hindsight, we should have put you forward for prefect."

"Ah, thanks, but I would be useless. No, it's a pity. Although I must say, I am thoroughly disappointed in this lot, especially the ones who promised their votes to you but didn't follow through on the day."

James shook his head and sighed. "You are so naive. They were never going to vote for me. The son of a country doctor with no connections... other than you, of course."

Charles laughed and punched James playfully on the arm. The bell rang for breakfast, and the boys made their way to the dining room. Mulligan was standing just inside the door.

"Thought you could take me, Langton," he hissed in James's ear as he passed. "I'm watching you."

James ignored him and carried on down to his usual table. Mulligan took his place opposite him and spent the entire mealtime glaring at James between each mouthful. Again, James ignored him, but Charles became increasingly agitated and tackled Mulligan.

"Now see here, Alfred, what is it with you and James? You are always on his back."

"If Langton stays away from me, I will leave him alone." Alfred Mulligan scowled at James. "Do you hear me, Langton? I don't like you. So just bugger off."

"That's ridiculous. James has never done anything to you," Charles retorted.

"He doesn't have to. I just don't like his type."

Alfred Mulligan pushed his empty bowl across the table, stood upright, glared at James, and then pointedly stared at Charles before turning abruptly and leaving the dining hall. Charles started to speak, but James put his hand up to silence him.

"Leave it. It's just not worth it."

Several other boys started to snigger as they, too, finished their stirabout and left the room. James felt shame burning somewhere in his stomach but dismissed it. He didn't know why the others didn't like him. And if James was honest with himself, he didn't care. He knew he was different from the others. The swagger and the testosterone-fuelled antics of some boys just didn't appeal to him. If that meant the likes of Alfred Mulligan didn't like him, so be it, for he had no wish to be in his company. The dislike was mutual.

"Charles, I know you mean well, but just leave it. The Mulligans of this world don't like me, but truth be told, I don't like them either. It doesn't bother me. I don't need to be liked. I have no desire to be popular. I just want to be left alone."

They were alone at the table. The other boys had followed Mulligan one by one.

"But I can't sit here and listen to that imbecile speak to you that way."

"Ignore him, Charles. I do."

James stayed out of Mulligan's way as much as possible, but it was inevitable they would clash at some stage. They shared the same classes, the same dormitory, and James felt Mulligan's malevolent eyes watching him at every turn. Nevertheless, he threw himself into athletics and quickly earned the respect of the other boys and the tutors. Mulligan's talents were more sedentary in nature, less open to admiration from the other boys. As James's popularity grew, Mulligan simmered. He glared at James from the sidelines at every meet and muttered insults under his breath every time James walked by. To the uninitiated, James appeared to be oblivious to Mulligan's dislike of him, but inwardly, James was seething. He spoke to Ellen about it during the Christmas holidays.

"I don't know what to do, Ellen. I am ignoring him, but it seems to have aggravated him even more. He barely hides the insults now. It is getting worse every day."

"Ignore him. Sticks and stones, young man. Sticks and stones."

James went back to school with added resolve and the first few weeks flew by uneventfully. February brought a light dusting of snow which carpeted the running track and the surrounding fields. James's breath crystallised in front of him as he ran tentatively around the frozen track. The dark winter nights had curtailed his training, and he was anxious to build up his speed again before the spring. He didn't see Mulligan watching him from the corner of the building until the last second. Instead, it was the contemptuous snort that caught his attention. Seconds later, James felt his feet slip out from under him. He was propelled backwards onto the track. His head hit the frozen ground with a crack which echoed in the chilly dusk. Dazed, he lay there, panting, the ice prickling his back and shoulders and extending its fingers into his entrails before the blackness overtook him.

When the blackness lifted, Charles was there, concern written all over his face, as he shook him, calling out his name. Several hands lifted him and carried him into the building, where the blackness came over him again. He woke once more and sat bolt upright as he saw Charles throw a punch at Mulligan. He felt the pain in his head explode and screamed out. He felt all eyes on him as he stood unsteadily like a newborn foal. Charles ran to support him, leaving Mulligan sprawled against the wall in the infirmary.

"That's right, Charles, run to your pet." Hate spewed out of Mulligan's mouth, but he was silenced by the other boys.

"Give it up, Mulligan."

"Shut up, Mulligan. Enough is enough."

Mulligan was shunned after that by most of the boys in their year. They found out he had been seen pouring water onto the track, purposely turning the spatter of snow into a dangerous patch of ice. He had made no secret of the fact he wanted to do harm to James. But he had underestimated the support James had gained by his prowess in the athletics team. James bore no lasting damage other than a severe headache for several days. The biggest change was in the attitude of the other boys toward him. They no longer tolerated Mulligan's muttered comments. It didn't stop Mulligan, but it did make his malevolence bearable.

Chapter 12

James, September 1874

James jumped out of the carriage, anxious to get back into the dormitory and start his third year in the Dundalk Educational Institute. He realised long ago he felt more at home in this building than he had ever felt in his father's house in Greenore. The same as the previous year, he had spent the last two weeks in Glassdrumman Hall and returned to boarding school from there along with Charles.

The following evening, they took their customary walk through the woods.

"And that's how I feel about it, Charles. It is my father's house, but it is not my home. I don't think it has been a proper home since my mother died."

Charles didn't comment. They took the same path through the woods every evening before prayers and had done since their first year. It was during those walks their friendship was forged. This evening the early September sun was still warm. The forest was alive with green moss, the sun dappling through the leaves, picking out wild flowers and disturbing the squirrels as they started their hoarding in advance of the winter months.

"I feel more at home in your house than I do in my own," James said.

"Then think of Glassdrumman Hall as your home. You are always welcome, you know that. My mother is always happy to see you, and I am glad of the company. I rattle around that house on my own during every school break. I can't bear it."

Charles nudged him, knocking him sideways off the path, and James laughed.

"We had great fun this summer. And I do appreciate your hospitality, honest I do. Those two weeks were the best part of the summer for me."

Charles went to answer him but stopped on James's signal, his head cocked to one side.

"Can you hear that?"

Both boys listened. They could hear voices, raised in a sing-song fashion, and they both strained to decipher the words. They picked their way through some undergrowth and emerged in the clearing beside the stream. It was a favourite location of theirs, off the beaten track and pleasant on a sunny evening. The stream emanated from the mountains bringing cool refreshing water and an excellent spot for catching minnows. A group of four boys were jumping up and down on the bank, alternating calls of "'fraidy cat, 'fraidy cat," and "pretty boys" while pointing and laughing at two young boys, no more than twelve, who were being held down by two older boys. They pushed their heads under the gushing water, held them down while they struggled, then raised their heads by gripping their hair, all the while shouting and laughing at them. The younger boys were choking and trying to kick out against their captors.

"Stop that." James ran out into the clearing. He pushed one of the older boys out of the way and helped the young boy to his feet. However, before getting the young boy upright, he was knocked into the water, and a melee ensued. Charles ran to his aid, and the older boys backed away.

"You didn't see what they were doing."

"Obscene behaviour."

"I don't care what they were doing. You have no right to treat another human being in that manner. You could have drowned those boys," Charles said.

The older boys mumbled as they turned away, their shoes squelching on the dry earth, and their rolled-up sleeves wet to the elbows. Charles and James helped the two younger boys to their feet. One wiped away angry tears while the other looked shamefaced. His cheeks red, his eyes looking everywhere but directly at James or Charles.

"Thank you." He offered his hand. "I don't know what would have happened if you hadn't come along."

He turned to his companion. "Come on, Nicholas, let's get out of here."

The two boys made their way back through the undergrowth to the comparative safety of the path, with James and Charles following behind. James wondered just what the two younger boys had been doing to bring so much wrath down upon them. He was familiar with the older boys. They were third-year students, and most were on the same teams as James and Charles. They trained together, sat together at meals, yet they weren't overly friendly with them.

That night after lights out, James lay awake, staring into the darkness as he mulled over the day's events. He was under no illusions. While everyone was friendly with Charles, they barely tolerated him and only when he was in Charles's company. James thought back to cricket games and training sessions. The other boys praised his speed on the track. They complimented his batting skills on the cricket pitch. But when he thought about it, he could not remember even one occasion when one of the other pupils engaged him in conversation. Then again, he reasoned, he wasn't exactly much of a conversationalist himself. He had to be his own company in Greenore. He had never learned the art of making friends or companionship until he met Charles. Charles was his only friend, the only person he felt he could talk to, the only other boy in this entire school he cared about or who cared about him.

His thoughts wandered to the young boys they'd rescued from the river. He did not doubt the older boys had seen the younger boys kiss, and he struggled with the knowledge. He had heard about those boys who only had feelings for other boys, dysfunctional boys who had no place in good society. He couldn't see the harm in it personally. He had never felt the attraction to the female form the way he knew Charles felt, particularly towards Amanda. He had met Amanda this summer. She was a perfectly pleasant girl, a friend, just as Charles was his friend. Not for the first time, James felt confused, awkward in his own skin, unsure of who he was or where he fitted in.

Chapter 13

Charles, Easter 1875

THE FOLLOWING EASTER, JAMES AND CHARLES TRAVELLED TO Glassdrumman Hall as usual. This year, there was extra excitement as Charles's parents were hosting a ball to celebrate their fortieth wedding anniversary. They were expecting family and dignitaries from as far afield as London. The party was to be held on Easter Monday, and Charles was looking forward to it. He knew James was more reticent and had tried to back out of spending Easter break with him.

"Come on, James. You can't abandon me this Easter. I am going to need you to fend off the cousins. It is, quite honestly, imperative that you visit this year."

James laughed at his friend.

"I am sure you will manage quite nicely without me."

But Charles insisted, so James gave in and promised he would attend, so at Easter break the two boys travelled to Glassdrumman Hall, ready to help prepare for the social event of the season. The family cook, Gladys, was usually their best friend. She liked nothing more than to whip them up a picnic to bring with them on their adventures into the Mournes. Gladys always fussed over them. She would ply them with her delicious hot chocolate and little pies that fitted precisely into the palms of their hands. They doubled up as hand warmers as well as filling their bellies until the fashionably late dinner time. Charles was suitably chastised when Gladys ran him out of the kitchen empty-handed on Easter Saturday morning. The kitchen was a frenzy of preparation. Gladys had no time, nor inclination, to satisfy the appetites of two teenage boys. The two boys set off for their trek without their normal picnic and with Gladys's admonishments ringing in their ears. Lawrence, the houseboy, caught up with them before they were even out of earshot with bread and cheese hastily prepared by Gladys, whose bark was worse than her bite.

"Give Gladys our thanks. I knew she wouldn't let us go hungry," Charles said. "Do you think she would have some of her little pies ready for us when we get back around mid-afternoon?"

Lawrence laughed. "You might get away with asking her, Master Charles, but I'm not going to risk it. She'll throw the rolling pin at me, the mood she is in."

The boys had a short walk planned. Spence's Mountain was to the rear of the estate. Smaller than Mount Donard, it was a pleasant walk, and the route they planned to take was short. It was a bright day, bitterly cold after a hard frost the night before, but a fine day for the 4th of April. They set out at a fast pace, barely stopping for breath, each wrapped up in their thoughts. The ball was two days away, and Charles told James that Amanda would be there as she was visiting her cousins over Easter.

"You're sweet on Amanda, aren't you?" James teased.

"I like her, yes, don't you?"

"Well, she is genuinely nice. And I think she quite likes you."

"Do you think so? She is pretty, isn't she? And intelligent too."

James laughed and pushed his friend on the arm.

"Oh, you are sweet on her."

Charles laughed back but said nothing. He turned back to the path and waved James ahead of him as the track narrowed. They had hiked further than they intended, but they still had plenty of time to return before nightfall. Ahead of him, Charles saw James's right foot slip off the track and heard his warning shout to avoid the ice, but it was too late. Charles slipped on the same patch of black ice. He felt his feet go from under him and his breath whoosh out as his head hit the track with a thump. Charles tried to lift his head, but then the blackness descended on him. He heard James calling his name as if he was miles away and felt his shoulders being shaken. A wooziness had overtaken his thinking, as Charles struggled to open his eyes. He felt them flicker and saw the outline of what looked like James towering over him, but the blackness returned, and he felt himself sinking into it. Charles became aware of the heat and a low mumble close by. He opened his eyes slowly, but the blue sky above him had been replaced by his bedroom ceiling.

"Charles." James was beside his bed. He could feel him gripping his hand. Then his mother's face came into view. She touched his face and smiled at him.

"Good to have you back. You have given us quite a fright."

His head felt too heavy for his body and a dull, thudding pain reverberated behind his eyes. He tried to sit, and James aided him, putting his hand behind his back and easing him upright. The doctor approached him and held up his fingers in front of his face.

"How many fingers can you see, young man?"

Charles sniggered. "Two, of course."

The doctor smiled and nodded while Charles heard his mother's relieved sigh.

"You have James to thank. How he got you down that path,

I will never know. He half carried you, half dragged you as far as the paddocks, then ran for help." Lady Best put her arms around James's shoulders. "These shoulders are stronger than they look."

Charles felt his eyelids grow heavy and his mother's hand on his as he drifted back to sleep. When he woke some hours later, he felt a different hand touch his. Softer, smaller and without the heavy gold rings his mother wore. He opened his eyes, saw Amanda in front of him, and heard her soft voice calling his name. She smiled, and he found himself opening up to the sunshine emanating from her, or was it from the window behind her? He wasn't too sure, but he felt a warm glow and a fuzziness that had nothing to do with his fall.

"Charles, how do you feel?"

"Better, much better." Charles smiled and pulled himself upright. He did feel much better. The earlier pain in his head was now no more than a dull ache, and his stomach was starting to growl with hunger pangs. When he said as much, James raced out of the room and down to the kitchen to find Gladys, leaving Charles and Amanda alone in his bedroom. Charles reached for Amanda's hand. Amanda took a step backwards, then glanced around the room before stepping forward again and placing her hand in Charles's.

"I was so worried, Charles, or rather we were all so worried. James has barely left your side, and your mother has been constantly at your bedside."

'Well, I feel fine now and really happy to see you…"

The door burst open, and Lady Best swept into the room. Amanda dropped Charles's hand and took a step backwards, but Lady Best only had eyes for her son.

"Charles, James told me you were awake again. How do you feel now?"

"I feel much better, Mother. Looks like I will be attending your party after all."

Chapter 14

Charles

On Easter Monday evening, Charles was dressed in his best suit, aided by his father's valet, at the Colonel's insistence. While Charles had initially argued he could manage perfectly well alone, he was secretly glad. Once he was dressed his chest swelled with pride as he envisioned his future as Lord of the manor. A future where Charles would take over the running of the estate and could, if he wanted, have a valet to look after him, to make sure he was always appropriately dressed, his necktie perfectly fixed, his cuff-links symmetrically aligned, and his jacket unfettered by rogue threads. Charles studied his appearance in the mirror as the Colonel's valet swept a fine brush over the back of his dress jacket. He held his head high and inhaled deeply as thoughts of his parents and their position in the community forced him to take a long look at himself. He was the future of this family, he thought, the sole heir. It was his responsibility to look after this house and this estate, to marry well and have children who would inherit from him.

A knock on the door heralded the arrival of James, dressed and ready for the ball in a suit his grandmother had ordered to have made for him some months previously. He looked handsome in an awkward sort of way, like a young calf, his limbs too long for his body and his hair tousled no matter how much he tried to dampen it down. The Colonel's valet took him in hand, brushing down his jacket and applying oil to whip his hair into a presentable shape, for which James uttered his effusive gratitude.

The two young men descended the staircase side by side. The gentle strains of the orchestra drifted out into the hall amidst the murmur of conversation interspersed with the odd tinkling laugh and deeper rumbles of cigar-smoking men. Charles and James looked at each other, smiled and made their way into the grand ballroom. The room was packed. Every person who had ever made the acquaintance of the Best family had been invited. The grace and generous hospitality of Colonel and Lady Best was renowned throughout the country. Everyone who could attend was there, dressed in their finery and eager to enjoy all that Glassdrumman Hall had to offer. The one exception was David Langton, who'd declined the invitation, pleading his heavy workload. Charles was thankful, knowing James would not have been comfortable under his father's critical eye.

Charles only had eyes for Amanda. The second he saw her he abandoned James and made his way over. He filled in his name on her card for every second dance and smiled at her as he led her onto the dance floor. When the first dance was over, Charles escorted her back to her table where James was waiting. He also filled in her card so that it was completely full, while Charles beamed his approval at his friend. The dancing continued into the small hours. When the orchestra finished playing and the goodbyes were said, a procession of carriages made their way down the gravel driveway. The lanterns on the sides of the carriages gave the appearance of a string of fireflies lighting the way to the village and beyond.

The ball was a tremendous success, the event of the season, and Mrs Best was extremely happy at breakfast the following morning.

"Charles, I see you spent quite some time with Amanda. A very pleasant girl, I must say. The Mitchells are a good family. Her father is in the same unit your father served in, you know."

Charles felt the heat rising from his neck upwards to his face and was sure his complexion was bright red to match the apples in the fruit bowl on the side table.

"James danced with Amanda as much as I did, Mother."

Lady Best didn't reply, but her expression told Charles she enjoyed his discomfort. He heard the clatter of James's teacup hitting off the saucer as he tried to contain his mirth. Charles rose from the table and went to the sideboard where a range of breakfast delicacies were displayed. He took his time making his choices, keeping his back to the table until he felt his colour had subsided. He avoided looking at James as he took his place at the breakfast table again.

"It was a wonderful party, my dear, well done," the Colonel said from his place at the head of the table. Mrs Best nodded her acceptance of the compliment and touched the corners of her mouth with her linen napkin, her smile bouncing back at her husband.

"Yes, it was a wonderful night, my dear. Thank you for allowing me free rein on the hospitality and thank you for being such a wonderful host."

Colonel and Lady Best raised their teacups to each other much to the amusement of Charles and James. Charles basked in his parents' mutual respect. He said an inward prayer that someday he would be lucky enough to have the same type of relationship with his wife.

Later that day, Charles and James met in the library. The day had turned wet, and both were reluctant to venture outdoors. There was a welcoming fire in the hearth, and both were feeling lazy after such a late night.

"Do you remember the first time you stayed here, and I showed you the library?" Charles asked from the depths of the armchair in front of the fire. James looked up from his place on the sofa situated at a right angle to him. His lean body was stretched out over the entire length of it with his nose firmly in a murder mystery series.

"I had never seen so many books in one room before. I am still in awe every time I set foot in this room," James said, waving his hand around the room. "So many books, so little time."

Charles couldn't suppress the grin. James's enthusiasm was infectious, even on a lazy day like today. He had read his way through the entire ancient Greek section and was now enthralled with murder mysteries. If he kept reading at this rate, he would have read more of these books than Charles had, or any of his family, for that matter. He glanced over at the sofa where James appeared to be wholly caught up in the book. Sighing, Charles stared into the fire. He had enjoyed Amanda's company last night. The idea struck him that perhaps he would like to see more of her, but he dismissed it just as quickly. They were only fifteen, for goodness' sake. They were too young to even consider anything more than friendship. He wound a piece of his hair around his index finger as he recalled how a curl of her hair had fallen loose from its clasp during the night, its chestnut colour tickling the whiteness of the nape of her neck. Her eyes were the colour of the lough on a summer day, and he had lost himself in their depths, only resurfacing when the music ended, and he had to escort her back to her table.

He had watched her dance with James but felt no pang of jealousy. To him, it was obvious James and Amanda were friends only. There was no spark between them, no attraction.

Or at least he hoped not, the thought sprang unbidden, and he glanced across at James, who was still engrossed in his novel.

"James, what do you think of Amanda? Do you like her?"

James glanced up. "What, sorry, what did you say?"

"Amanda, do you like her?"

Charles searched his friend's face with anxiety clutching him, like he had never experienced before. His concern was dispatched with James's laughter.

"Amanda is a lovely person. I am sure we will be great friends. But if you are asking if I like her in the manner I think you are asking, then the answer is no. Now can I please return to my reading? You have interrupted me at a most inopportune moment as the murderer is about to be revealed."

Charles sighed and picked up the newspaper, a smile on his face as he scanned the headlines, unable to concentrate on anything but the memory of Amanda in his arms as they skimmed around the dance floor.

Chapter 15

Charles, September 1875

CHARLES HAD NEVER GIVEN MUCH THOUGHT TO HIS FATHER'S role on the Board of Governors. He was there at the prize-giving ceremonies and on special occasions. Charles always felt a particular pride when his father took his place at the podium to speak. While Charles was aware of the history of their school, it was only in his fourth year he came to understand the implications of its background as a Charter School. In his first year, Charles had heard unkind remarks from some of his fellow pupils aimed at foundation boarders but chose to ignore them, putting their comments down to ignorance and pettiness. He had never differentiated between the foundation or paying boarders himself, and neither had James. It was one of the qualities Charles admired in James, his ability to treat everyone he met with respect. Originally, he had presumed James was a foundation boarder, incorrectly, as it turned out. It was only when they got to know each other better that James had confided in him his grandmother covered the cost of his tuition.

"The foundation pupils must pass an entrance exam. They are all, to a boy, smarter than us. What right has the son of an army officer or any landed gentry to look down on someone smarter than themselves?" Charles had said to Isaac Paterson.

"They shouldn't be going to the same school as we attend. I will speak to my father. It's just not good enough for the sons of the upper classes to be educated side by side with the sons of the working classes."

"Rubbish." Charles was livid. "Such utter twaddle. If you feel so strongly about it, then maybe you should move to another school."

There were murmurs and mutterings from the other boys, divided by their upbringing, and all aware Charles's father was on the Board of Governors. They never really discussed it again, and Isaac Paterson was still a pupil. Charles and James avoided his company, finding him a bore and a bully. It was just before the Christmas break that Isaac crossed their paths again. Charles and James were returning from their walk. The dark evenings had curtailed their walks in the woods, and they had switched to a route around the perimeter of the school grounds. As they rounded the corner at the rear of the kitchens, they heard a voice jeering.

"Stupid little urchin. You're not fit to polish my shoes, and you think you can attend my school."

Charles watched in horror as Isaac swung a punch straight into the face of a young boy who could not have been more than twelve years old. James took off at a run from beside him, shouting as he ran.

"Leave him alone, you bully."

James was stopped by Isaac's fist into his chest. He bounced onto his back with a dull thud. Charles felt his world go into slow motion and heard silence except for the roar from his mouth that sounded like it came from someone else. He felt his rage explode inside his head as he charged forward. Charles knocked Isaac to the ground and straddled him, fist raised, ready to beat some sense into him when he felt someone grab his fist, preventing him from raining blows down on top of Isaac. He looked up, dazed to see the young boy panting and holding on to Charles's fist with both hands.

"Stop, stop." He was crying. His tears mixed with the blood pouring from his nose. "He's not worth it, stop."

Charles could hear his heart thumping as his rage subsided and the earth went into a silent slow motion. The angry red vision cleared from his eyes, and he glanced from the boy's tears to James's prone figure five feet away. Charles raised himself slowly and stood over Isaac, who lay whimpering on the ground, pleading for mercy. Charles spat on the ground to the right of Isaac's head and stepped over him to go to James. Charles and the boy helped James to his feet but then all turned, dismayed at Isaac's vile shrieks. He had pulled himself upright, clutching his chest where Charles had hit him and was shaking his fist at them.

"Look at the both of you. That lad is more of a girl. Help your girlfriend, Charles, help him or her up. Charity cases and losers, that's what you are."

A red tide of anger descended on Charles, and he launched himself at Isaac again with a deafening roar. The two rolled around the ground, tearing at each other and punching when they got an arm free. A crowd gathered, baying for blood like savages around fighting cocks. James and the young boy watched, horrified but unable to stop the spectacle.

"What is going on here?"

The crowd parted as the Master pushed his way through and silence fell as the crack of the cane on both warriors' backs stopped the fight. Using the thumb and forefinger of each hand, he pinched the top of the ear of each fighter and marched them off to his office.

Later that night, Charles returned to his bunk just before lights out. His right eye was starting to show shades of black and purple, and his knuckles were raw, the skin ragged and broken. He gave an imperceptible shake of his head at James and slipped into bed without comment. Charles pulled the covers over his head and said a silent prayer. His father would not like this, but he prayed he would understand. That Isaac was a vile creature and a bully. The young foundation boarder he had been beating up was a newcomer and the son of one of Isaac's father's servants. Isaac had no right to beat him up or berate him, but it was his attack on James that had caused Charles to lose his temper. How could he explain that to the Colonel?

As it turned out, Colonel Best waited until the Christmas festivities were over before taking his son to task over the school incident. He summoned Charles to his office.

"I had a meeting of the board on the last day of term," he said. "And a private meeting with the Master afterwards."

Colonel Best looked pointedly at his son. "Do you know what he told me?"

"No, sir."

"The Master informed me my son had been engaged in fisticuffs with another student. He also informed me you refused to say what led to the incident."

Charles remained silent, unsure how to react or what he could say.

"There is no excuse for resorting to that kind of behaviour, Charles. Not only have you let yourself down, you have also let this family down."

Charles sat with his head bowed. His chair was in front of his father's highly polished walnut desk with brown leather trim that he had brought back from India. The walls were adorned with tapestries depicting elephants and brightly coloured birds. In the corner stood a suit of armour, a throwback to his family heritage and in the other corner, a Buddha carved from dark wood and polished to a high sheen. Charles had debated with himself for the last few days over what he should say to his father but had decided it was best just to apologise and promise it would never happen again. If he told his father about Isaac bullying the young boy, it could lead to corporal punishment and maybe even expulsion for Isaac, and Isaac would not allow that to happen without spouting vile comments about Charles or about James, and he did not want those vile comments repeated.

"... bully... Are you listening to me?"

Charles realised he had not heard a word his father had said and looked aghast.

"Sorry... sorry."

"What I said was Rev. Turner seems to be of the opinion young Isaac is a bully who habitually threatens young foundation students. He suggested you may have taken offence to his latest attack. Is that the case?"

Charles gulped. His headmaster knew more than he thought. He hesitated and looked up at his father, then down at his hands twisting as he wrestled with his conscience. He felt his father pat his hand.

"Fine, Charles. I respect your silence. No one likes a tell-tale, and I respect that. You will go far in the military if you retain that attitude. On the other hand, young Isaac will not be getting an exemplary reference from the Educational Institute, and not because of this incident."

He hesitated as Charles went to protest.

"No, no, because he has proved himself to be a bully, and one cannot tolerate that type of behaviour. He will get a reference, but anyone worth their salt will know from its omissions the type of person he is."

Colonel Best waved at Charles to dismiss him, and Charles left the room without another word. He closed the door behind him and rested against the wall, exhaling, then grinned. He hadn't anticipated that.

Chapter 16

Charles, 1876

"PROUD OF YOU, SON, WELL DONE."

Colonel Best shook his young son's hand. Charles beamed at his father. The grounds of the Dundalk Educational Institute were resplendent in the summer sun, the trees providing a dappled canopy of shade. Charles kissed his mother's proffered cheek.

"Yes, well done, son. Your father and I are so proud of you for following in his footsteps." She smiled at her son. "We will miss you so much when you go into training."

"Margaret, he will do just fine in the army."

Colonel Best smiled indulgently at his wife as he tapped his son's shoulder with the polished ebony top of his favourite walking cane. A souvenir from India.

Charlie basked in his parents' approval in the sunshine, watching other family groups standing around having the same conversations, smatterings of laughter carrying on the light breeze. At the edge of the courtyard, under the shade of a large oak tree, James and his father stood alone like gate-crashers at a wedding. James was beside his father, his face devoid of all emotion and a space between them as if carved from ice. David Langton, red-faced with a whiskey nose and a scowl engraved into his features, stared at the other families from under his thick eyebrows. Charles excused himself to his parents and walked over to join them at the edge of the courtyard.

"James." He held out his hand in greeting. "Congratulations, my friend."

James smiled in return. "Thank you, my friend, and congratulations to you."

He turned slightly, bowed and spoke to his father.

"Father, I'm sure you remember Charles Best."

David Langton fixed his eyes on Charles and shook his hand.

"Yes, of course, the heir apparent to Glassdrumman Hall. I believe you are taking up a commission. Well done. Of course, James will be going to Trinity College in Dublin to study medicine."

David withdrew his hand, rubbed it on his trousers and eyed Charles with a glassy stare. Charles was struck by the similarity in colour with James. The same solid grey, but the similarity ended there. Years of hard work and whiskey had taken their toll on David Langton, and his eyes reflected his unhappy soul. David Langton exhaled and rocked on his heels, looking around him as if unsure of what to say next.

"James, you're still joining me for two weeks in August at the country estate?"

Before James could answer, his father spoke up. "He will not. James has work to do. We have a country practice that is too big for me. James will be starting his training tomorrow. He has no time to be gallivanting around the country."

James shrugged at his friend, and Charles could see his eyes pleading for understanding.

"Not to worry, James, you know where I am if you get a

chance. Good luck with the medicine. I hope it goes well for you."

Charles made his way across the courtyard back to his parents' smiling faces, leaving James and his father alone together in the dappled shade of the oak tree.

"David Langton is his usual belligerent self," he told his father.

"James is a fine young man, Charles, and I am glad you call him a friend, for with a father like that, he needs a friend. Is David Langton still insisting that James study medicine?"

"He is, Father. James has been accepted and starts in September. In the meantime, his father wants to show him the ropes in his practice, so James will not be joining us this summer after all."

Margaret tutted. "Maybe I should have a quiet word. The man is more to be pitied. He never got over the death of his wife in childbirth. She was so young, so beautiful. It was such a tragedy."

Before either the Colonel or Charles could say anything, she strode out purposefully towards James and David with her son and husband scrambling after her like ducklings after their mother as she cut a swath through the assembled groups.

"David, how lovely to see you." She held out her hand. David Langton's eyebrows rose in surprise, but he took her hand and kissed it.

"Margaret." His response was curt and matched by the Colonel.

"David." The Colonel shook David Langton's hand. "James, we wanted to congratulate you in person. Well done on graduating today."

James smiled at the Colonel and Lady Best. "Thank you, sir, ma'am, you are very kind."

"The boy has been accepted into medical school."

David's gruff tones cut across the smiles. "He is starting his training straight away with me on the peninsula. Hands-on, the best training you can get."

"Yes, so I believe. But I hope you will allow us the privilege of entertaining James for a few weeks this summer. We have always enjoyed having James in our home, and this will be the last year the boys will have any time off together. In September, James will be in medical school, and Charles will be in the army," Margaret said.

Her serene smile was at odds with her iron will hovering underneath.

David Langton was no match for her, and he scowled as he reluctantly agreed James could join them for the last two weeks in August.

"Let's go, James. We have wasted enough time today with this frivolity. We have work to do. So, if you will excuse us, Margaret, Colonel, Charles?"

They said their goodbyes and watched as James followed his father out of the courtyard and onwards to the gates.

Chapter 17

James

James tried to get involved in his father's practice. He cared about the patients; it was his father he couldn't stand. James picked up a lot of practical information shadowing his father as he did his rounds. He was good with people. They opened up to him in a way that was impossible with his father. David Langton lost any people skills he may have possessed the night his beloved wife died. James believed that in his father's troubled mind, it was the fault of his patients he was not with Janet when her labour began. He heard his father in his drunken rants shout that if he had been at home, he could have anticipated the danger she was in and would have been able to prevent her death. James heard his father blame everyone for his wife's death, and on his rounds, he let them know it. Thanks to his sullen and short-tempered behaviour, he lost the respect of the people he had sworn to help. His practice shrunk as more and more people shied away from him, preferring to travel further afield for medical advice. David Langton was only called for serious emergencies and only if there was no other choice, for he had been known to show up at a patient's farm worse for wear, with whiskey breath and bloodshot eyes.

At home, David made James's life a misery. David Langton never spoke to his son, preferring only barked instructions, and thumped him for the slightest infractions. James feared for Jane's safety at times, but their father always shied away from her. Her presence was always guaranteed to quieten him. It was as if her silence frightened him. There were nights, particularly after a violent outburst from their father, that James would sit in Jane's company, comforted by her serenity. There was a sense of peace around her, an aura that soothed his spirit and calmed his battered heart. James would lay with his head in her lap while she stroked his hair, the wild mane of vibrant curls they had both inherited from their mother.

While Jane held his heart, Ellen, their housekeeper, was his only friend in the Langton household and the only person he could ask for advice. He confided in her.

"I thought medicine was for me, Ellen, but I am starting to have my doubts. Why should I study to take over my father's practice? I can't stand the man. I can't stand this house. I don't know how much more of this I can endure."

Ellen listened to him and sympathised, but there was little she could do. The portrait of his mother hung in the parlour. She had been a beautiful woman, a russet-haired beauty with dark eyes and a ready smile. James often wondered how different his life would have been if she had lived. How different his father would have been? He sometimes heard him, in the middle of the night, full of whiskey, crying, imploring his wife to come back to him, his raw grief spluttering and roaring around the house, banging off the walls and ceilings and enveloping them all in a dark shroud of misery.

During the day, David Langton was surly and unforgiving. He insisted James accompany him on his rounds but barely spoke to him other than to bark orders. On his return, he locked himself away in his study, never once even bidding the time of day with his daughter. If James dared to challenge him or question him in any way, he felt his fist and his fury. James couldn't wait to escape but felt guilty about leaving Jane there in that house with only Ellen for company.

"Why do you stay, Ellen? Why put up with that man's moods?"

Ellen looked at him from where she stood, her fingers continuing to knead the dough on the scrubbed oak table, and gave a short snort.

"Sure, where else would I go, sir?"

"I'm sure there are many fine houses who would be glad to have you, Ellen."

"No, I don't think so, young sir." Ellen gave a wry smile as she continued to knead the dough with the palm of her hands. "I am quite happy here. I have my private room, as does Mick, and I am my own boss, more or less. The Master might not be the most pleasant employer, but he leaves me well enough alone as long as I look after Jane and make sure there is food on the table and the house is kept clean. I made a promise to your mother I would look after both of you, and I intend to keep it."

James sighed and acknowledged Ellen was right. She was happy enough in this house. So was Jane, if he was honest with himself. It just wasn't for him, and the sooner mid-August came around, the better, and he could make his escape to Glassdrumman Hall and after that to his mother's home city of Dublin.

Chapter 18

James, 1876

JAMES INHALED THE SUMMER AIR AS IF IT WAS HIS LAST BREATH. The hum of bees in the golden grasses flitting from flower to flower mingled with the gentle breeze that brought salty tangs from the sea shimmering in the background.

"Can you smell it, Charles? There is nowhere else like it in this world of ours."

James was sitting cross-legged, making a daisy chain, his long fingers piercing thin slits in the green stem of each flower and threading through the next. One eye looked out from under the cap, which sat sideways on his red mane, shielding his face from the sun. Charles smiled back at him, an open, engaging smile, and James felt his heart melt and a strange stirring within him. James cleared his throat and turned back to the view, appalled at the feelings stirred in him by the sight of Charles's smile.

James stood and offered the daisy chain to Charles. "Take this, my friend, something to remember me by except it will be dead by the time we get back to the house."

He laughed as he punched Charles playfully on the arm.

"Say goodbye to that view. Next time you see the Irish Sea, you will be crossing it. Sandhurst awaits you, my friend."

Charles sighed. "Tell me I am doing the right thing. I know Sandhurst is a family tradition for us Best men but is it right for me?"

James followed Charles's gaze out to sea. "Only you can make that decision, Charles. Your brother went to Sandhurst. He fulfilled the family obligation. Just because he died doesn't mean you have to follow suit. You have your own destiny to carve out."

"Yes, but the Colonel wants his son to follow in his footsteps. If George were still here…"

"But he's not, I know. But the Colonel has lost one son in service to his King. Why risk another one?"

"It was dysentery that killed George in India. If he had been killed in battle, maybe it would have been different." Charles sighed.

His shoulders slumped as he stared down at his feet, not noticing the beetle writhing on its back, trying desperately to right itself before some predator saw its predicament.

"The Colonel will be looking for us. We should get back, or your mother will send out a search party." James tapped Charles gently on the shoulder, causing him to jump.

A nervous laugh escaped Charles, and his face coloured as he felt James's touch.

"You are one to talk," Charles said. "You are only going to study medicine to please your father."

"No, I want to do medicine. I just don't want to go back to the Cooley Peninsula when I'm qualified. I cannot stand that man. Honestly, I cannot wait to get away from him forever. If it wasn't for Jane, I would never go back there."

"Both of us trapped by our parents' expectations."

Charles's face hardened, and he flung the daisy chain with the force of a hand-baller, but the wind caught the inoffensive chain of wild flowers, and it fluttered to the ground five feet from them. Both men laughed, the tension relieved, friendship and good humour restored.

In the evening sunshine, they made their way down the mountain to Annalong Valley. It had been a great two weeks, and both were energised and recharged, ready for the challenges ahead.

Lady Best was waiting for them in the drawing room and ordered them upstairs to dress for dinner before the Colonel came downstairs. They washed quickly, changed and managed to get back to the drawing room at the same time as the Colonel.

"Evening, Mother." Charles kissed his mother's proffered cheek before accepting the aperitif offered on a silver tray by Giles.

"Thank you, Giles." Charles turned to his father. "Lovely day today, sir. We trekked over Spence's Mountain. Splendid views out to sea and back to Mount Donard."

"Good man, good man." The Colonel settled into his wing chair. "It will look a bit different next time you are home."

"It will, sir."

A gentle gust blew the sheer curtains inwards. The fire flared in the breeze, for the drawing room retained a coldness that the fire struggled to dispel even on the warmest of summer evenings. Lady Best wore a light shawl over her shoulders as she sipped her sherry, her armchair directly in front of the fire.

"James, how did you enjoy your walk?"

James accepted his drink from Giles before sitting opposite Lady Best.

"Delightful, Lady Best. It was a beautiful day."

"Tell me, James, are you looking forward to residing in Dublin?"

"Yes I am. I will be going home tomorrow and plan to

move to Dublin the following Tuesday. My grandmother has my room ready for me. I see no reason to delay."

"Dublin is very different from what you are accustomed to. It is a beautiful city, and I hope you find it welcoming. I have some contacts there I will put you in touch with. My cousin Lady Morton has a residence in Merrion Square, which if I recall correctly is quite near to Trinity College."

"Why, thank you, Lady Best," James said.

"Do you know anyone in Sandhurst, Mother?" Charles said.

"Now, Charles, military college is a vastly different experience than studying medicine at Trinity. Having said that, yes, I do have connections in Sandhurst, as you well know, and I have already been in touch with my cousin Gerald on your behalf."

Charles raised his glass to toast his mother, and James and the Colonel joined in. They were interrupted by Giles informing them dinner was served. James smiled at Charles and winked. He'd admitted to Charles earlier in the week that despite being a frequent guest in Glassdrumman Hall, he was still overawed when Giles called them for dinner. The household James had been brought up in was very different from the atmosphere Charles had grown up with at Glassdrumman Hall. James often wondered how someone of his mother's standing had ended up on the Cooley Peninsula with a country doctor. Janet Cantwell had been from the upper classes in Dublin, a débutante with plenty of admirers. Yet, she chose David Langton. James realised that at that time, his father had a successful practice and a certain standing in the community, but it had disappeared after her death. He wondered if it happened immediately or was his father's demise more gradual like a dripping tap. All his self-respect disappearing bit by bit, year after year.

In the Langton household, no one met for drinks before

dinner. James and his sister ate in the kitchen with their live-in housekeeper Ellen. The dining room with its formal mahogany table, gilt mirrors and heavy damask curtains was only used when his grandmother visited twice yearly to check on her grandchildren. It always smelled slightly of dust and neglect despite Ellen's efforts to keep it aired. David Langton rarely showed his face at mealtimes, preferring to eat at his desk with his whiskey for company. Dismissing his thoughts with a shake of his head, James followed the others into the dining room, where the evening meal was waiting to be served.

"My compliments to the cook, Giles, dinner was delicious as always," Charles said, and the others mumbled their agreement. Lady Best excused herself and retired upstairs while Colonel Best retired to his office with a brandy and a fat cigar. Charles and James were left to their own devices. The library beckoned, and they spread out in front of the blazing fire, sated and content after the large meal.

"It's been a great two weeks, Charles, but I'm looking forward to getting to Trinity and getting started."

"Good, I'm glad. You will have a wonderful time. Enjoy it. Medicine is your forte. Forget about your father until you graduate. Then you can make your decision. You don't have to go back to Greenore. You don't have to take over his practice."

"It's what he expects, though."

"And I repeat back to you what you said to me. You need to follow your own path. Get your degree. Become a doctor. You don't have to go back to Greenore."

"And like you said to me, I must do what is expected of me."

Chapter 19

Charles at Sandhurst

'Lights out.'

Charles felt like he was back in the Institute. He lay flat on his back and relaxed into the horsehair mattress, wriggling his way into the least uncomfortable position. He hated it here. He was an outsider, and the other cadets were intent on making sure he didn't forget that. He was accustomed to being different. Growing up as the heir to the Glassdrumman Estate in rural County Down, his cultured accent had born no resemblance to the accents of the local village children. Charles had never given it any thought. Here, they mimicked him, called him names. He had never considered being born in Ireland made him different. His ancestry was British. His father and brother had served in the British Army. His father still used his rank. His mother was from a long line of British officers who served in the Crimea and India. Charles nearly laughed out loud at the thought his family had the longest and most illustrious of any of his fellow cadets when it came to military service. Tiredness ached through his bones, and his eyelids felt heavy. *Two more months and I will get home for a two-week break,* he thought, and the idea of seeing James and Amanda brought a faint smile and a warmth to his heart that helped him fade into an exhausted sleep.

The following morning brought a letter from Amanda. Charles smiled at the petite and exact handwriting, perfectly aligned in the centre of the heavy cream envelope. So typical of Amanda, he thought, exact and undemanding. Charles placed the letter in his locker on top of the growing pile tied up with an old shoelace. Something to look forward to later when the day's training was done, and he could relax and lose himself in her words. She wrote to him regularly. If he was honest with himself, it was Amanda's letters that kept him going. She wrote breezy, carefree letters about her life in Belfast, making the most mundane of everyday activities an adventure. Her letters always made him smile and put warmth in his heart that lasted for hours despite his testosterone-fuelled companions. James's letters were tied up beside Amanda's, a bundle of equal height but varying colours and sizes. The handwriting was large and flowery and filled the page, practically shouting out his adventures in Trinity, his fellow students and his latest passion, the drama group. Charles closed his locker with a sigh, lifted his cap and made his way to the parade ground.

It was Sunday morning before Charles got the opportunity to read his post. He had three letters to open. The first was from his mother reminding him the annual cricket match would be held during his leave at home.

I hope you will wear your uniform for the fête after the cricket match. Your father and I are enormously proud of you, son, and are looking forward to seeing you in the uniform your brother wore so proudly.

That is the only reason I am here, Mother, he thought to himself and sighed as he folded the page and replaced it in the envelope. The next letter was from James. Charles laughed aloud at James retelling his role in the play his drama group had put on in Trinity. He felt a twinge of envy at the fun James appeared to be having. Military college was many things, but the word fun could never be used in any description. But he was also glad for his friend. James had been so unhappy at home. The relationship with his father was no better. If anything, it was worse.

I do not envisage myself ever returning to Greenore, Charles. I am enjoying Dublin. There is so much to do, so much to see. Greenore may be beautiful, but that house and that man are poison, and I have no desire to return. My grandmother has introduced me to a new circle of people, and Trinity College has opened my world. I hope you can meet me here sometime so I may introduce you and maybe entice you to stay.

At least he surmised the word was "stay", for the paper was so ink-stained parts of words had been covered up, and Charles had to decipher the meaning. He smiled as he folded the ink-stained sheets and rose to clean his hands before he could even consider opening the pristine last letter.

Dear Charles,

I hope this letter finds you well.

So formal, Charles smiled to himself, *so typical of my Amanda.* He sat upright. In his thoughts, he had called her "my" Amanda. He settled himself back onto his bunk as one thought tumbled out after the other. She was his Amanda. Maybe it was time he spoke out. Perhaps she didn't feel the same way. He reread the letter. It was very formal. But Amanda was very formal. She wasn't about to spill out her heart to him on paper. Well, that's if she had any feelings for him. Now he was confused. Did she care for him, or did she write out of some sense of duty? The dreaded word, duty, it was his sense of duty that had landed him here, in a place he hated, away from family and friends, and Amanda and James. He wondered why he always lumped Amanda and James in the same thought. *Well, they are your best friends, Charles,* he scolded himself. Did he love Amanda? Did he love her enough to spend the rest of his life with her? To provide for her. To have children with her.

He decided August was the perfect time to test it out. He would spend some time with her. Ascertain if she felt the same way about him as he thought he might feel about her. His initial training would be over then, and he would know where he would be posted. Maybe then he would ask for her hand in marriage. His parents would approve of his choice. They were very fond of Amanda. Charles knew he was an eligible bachelor much in demand in the social circles his parents moved in. He wondered if those social circles extended to Dublin society but had no doubt they did. Wasn't James's mother originally from a good family in Dublin? He gave a lot of thought to his reply to Amanda's latest missive and made sure to mention the annual cricket match.

I hope you are staying with your cousins again this year. I look forward to seeing you at the annual cricket match and afterwards at Glassdrumman Hall. It will be good to see you and James again.

He reread his words, checking to see if he had the balance right. He wanted her to know that he was looking forward to seeing her, but he didn't want to sound overly demanding. Happy with what he had written, he sealed the envelope and headed to the orderly room to post with the others.

A few weeks later, Amanda's reply took his breath away.

Charles, I have missed you so. August cannot come around soon enough.

Charles felt as if his heart would burst open, and he could feel his grin stretching his skin from ear to ear. Amanda missed him.

Chapter 20

James

The moment James walked through the gates at Trinity College, he fell in love with the place. He emerged from the archway onto Parliament Square and stood looking around him, transfixed. Students, his age and older, milled around him, some sure of their way, striding purposely towards the buildings, others like himself, standing in awe. Once again, he thanked God for his grandmother's generosity. He had no doubt his father had drank any and all proceeds from his practice long ago. James had talked to his grandmother at length the previous evening. She had advised him to study hard, earn his degree, but leave consideration of his future until after he had qualified.

James dismissed the imagery from his mind and concentrated on what was in front of him. His future lay there in the vibrant green of the grass and the grandeur of the buildings. He couldn't stop the smile that rose from inside him as he lifted his bag and made his way to the medical facility. He settled into student life as if he had been born to it. Every evening he returned to his grandmother's house, where she fussed over him and introduced him to Dublin society.

Dublin had a much grander social mix than anything he had encountered before. He enjoyed the social aspect of city living. James joined the Dublin University Cricket Club and quickly became one of their stalwarts. He made friends and learned so much more than medicine. His fellow medical students were an eclectic bunch from across the country, but he noticed their accents were all broadly similar, including his own. He wrote to Charles every week, a running commentary of his daily activities and the people he spoke to. Every Monday evening, he raced back to his grandmother's in anticipation of the latest missive from Charles. He retired to his room straight after dinner, pleading tiredness so he could savour every word his friend had written. What he read worried him, for Charles hated Sandhurst almost as much as James loved Trinity. James wrote to him, imploring him to talk to the Colonel, to tell him how unhappy he was, but Charles replied it was his duty to become the officer his parents expected.

Mrs Cantwell threw several soirées in an effort to introduce her grandson to a suitable young woman. James was flattered by the attention. One look in the mirror confirmed he was a good-looking man. He had grown tall and slim with a shock of auburn hair that refused to be tamed. His beard and moustache were full and rich, kept under control by a reliable barber. His grandmother's daily praise boosted his self-confidence. He learned to converse with people and lost the shyness which plagued him as a younger man.

He was a popular guest in Dublin society, but he conceded to himself his problem was not his looks or his background. He just wasn't attracted to these society women. While he admired their dresses and hairstyles, loved their shoes and shapely ankles, they didn't arouse him. It struck him he would have made a better woman than a man, and Isaac's words came back to haunt him. Sometimes when he retired at night, he tossed and turned in his single bed and his thoughts turned to Charles and Amanda. He envied their relationship, and he admitted to himself he wasn't attracted to any woman. He couldn't talk to anyone about it, even Charles. He wondered if he was homosexual but dismissed the idea. He loved Amanda like a sister, but he also loved Charles. At the end of the day, he felt more comfortable in women's company, more in tune with women.

One night when his grandmother was at the theatre, he went into her room and raided her wardrobe. They were of similar build, although he was much taller. He swept his hair back and fastened it with a clasp he found in her jewellery box. He tried on one of her dresses, a delicious concoction of cream lace and satin. It was too tight and wouldn't fasten properly, but it was gorgeous. He could barely contain himself as he shimmied first one way, then the other, admiring the swish of the fabric as it brushed his ankles. A noise downstairs made him freeze in place like the mannequin in his anatomy class. He hurriedly removed each item and returned them to their rightful place. He crept back into his own room, the fear of detection making him shiver like a man with a fever.

A few weeks later, a sign on the college noticeboard took his attention.

Trinity College Drama Society. New members needed.

After class that evening, he went along to the meeting and immediately became involved in the drama society. They were actively recruiting someone to look after their wardrobe department. James seized the opportunity. He had never considered going on the boards, so to speak, but it didn't take much persuasion from the others to audition for the part of an elderly duchess in their latest drama. It meant shaving off his beard, but he didn't give it a second thought. When the barber had finished, he looked into the mirror and saw his sister's face. That brought a smile to his face and a determination he would be the best duchess the drama society had ever put on stage. He felt the flutters of excitement in his stomach as he pulled on the dress that night. As he fastened it and smoothed it down over his hips, he finally felt at one with his body. Not gangly, not uncomfortable, just at peace.

The new play went down well with the other students. James bowed to rapturous applause in the college theatre every evening. Backstage, he was reluctant to remove the gown. It was a beautiful piece, green velvet with mother of pearl and a flowing skirt which he admired in the mirror before the others joined him. The other players teased him.

"James, if I didn't know better, I would ask for your hand. You are a fine-looking woman in that gown. You could leave here tonight in that, and no one would be any the wiser."

James had laughed and lowered the tone of his voice to sound even more masculine than usual. *No need to bring attention to myself,* he thought. *Maybe this play-acting has gone too far.* His grandmother attended the play the previous evening, and she had commented on his appearance. He heard the undertone of concern. As he walked home alone, mulling over his performance, he considered leaving the drama group.

In the end he decided against it. Instead, he volunteered to look after the group's entire wardrobe. His grandmother had loads of space where it could be stored until needed again. His offer was gratefully accepted. That night, as he walked back to his grandmother's, he mulled over his role and decided to audition for a male role in their play next year. Perhaps that would deflect anyone from thinking about their comments. Perhaps they had meant nothing more than a compliment to his acting ability, but he didn't want to risk it. Crossdressing was a dangerous pastime, and he didn't want his name associated with it. His grandmother would be apoplectic. Besides, now he was storing the wardrobe, he could dress in the privacy of his own room any time he felt like it. He couldn't stop the little glow of happiness that spread from his stomach to his head, and he smiled into the darkness.

He had a lot to look forward to this summer. The term would end within the next few weeks, and Charles would be home the month after. He had lots to talk to Charles about on his visit home. Charles was to return to Glassdrumman Hall in August for two weeks, and James was looking forward to his annual visit. It had been a year since they had seen each other, although their weekly letters kept them up to date. He missed Charles, and he missed Glassdrumman Hall.

Chapter 21

Charles

Charles Best stood on the platform as the train from Dublin pulled into the station in a smoky haze. He had ridden out in the carriage from Glassdrumman Hall to collect James, unable to contain himself at home until he met his friend again. The steam from the engine engulfed the platform as the doors opened, and Charles strained to see the passengers disembark. At the other end of the platform, he saw a tall figure striding towards him with an air of confidence about him that made Charles look twice. It was his hair he recognised first. That auburn mane was as flamboyant as ever, but everything else about James had grown up. Charles grasped the outstretched hand and shook it vigorously.

"James, you are looking well, old boy."

James's smile stretched from ear to ear as he shook his friend's hand and clapped him on the back. Charles felt the strength in his grip and the pleasure in James's voice.

"Let's get out of here. Glassdrumman, here we come."

By the time they reached the estate, they were as at ease with each other as if they hadn't spent the last year apart. Their friendship forged over five years of boarding school reblossomed in minutes. At dinner that night, Mrs Best listened to James's recanting of Dublin society with rapt attention. He told stories of his drama group and the fun they had with the play. He told stories of dinner parties and soirées and described in detail the apparel and latest styles of the upper echelons of Dublin society. Mrs Best was enthralled. Colonel Best was amused. Charles listened, amazed by his friend's bonhomie.

The next day dawned bright and warm, the perfect day for the annual cricket match. Charles and James were both playing for the Hall and looking forward to it.

"I haven't played since I left Ireland. I think I may be quite rusty." Charles laughed.

"Not to worry. I'm on the college team, so my skills have improved considerably. Do you remember the very first year I played? I couldn't even hold the bat."

Charles laughed. "You had no clue about the rules. Now here you are years later, playing for one of the most prestigious colleges in the British Isles."

The Glassdrumman Hall team won by a comfortable margin, significantly aided by James's abilities on the field. Charles felt a slight tinge of jealousy as his teammates crowded around James, clapping him on the back and congratulating him, but that turned swiftly to pride at his friend's achievements. On their return to the grounds of the house, they changed quickly and returned to the front lawns, where the fête was in full swing. Crowds thronged the various tents nibbling on watercress sandwiches, smoked salmon and devilled eggs. Local girls hired for the day walked through the crowds with jugs of fresh lemonade. Charles spotted Amanda as soon as she arrived, and nudged James. She looked beautiful in her white dress and summer boots as she delicately picked her way across the lawn to greet them.

"Charles, how lovely to see you." She presented her hand for his kiss. Charles held on to it for as long as he dared.

Thanks to the letters they had exchanged for the last year, he had grown extremely fond of her. James hugged Amanda like the old friend she was and demanded to know what she had been up to for the past year. Charles couldn't take his eyes off her. He fancied she kept stealing glances at him. The three friends found a bench on the corner of the lawn and sat gossiping like old women for the rest of the afternoon. James volunteered to bring plates of food for them and excused himself with a wink to Charles. Alone, at last, Charles was suddenly nervous.

"Your letters have been wonderful," he said, looking down into her eyes. He had forgotten how dark they were, like bottomless pools.

"Yours too. I treasured each one."

Amanda coyly lowered her gaze and played with a blade of grass in front of her.

"I really enjoyed hearing about England and your life there."

She looked at him and smiled, and he felt his heart miss a beat. They chatted back and forth, exchanging smiles and glances that convinced Charles that perhaps Amanda could feel the same way about him as he felt about her. James returned with plates of food and left again for water and lemonade. Charles and Amanda were surprised to note the sun beginning its decline when James returned sometime later. Amanda's cousins also approached them. They had been sent to fetch her by her aunt, who had been watching the young couple from her viewpoint in a tent on the far side of the lawn.

That night as they sat under the stars on the back veranda, Charles told James he thought he was in love with Amanda. He was taken aback when James burst out laughing.

"I could have told you that. You two have been dancing around each other for years. She is the one for you."

"But what if she doesn't feel the same way, James?"

"She does, believe me, she does. Amanda spent all afternoon with you. She didn't take her eyes off you for a second."

Charles paced up and down the veranda, his thoughts whirring in his head. He had one more year to complete his officer's training, but after that, he could be posted anywhere in the world. Would Amanda be willing to marry someone who couldn't commit to living in Ireland on a permanent basis? He shared his concerns with James.

"She has been brought up in a military family, Charles. Sure, isn't her father a soldier? Isn't that why she spends her summers in County Down? She understands the military way of life."

"Yes, but what if she doesn't want that for herself? Do you remember, years ago, she complained she hadn't seen her father in over six months? She said it wasn't a life for a family."

"She was a child then and besides, you are no ordinary soldier. You are the heir to this estate, and that is something solid, something every woman in the parish and beyond is aware of. You, my man, are what's known in society circles as quite the catch."

Charles laughed at his friend's description and conceded that perhaps he was right.

"But what do I do now? Do I declare myself, or do I wait until my training is complete and I get my posting?"

"I don't know. I can't advise you there. But the one thing I will say is to do what you feel is right. You will know when the time is right for you and Amanda."

The two men retired to their rooms, each thinking about their future.

Chapter 22

James

James returned to Dublin and back to his second year in medical school. He studied hard, but he made sure to leave time for socialising. The drama group met on the second week and started planning for their next production. This year James was playing a hard gambler and a womaniser. He was looking forward to the role. The group started investing in new costumes, which James brought back to his grandmother's for storage until they were needed for the dress rehearsal.

On Thursday evenings, James got into the habit of staying home. His grandmother played bridge at a friend's house, leaving shortly after dinner and returning three hours later, tired and topped up with sherry. James looked forward to those evenings. His grandmother had kindly allocated a spare room to store the drama group's wardrobe. The room was down the hall from his own bedroom. He started checking the costumes for signs of moth infestation or mould on the pretence of essential maintenance. One evening, he couldn't resist trying on the green velvet. Slipping into the dress, he caressed the soft velvet as it touched his skin. He held his hair back as if it was combed into a clasp and admired how it felt.

Swinging back and forward, he felt the swish of the fabric against his ankle and the pull on his hips. He loved how it made him feel. The next Thursday night, he locked the door and spent some time dressing in his favourite green velvet gown again and styling his hair with a pearl clasp. He looked in the mirror and liked what he saw. Then it hit him. He didn't feel like a man dressed as a woman. He felt like a woman.

For the next few days, he was haunted with memories of how comfortable he felt in women's clothing and fear of what that said about him. He swore he would never do it again, but the following Thursday night, he couldn't stay away. As soon as his grandmother left the house, he crept down the corridor and turned the key in the door. The green velvet gown beckoned, and he caressed it lovingly before donning it. He fastened his hair with a silver comb and looked at his reflection in the full-length mirror from every angle, admiring the curve of his neck and the sweep of the gown as it tickled his ankles. He imagined himself at society gatherings in his female persona, smiling, conversing, living the perfect life. James became so caught up in his fantasy that he was surprised to hear the sound of his grandmama returning. He checked the door remained locked, sat back and listened until the house fell silent again. With a sigh, he removed the silver comb, hung the dress back on its padded hanger and returned to his room.

That night he slept fitfully. He woke early and left before his grandmother rose. It was a busy day in college with lectures, but he had trouble concentrating. Halfway through the morning, he was called out of his lecture by a harassed-looking professor who instructed him to go straight to the provost's office. James was puzzled and a little scared. Had they somehow found out he liked women's clothing? Had someone from the drama group said something? He knocked on the door and waited, fear causing him to sweat under his oxters and at the nape of his neck. Finally, the door opened, and the provost led him inside.

Afterwards, he couldn't recall precisely what was said. His only memory was that he was bowled over by grief. His precious grandmother was dead. She had died in her sleep, alone in her bed while he tossed and turned only yards away. It was her lady's maid who found her when she brought her tea tray upstairs at ten thirty, the same time she brought her tea tray every Friday morning. James couldn't remember walking through the front gates of Trinity College. He couldn't remember the short walk to his grandmother's home through the city streets. His next memory was seeing his grandmother's corpse laid out the following day. Her chalky face was like a plaster shell of her former self, her eyes held shut by pennies. James felt cold and a deep pain in his chest weighed him down and threatened to buckle his knees from under him. He couldn't concentrate. He could see people's lips moving as they spoke to him through a thick fog. They were offering their condolences, and he knew he answered them, if a curt thank you was an answer.

His father clapped him on the back and offered his hand. James accepted it without comment and moved away. He could feel his father's eyes on him but continued to ignore him, concentrating instead on speaking to the minister about the service. He wasn't surprised to learn his grandmother had left detailed instructions on her funeral arrangements and he was actually quite relieved. He was even more relieved when Charles's arrival was announced. James rushed to the door, hand out to accept his friend's hearty handshake and commiserations, grateful for his support.

"Thanks for coming, Charles. I know grandmama left instructions, but I want to ensure her funeral is done properly. Grandpapa died long before we were born, and she practically brought up Mother single-handedly. Then when she died, well, my poor grandmama. We were all she had left."

James felt the weight of his grandmother's expectations and gratitude for the life she had given him. James knew he and his sister would have had vastly different lives without his grandmother's interference.

"Chin up. I'm here now. Tell me what you need."

James was grateful for Charles's support and, with his help, got through the funeral arrangements. Writing the eulogy was the hardest part for him. He struggled to find the right words to describe his grandmother, to put into words how much he had loved her.

"It was unbelievable the difference she made to that house. We counted the days between each visit. The Christmas ones were the hardest. Even though she loved our mother or maybe because she had loved her, she made sure that we had our presents from Father Christmas. She made sure we felt loved. My father drank himself into oblivion in the run-up to New Year's Eve. He absented himself from our lives as if he blamed us for her death."

James hung his head, wringing his hands as grief swept over him. He felt Charles's arm across his shoulder and the silent support he offered.

"It was grandmama who organised a tutor for me, who sent me to the Dundalk Institute, who paid my fees in Trinity. Without her, I have nothing."

James didn't care who saw him cry. The fat tears plopped off his face onto his hands which appeared to take on a life of their own, twisting and turning together. As he looked down on them, they looked to him like his grandmother's hands, and he took strange comfort in that. A shadow fell over them, and he felt his father's rage before he lifted his head. David Langton stood over them, his eyes aflame. He leant over and whispered in James's ear in a clipped voice as cold as the Atlantic in January.

"Stand up, boy. Behave like a man."

James obeyed, wiping his sodden cheeks with the handkerchief Charles hastily provided. He felt sick and started to waver, suddenly dizzy. His father looked at him from under his bushy eyebrows in a manner James knew meant *you better not.* So, James pulled himself upright, shook his head to dispel the lightness and promptly lost consciousness. When he woke up, Charles was beside him and helped him to his feet while his father stood over him, quivering, his displeasure written in every line in his face.

"I suggest you retire. Tomorrow will be a long day. I will see to the eulogy." David Langton held his hand out for the notes James had written. James handed them over without comment. He knew there was no point. If his father had decided he would do the eulogy, then that is what would happen. James knew better than to argue.

"I didn't want to do it anyway," James said, as he left the room and made his way upstairs. He locked his door and sank onto the bed, allowing his grief to wash over him. A knock on the door stifled his cries.

"James, it's me, Charles. Let me in."

"Leave me be. I just need some time alone."

"But James."

"Please, Charles. Call on me in the morning."

He heard Charles's footsteps move away from the door and succumbed to his grief once again, crying until he could cry no more and fell into a deep, troubled sleep. In his dreams that night his grandmother was dressed in a green velvet gown, her silver hair held back in a clasp the same colour. She scolded him, her finger wagging at him, saying, "I am so disappointed in you, James." He woke with a start and looked around him, then opened the curtains to reveal a dull, damp day. The clouds hung tiredly as if unable to lift themselves over the rooftops. The banging on his door made him jump. He opened it, allowing Charles to enter the room.

"I said I would call you for breakfast. Come on, get washed there, old boy, and meet me downstairs in five."

James forced himself to go through the motions. He ate, and he drank, and he spoke when spoken to, but he studiously avoided his father. James was conscious of Charles beside him and was grateful beyond words for his presence, especially at the graveside. He sat through the funeral service in a daze, hearing nothing, and focused only on the ornate oak coffin placed in front of the altar. He felt Charles's support and his father's disapproval as they followed the hearse on the short walk to his grandmother's final resting place. Finally, the heavy clouds could no longer hold their load, and they emptied. Sheets of grey coldness lashed across the graveyard and danced in the mud around the open grave. The minister's final words were drowned out by the explosions of rain beating off the sizeable black umbrella his assistant held over him. James stepped forward and stared into the grave as the first shovel of soil landed on top of the coffin. The icy rain stabbed his head and face like tiny needles piercing his skin. The assembled mourners started to move away, anxious to find shelter from the biting wind and rain. He felt a tug on his sleeve and turned. Charles held his umbrella over him and his hand out to guide him back to the path and out of the weather. James nodded and followed his friend.

The rest of the day was a blur. The funeral party retired to his grandmother's home for refreshments and milled around, speaking in muted tones of her warmth and her strength of character. James accepted their condolences over tea and sandwiches, with Charles constantly by his side. He kept an eye on his father's whereabouts and purposely moved from room to room to avoid being in close proximity to him, but he couldn't avoid him altogether.

"Well, James. I am sure your grandmother has left you well provided for. So, knuckle down to your studies. You are needed in Greenore."

James felt a sudden surge of anger.

"Why, Father? Why would you want me back in Greenore when you can't stand to look at me?"

David Langton stared back at him, his watery eyes half closed under dark-grey eyebrows, his voice a guttural growl.

"You will do as you are bid, boy."

James took a step towards him, fists clenched and anger rushing in his ears, deafening him to the silence that had engulfed the room. Charles deftly stepped between them.

"Gentlemen, this is neither the time nor the place. James, I believe you are wanted in the drawing room." The fog lifted from James's eyes, leaving him trembling with suppressed rage. Flashing a look of pure hatred towards the man he called Father he allowed Charles to lead him away. His anger deflated as he left the room, his heart beating in his throat, choking him. His chest hurt, and he struggled for breath. They got to the corridor leading to the servants' quarters out of sight of his guests, before James bent over, clutching his chest. He felt Charles's arm on his and allowed him to lead him down the corridor and out the doorway into the kitchen garden. There, in the midst of the herbs, his breathing gradually returned to normal. The rain had stopped, leaving the night air cold and damp. Puddles floated under their feet, soaking their already wet shoes. Charles lit a cigar and handed it to James before lighting one for himself. The two men stood in companionable silence, the acrid smoke billowing around them in the dark. James coughed and then took another drag, wallowing in the peppery taste on his tongue.

"I loved her, Charles." James looked down at the puddle beneath his feet.

"I know, old boy, I know." Charles nodded and puffed again on his cigar.

The back door opened, and the light spilt out into the yard.

"Pardon me, sir, but the minister is leaving, and he would like a word."

James dropped the remnants of his cigar into the puddle and smiled as the red glow extinguished in seconds.

"Pity I couldn't extinguish my feelings about my father that easily," he said, patting Charles's shoulder as he made his way inside to speak to the minister.

The next day James wandered from room to room, feeling the emptiness. Charles had left early to catch the first boat to England. His father left shortly afterwards without a word. James couldn't face going back to college. Not yet anyhow. He knew he needed to talk to Jane, but he couldn't face that yet either.

Chapter 23

Charles's Proposal

THE COMMISSIONING CEREMONY WAS A DAY OF GREAT POMP. Colonel Best was resplendent in his dress uniform. He wasn't alone. There was a preponderance of dress uniforms, with most of the fathers of the young newly commissioned officers still serving and a few like Colonel Best long retired. Charles was conscious of his parents watching him intently as he and his fellow cadets finished their elaborate foot drill. When the ceremony was completed, and his ceremonial sword was back in its case, Charles rejoined his family.

"Well done, son." The Colonel shook his son's hand.

"Yes, well done, Charles. You look resplendent in your uniform." Lady Best beamed at her son, her eyes sparkling with unshed tears.

Charles felt the weight of his parents' expectations, but he shrugged his feelings aside and revelled in their approval. It was worth it to see his father's obvious pride and his mother's beaming joy as she nodded approvingly at his uniform. They were dining in the officers' mess that evening, and he was looking forward to it.

"Did you get your posting yet?" the Colonel inquired.

"Yes, sir. We are shipping out to British Natal in a few months. I have a few days' leave before I join my unit in Southampton, so with your permission, I might travel home with you tomorrow."

"Africa. How exciting." Lady Best checked her gloves. "I believe only the finest diamonds come from there."

"Perhaps I shall bring you one back, Mother."

Lady Best laughed as she slipped her gloved hand through her son's arm, and they commenced the short walk to the evening festivities. Charles was looking forward to getting back to Glassdrumman Hall, and more importantly to seeing Amanda again. Her last letter had arrived only the day before, informing him she would be staying with her cousins for a few days. The timing was perfect, he thought. It was as if it was meant to be.

"Did I mention I have been in touch with Amanda?"

His mother's rapt expression told him everything he needed to know.

"We have become quite good friends, and I am thinking of speaking to her father." Charles felt his face colour as he waited on his parents' reaction. He should not have been concerned. His father shook his hand vigorously.

"Lovely young woman. Her father is on the school board, you know. Yes, yes, good family. I must say, Charles, I am most impressed."

Lady Best leaned towards him and kissed him on his cheek.

"I am delighted. Amanda is a smart choice of a wife for a young officer. She is a lovely girl. I'm just surprised it has taken you so long. You two were made for each other."

Charles was elated. This was the best day ever. The only cloud on his horizon was the absence of James. He wondered where his friend could be. He hadn't heard from him in six months. The last communication he had with James was a month after his grandmother had died. She had left everything to him, her house and sufficient income for him to continue his studies. James had been happy, or so he thought, but shortly after that, James had disappeared. The house was locked up, the staff paid off, and James dropped out of college. Charles was worried about him. He had made inquiries, but he hadn't been able to locate him. Charles continued to write, hoping somehow one of his letters would find him. The letters were never returned, but he never received a reply.

He put all thoughts of James aside the following night when they arrived back to Glassdrumman Hall. His priority over the next few days was Amanda. He wanted an answer from her before he set sail for Africa. They could plan a wedding for his return in two years. After breakfast, before he set off to call on Amanda, his mother called him into the library. She sat before her writing bureau.

"Charles, I just wanted to tell you how proud your father and I are of you. We do realise you may have gone into the military more out of a sense of duty than any deep desire to serve, but you will make a good officer. You have grown into a fine young man."

Charles was touched by his mother's words.

"Let's just hope Amanda agrees with you, Mother."

"Oh, I think she will, my son. I want you to give her this."

Charles accepted the oval velvet box from his mother.

Curious, he opened it. Inside was a gold band studded with three small sapphires. It was delicate and pretty and looked as if it were meant for Amanda's hand.

"It was my promise ring. Your father gave it to me when we became betrothed, and I wore it until he bought my engagement ring. He went away to serve his country just as you are, and we wanted to pledge our troth before our official engagement. So, I suppose what I'm trying to say to you is I would be honoured if Amanda wore it."

Charles kissed his mother's cheek, suddenly humbled by his

mother's gesture. He closed the box carefully and placed it in his inside pocket.

"It is beside my heart, Mother. Thank you."

"Now go."

Lady Best turned back to her writing bureau. Charles bade his leave, filled with confidence and suddenly overcome with the need to see Amanda. He loved her; he was sure of that. She was perfect for him.

One look at Amanda's face as he entered the drawing room told him everything he needed to know. His delight at seeing her was mirrored in her eyes. He kissed her hand and shook hands with her parents under the watchful eye of her aunt, a staunch supporter of Charles and Amanda. Over dinner, he charmed them with stories of life as a young officer and his plans for Glassdrumman Hall. Then, over cigars and cognac, he sought out the company of Amanda's father and asked for his daughter's hand in marriage.

"My boy, I thought you would never ask."

There was handshaking and backslapping, and Charles felt as if his face would break open with the breadth of his smile. The next day he called before lunch and met with Amanda in the drawing room. Even with her father's approval, he suddenly felt apprehensive, nervous she would refuse him. Amanda was quiet, staring out the window towards the lawns, her fingers intertwined in front of her. She turned as he entered, the window framing her in sunlight. He swallowed as his mind blanked, and he stumbled forward as if he had tripped over some unseen obstacle.

"Charles, whatever is the matter?"

He strode over to her and took her delicate hands in his. He looked down into her eyes, and as he saw the dawning realisation on her face, he made his decision and bent down on one knee.

"Amanda, will you do me the honour of becoming my wife?"

The rest of the afternoon went by in a blur for him. Amanda's definite yes was drowned out by his whoop of delight, which summoned the remainder of the family who delighted in the news. Champagne was popped, and plans were made. Amanda was thrilled and overcome with emotion when Charles gave her the promise ring. As he put it on her finger, he promised her he would buy her the finest diamond he could find in Africa.

"All I need is for you to return to me, my love."

Charles felt the happiest he had ever been. He had three more days before he had to return to England and those days were full. His parents invited all of Amanda's family to a shoot the following day and dinner that evening to celebrate the engagement.

Little did he know what lay ahead.

Chapter 24

Charles

Even the dull and dreary weather couldn't put a damper on Charles's spirits as he prepared for the shoot. The mountains were hidden behind a low cloud which hung over the estate with no break on the horizon. The weather didn't influence the shoot. There were ten men taking part, all experienced, most either serving or ex-military, including Amanda's father. The ladies saw the men off then retired to the drawing room to discuss wedding plans. Charles waved goodbye to Amanda and followed his father and the other men to the chosen location on the estate. There had been numerous shoots hosted in Glassdrumman Estate over the years and this one was not exceptional in any way. The participants chatted leisurely about the current situation in South Africa and in India and the idea of Home Rule in Ireland.

The shoot started uneventfully. Loud bangs by the groundsmen rustled the grouse out of their hiding places. As they rose in the air squawking their disapproval a volley of shots rang out with varying results dependent on the skill of the shooter. The men claimed their spoils, congratulating each other on their fine shot. The bonhomie turned to shock and horror as, in turn, their attention was drawn to the body on the ground. Silence descended as they took in the sight before them one by one. A gaping hole rapidly filling with blood covered the Colonel's chest. His eyes were open and staring. His gun lay in pieces around him. Charles ran to his father and knelt beside him, shocked into silence. He could hear the murmurs.

"A misfire."

"The bloody thing exploded."

Charles felt a hand on his shoulder and allowed himself to be led away. His legs felt like lead, his brain numb. He spread his hands out in front of him, shocked to see them stained with his father's blood. He gratefully accepted the thimble of brandy offered, the hot liquid burning its way down his throat and setting his insides on fire. The vision of his father's bloody body was imprinted on his brain, and he shook his head to dispel it. He heard Arthur the gilly instruct the boys to gather up the rifles and return them to the cart. Slowly the cotton wool in his head cleared.

Charles took a deep breath and assumed the mantel of leadership he was born to. It was his responsibility first and foremost to inform his mother. Arthur understood without being told and led his horse to him. Charles and Arthur rode back to Glassdrumman Hall, leaving instructions on the removal of his father's body. Arthur went to stable the horses as Charles made his way inside. He opened the door to the library and slowly moved to where his mother sat, at her desk at the open window.

"Charles?"

Charles saw the confusion on his mother's face, heard the unspoken question in her voice. He knelt in front of her and took her hand in his. He could see the fear in her eyes and closed his.

"It's Father. He is dead."

The rest of the week passed in a blur for Charles. The death of Colonel Best came as a shock to the whole community. He had been a popular landlord with a reputation for fairness and good management. Charles supported his mother as best he could but also felt the weight of his inheritance on him. On his father's death, Charles became Master of the Estate with all the responsibilities that entailed. Amanda and her family were of great assistance, and he was grateful to her and thankful for her support. He missed James dreadfully. There was no word from him. Charles sent a telegram to his Dublin address expecting James to arrive on the next train. There was no reply. The papers had all reported his father's death, but there was silence from James.

"I don't understand it, Amanda. James Langton is my best friend in the world. My father treated him like a son. Where can he be?"

When it came time for Charles to return to England after his extended leave period, he was reluctant to leave his mother alone and was grateful to Amanda who offered to stay at Glassdrumman Hall to keep her company. Lady Best would have none of it.

"I am not some frail little old lady who needs assistance. I may be heartbroken, but I am not senile. Charles, you need to get back to your unit and Amanda, while I appreciate your offer, you do need to get back to your own home. You have wedding plans to make."

Charles relented. With a sinking heart, he said his goodbyes to his mother and to his fiancée before setting sail for England and back to his unit.

Act 3

Chapter 25

Agnes and the Nightingales, 1878

Agnes was so excited she could barely breathe. It had taken all her powers of persuasion to get her father to agree to send her to the Florence Nightingale School of Nursing. Since she was a small child, she had been enamoured by the story of Florence Nightingale. At night she dreamed of administering to wounded soldiers. Agnes could visualise herself smiling sweetly by lamplight as she mopped their brows and uttered assurances to them. She couldn't wait to begin training. Unpacking her belongings into the small bedside locker, she looked around her dormitory. Four beds lined up against each other on opposing walls, each with a locker. Propped against the middle wall sat a wardrobe with the door open and four hangers just waiting to hold their uniforms. Beside the wardrobe, a dresser held a large jug and washing bowl in pale blue, the only colour in the spartan room.

Agnes was unprepared for the burst of energy that filled the quiet room as the door opened. In front of her stood the liveliest creature she had ever seen. She was the same height as Agnes, which was taller than most women, with broad shoulders and a determined tilt to her chin. Her chestnut hair appeared to be fighting its way out of its clasps, and her eyes danced with devilment or merriment. Agnes wasn't quite sure which. She dropped her bag at the door where she stood and looked around her.

"Hello, I'm Emma Durham. Dear me, this room is a bit grim," she said with a grin.

"Agnes Rickman, pleased to meet you."

Emma flung herself on the bed beside Agnes and groaned.

"Agh, they don't believe in comfort here, do they? This mattress has seen better days."

They both jumped at the sound of a yelp and a clatter and turned to see two young women in a heap on the floor, having fallen over Emma's abandoned bag.

"Oh my, I am so sorry." Emma leapt up to help. "I just dropped my bag without thought. Are you hurt?"

"Well, if I am, I have come to the right place."

The women laughed as Emma helped them to their feet and introduced herself.

"Yvonne Horner, pleased to meet you, and this is my friend Mary Armfield."

The four women chatted as they unpacked. Agnes was thrilled to meet three like-minded people, feeling as if she had finally found her place in the world. Her father, a successful merchant, had vague notions of marrying her off, preferably to the landed gentry, but wasn't surprised when she told him of her ambitions. Her mother had encouraged her, expressing her pride in her youngest daughter's calling. Her older sister had been supportive, and it was her intercession that eventually won their father over. So here she was, eager to start, sharing a room with these three women, confident she would become the best nurse ever to graduate from St. Thomas'.

That evening they met the other students, thirty in all, who all had ambitions to become nurses. Agnes was fascinated. In her sheltered upbringing, she hadn't realised how many other young girls had been inspired by the story of Florence Nightingale. They were from all walks of life. Many were not unlike herself in that they had a middle-class upbringing. Others were of the upper classes, women who had reasonable expectations of marriage and an excellent standard of living but had shunned that way of life in favour of nursing. The lower classes were also represented. These women saw nursing as a way of escaping from poverty or servitude. During a discussion in the nurses' lounge, Emma summed it up for Agnes and the other young women.

"At the end of the day, we are all here to learn, to train, to be the best that we can be. If a man can have ambition, why can't we, as women? Florence Nightingale has made an enormous contribution to the medical profession. We can do the same if we put our minds to it."

"Yes, but Emma, if a handsome young man swept you off your feet and was financially in a position to keep you, surely you would choose him over nursing. As women, we cannot have careers. Surely the idea is to meet someone who will care for you and who you care for?" Yvonne hoped to meet a dashing captain and live in India or some other far-flung place in the Empire.

"Ideally, yes, maybe there is someone for everyone but, ladies, what if you never meet your Mr Right? What if he doesn't exist? Do you depend on another person for your happiness, for your personal fulfilment? Or do you find your own niche in life?"

Agnes nodded her agreement. After listening to the stories of some of her fellow trainees, she was grateful to her mother for her insistence her daughters receive an education. For the first time, she realised how radical her mother was in her quiet way. Most of the women had been taught little beyond reading, writing, simple arithmetic and needlework, the skills required to run a household. Agnes and her sister had been taught algebra and geology, geography, history and the languages French and Latin. She felt privileged and was happy to share her knowledge with the others in their spare time in the nurses' lounge.

Over the next year, Agnes worked hard. She soaked up everything she was taught and, in her free time, pored over medical journals and periodicals in the nurses' lounge. It was a busy time, and the months flew by. Agnes looked forward to graduation but was even more excited at the prospect of her interview with her hero. Every student was interviewed by Miss Florence Nightingale in person before final certification. Like her fellow trainees, Agnes was nervous, aware this interview could make or break her career. Miss Nightingale lived in a flat on South Street in Mayfair. She had a hands-on approach to the training school set up in her name and personally vetted the students regardless of her own ill-health.

"Imagine, tomorrow we meet Florence Nightingale, the Lady with the Lamp."

Yvonne's awestruck whisper sent a shiver of anticipation through Agnes.

"What if I get so overwhelmed, I cannot speak?"

Emma blew out her cheeks and shook her head. "Not a good idea. The Lady with the Lamp may be an invalid, but she is as sharp as a tack. If you don't impress her, she may oppose your certification."

Agnes shivered. "But she must be a compassionate woman… otherwise, how could she have earned the respect she commands? She wants us to finish our training. She wants her nurses out in the world, promoting her good work. This is my bible." She showed Emma her copy of Miss Nightingale's book, *Notes on Nursing*. "I think I know every word by heart, yet I still read it. It reminds me of why we are here, the reasons we have been inspired by her."

The following day, as Agnes sat in the same room as her

hero, she tried valiantly to follow her own advice. She could feel her insides shaking, but her voice was steady as she answered Miss Nightingale's questions, who sat opposite her on a hard-backed chair with her notebook in her hands. Agnes never took her eyes from Miss Nightingale's face, which in Agnes's view, showed her personality traits. There was a kindness in her eyes, a warmth which told of her compassion and gave comfort, balanced by the tightness of determination across her lips, a steely line that portrayed her strong will. Agnes was in awe of this woman, now approaching her sixties. Miss Nightingale had made such an impact on the world, not only in nursing but as a statistician, and she now sat in front of her and spoke to her of what she could accomplish if she put her mind to it. Agnes left the room inspired.

The class of 1878 received their certification a few days later. They had a week free before taking up their posts. Agnes and her colleagues were all assigned to St. Thomas' and were eager to start. Her father had sent his carriage to collect her, and she made her way across the city to her home with her certificate safely stored in her bag. Her mother was sitting in the parlour, her needlework in her hands. She leapt out of her seat, spilling thread onto the polished parquet floor, and hugged her youngest daughter to her.

"I am so proud of you, my darling. Come, sit and tell me all about Miss Nightingale."

Agnes basked in the sunshine of her mother's approval as she led her to the couch by the fire. The next hour flew by as she relived her training, describing the other trainees, the hospital and her meeting with Florence Nightingale. As Agnes talked, her mother sat beside her, probing, listening, and occasionally laughing. When she spoke about her encounter with Miss Nightingale, her mother sat up straight, wide-eyed and wrapped Agnes's hand in hers.

"Oh, Agnes, how wonderful," she said in a choked voice

with a bright sparkle in her eyes. "To meet someone so special must have been wonderful."

Agnes nodded. "It was, Mother, it was. I was so nervous, I thought I might not be able to speak, that I would open my mouth and no words would come out, or worse still, that I would speak complete gibberish. But she put me at ease. She was so inspiring. I just hope I can live up to her faith in me."

"You will, my dear, you will." Her mother looked into her eyes. "You have grown into an amazing young woman. Your father and I are so proud of you."

Agnes beamed at her mother. She could feel her happiness bubbling out of her and filling the room. The door opened, and her father walked in.

"Welcome home, my pet, and congratulations."

Agnes raised her cheek for her father's kiss before the conversation returned to the achievements of Miss Nightingale. Agnes was surprised by her father's knowledge.

"My daughter wants to follow in the footsteps of Miss Nightingale, so I made it my business to find out everything I could about her. I am very proud of you, my dear. Well done." Mr Rickman raised a glass to his daughter.

Chapter 26

Agnes

Agnes loved the hustle and bustle of St. Thomas' Hospital. It perched on the banks of the Thames in the heart of the city. Recently built, it was a testament to the influence of Miss Nightingale, for it was she who'd advised on the design. Seven large separate buildings were connected by walkways, fully utilising space and light. The wards had full-length windows at specified intervals, with the beds set between to encourage good ventilation. Each ward had individual washing and sanitary facilities separate from the kitchen and linen storage.

Agnes was assigned her room in the nurses' quarters and set about making it as homely as possible. She brought her writing desk and books from home and rearranged the few pieces of furniture, placing the desk in front of the garret window to get the most of what little light managed to creep in. Emma was in the next room with Yvonne and Mary just down the hall. They worked hard on their shifts and on their time off, caught up on sleep and reading, and found time to venture to the theatre. Once a month, Agnes travelled home to her parents' house and filled them in on her adventures. Her mother lapped up all the details while her father merely inquired if she had met any handsome doctors yet who might sweep her off her feet. While Agnes was aware of the young doctors in training in St. Thomas', she had yet to meet one who held any appeal for her.

She was enjoying her work at St. Thomas'. Sometimes it could be difficult dealing with some very tragic cases, but nothing prepared her for the horror of the influx of victims from the sinking of the SS *Princess Alice* in the River Thames. Over one hundred survivors: men, women and children arrived into the care of the hospital with a myriad of complaints, ranging from broken limbs, cuts and bruises to severe infections.

"The bodies are lined up; the morgues cannot cope. Hundreds of bodies with many hundreds more still in the water," Emma told her as they compared notes. "The pollution in the Thames caused horrific damage to some of the bodies."

"Those poor people," Agnes said. "Oh, Emma, it could have been us. We were on the same ferry only last week."

"And it was such a lovely day too. God rest their souls."

The women fell into bed, exhausted by the events of the day but painfully aware they were needed back on the wards by sunrise. The ward Agnes was assigned to was full of women of all ages. One elderly lady was very poorly, and Agnes made sure to check on her regularly, feeding her sips of water and mopping her face and hands. An infection from the sewerage-laden waters took its toll on her, and she was getting weaker by the hour. Agnes spoke to the woman as she tended to her. She told her about the climbing roses which scrambled on the archway outside the window of the ward, the sweet fragrance masking the stink of the Thames. She felt a shadow fall over her and looked up, startled, into the eyes of the most handsome man she had ever seen. He was resplendent in red, his collar buttoned right up to his strong chin. His full lips were partially covered by a neatly trimmed moustache, and he had a tousle of fair hair. His startling blue eyes clouded as he bent over the ailing patient.

"Mother, it's me. It's Matthew."

"She has been asking for you. Would you like to sit here with her, mop her brow? The coolness may help with her fever," Agnes said.

She settled the young man beside his mother and returned to her other patients. Agnes was grateful for her training in the hours that followed. Each of her charges was sick with fever. She moved from bed to bed, administering as best she could. St. Thomas' was a modern hospital designed to prevent the spread of infections and practised the very latest nursing techniques as advised by Miss Florence Nightingale. But all of that wasn't enough to save some of their patients, particularly the elderly. Several died before Agnes's shift was over. Those who died were the old and infirm and those who had been in the water longer. Their bodies were moved to a makeshift morgue, and their beds were scrubbed, remade and filled with more victims of the disaster. That night Agnes fell into bed exhausted from her efforts only to rise a few short hours later to return to the ward. Matthew had remained at his mother's side, who was showing signs of improvement.

"Oh well done, Matthew. I do not doubt that you have inexorably aided your mother's recovery."

Agnes smiled at him as she checked her patient, relieved to see her temperature falling and her breathing returning to normal.

By the end of her shift Agnes ached from head to toe. But there was reason to be grateful. No more deaths. All her patients showed signs of improvement. She felt the horror of the last two days recede, and the first stirring of hope lifted her heart. The handsome young soldier had left earlier in the day but arrived back just as Agnes was leaving the ward.

"Nurse, I am so glad I caught you. Will you allow me to escort you?" He bowed, and she blushed.

"Why certainly, sir, but I am not going very far."

Matthew walked her the short distance to the other side of the hospital grounds, and they found out they had a lot in common. Matthew was a doctor in Netley's Royal Victoria Military Hospital near Southampton. They talked about the disaster and the horror of the hundreds of people who had died. Matthew told her all about his mother, a widow who was recovering from her ordeal and his father, who had been killed in the Crimean War. They tried to avoid talking about his impending posting to South Africa.

"Who will look after your mother?" Agnes asked.

"I am hoping she will be fully recovered before I leave. Although my aunt has offered to move in with my mother until I return."

Every day followed the same pattern. Agnes worked long, hard shifts and Matthew escorted her back to her quarters in the evenings. At night in her single bed, Agnes found herself dreaming of Matthew. She woke, remembering how his eyes crinkled around the edges when he laughed. She dreamed of how he ran his long fingers through his straw-like hair when he was distracted, leaving it standing straight up like a scarecrow. The other women had begun to tease her about her "beau", a charge she strenuously denied. But she found herself daydreaming about him, imagining how it would feel to hold his soft hands or kiss those full lips. Then she dismissed those thoughts as ridiculous fantasies unworthy of her and scolded herself for thinking like a silly débutante instead of the career nurse she saw herself as.

She talked it over with her mother on her next trip home.

"You must bring him to meet us, my dear." Mrs Rickman was insistent, so Matthew accompanied Agnes to her home to meet her parents the following week. Agnes didn't know what she wanted her parents to think of Matthew. Part of her hoped they would disapprove of him in some way, after all, he was a few years older than her. If her parents disapproved of the age difference, that would give her an excuse to have nothing more to do with him. Another part of her wanted them to see how wonderful he was. Matthew charmed them. He was kind and mannerly, telling witty stories about his military training and sweet anecdotes about his mother and her charity work in Southampton. Agnes was hooked, and her parents approved.

During their nightly strolls through the hospital grounds, they made plans. Agnes was fascinated by the idea of a military hospital and curious to see what Southampton might have to offer, so on her next day off, they travelled to Netley. The moment she saw the impressive red-brick building, she was enthralled. That evening, she arrived brim full of information for Emma, Yvonne and Mary. There were opportunities for nurses at Netley, which appealed to all four women. They all enjoyed their work in St. Thomas', but Netley would present a different set of challenges.

"And Matthew, where does he fit in?" Emma asked.

"Yes, Agnes, what about Matthew?" Yvonne and Mary chimed in.

"Matthew is a perfect gentleman." Agnes smiled. "He may work in the hospital, but he travels to South Africa soon for an extended tour of duty. My interest in Netley is purely to further my nursing career. Matthew is not a factor in that equation."

Agnes was indignant at the outbreak of laughter her comment brought but couldn't stop the smile that broke out, and she laughed with her new-found friends. They were right, she thought. While Matthew wasn't her only reason to relocate to Netley, he certainly was the reason for looking at Netley in the first place.

Chapter 27

Agnes

AGNES THOROUGHLY ENJOYED WORKING AT THE ROYAL Victoria Hospital in Netley. She felt it was what she had been trained to do. After all, Florence Nightingale had earned her reputation during the Crimean War nursing soldiers. Agnes felt she was finally doing what she was also born to do. The fact that she saw more of Matthew was an added bonus. She smiled as she spotted him from her vantage point at the window. She would recognise his walk anywhere. Long, confident steps, his head held high and his back straight. Even out of uniform, he had the bearing of a military man as he strode across the lawns in the direction of the hospital. He was such a gentleman. He insisted on escorting her and her friends to and from their quarters anytime he wasn't on duty. Some of their shifts were intertwined, so she got to work with him inside the hospital as well as socialise outside of working hours.

"I got my orders today. We ship next month."

Agnes searched Matthew's face for his usual smile but saw only anxiety.

"What is it, Matthew? You have been waiting for this. Why do you look so worried?"

Agnes was puzzled as Matthew turned away from her and paced up and down, running his fingers through his hair, his eyes downcast.

"What is it?" Agnes was worried now. She had never seen Matthew so agitated before. Even when his mother was ill in St. Thomas', he had been the epitome of calmness. On the most traumatic of days in Netley, he had never once shown any signs of anxiety, taking charge under pressure and leading by example. She couldn't believe her eyes when Matthew stopped pacing, looked at her and took her hand. She could feel his pulse racing but not as much as hers when he dropped down onto one knee with her hand still in his.

"Agnes, will you marry me?"

Agnes was dumbfounded. She felt her mouth open in shock and had to make a conscious effort to close it, like a dying fish in the Friday morning market at the docks. She laughed as that image flashed into her head and then watched his face freeze while his grip on her hand tightened. She smiled down at him.

"Oh, Matthew, yes, of course, yes."

Relief swept over Matthew's face followed by a beaming smile.

Sweeping her into his arms, he swung her off her feet. She squealed as he spun her around, holding her closer. The commotion caught the attention of those around them, and cheers reverberated together with rapturous applause as the news spread. The banns were read, and within three weeks, Agnes and Matthew Williams were set to marry in the military chapel in Netley. It all happened so quickly she didn't get time to think. Then, the night before the wedding, she voiced her niggling concerns to her mother.

"Do I love him enough, Mother? I know if I had to choose between nursing and Matthew, I would choose nursing."

"Agnes, I know you are scared, but Matthew is a good man.

He will not make you choose. Having said that, you must realise when you have children, you will feel differently. You will want to be a wife and mother. Being a mother is the most important position any woman can aspire to, and you will make a great one."

"But, Mother, my training, my career. I want to continue nursing. I am good at it. Matthew and I work well together. This has all happened so fast. Maybe we should have waited until after his return from the Cape, give us both some time to think."

"Oh, my darling girl. You are nervous. Every bride gets nervous before her wedding. Why, the morning of my wedding to your father, I practically begged my mother to call off the whole thing, but I didn't, and here we are, the sky didn't fall in, your father and I have been very happy."

Agnes tried to bury her reservations and get some sleep. She dreamed of travelling with Matthew to some far-flung corner of the world, in Africa maybe or China. They could set up a small hospital, administering to the locals, fulfilling her dreams of being a second Florence Nightingale. She woke refreshed and eager to start her new life as Mrs Agnes Williams. Her dress was hanging in front of the mirror. The early morning light shone through the window, illuminating the delicate Carrickmacross lace. Originally her sister's wedding dress, it was adjusted to suit her frame by her mother's dressmaker. She couldn't wait to put it on and walk down the aisle to Matthew.

Matthew was resplendent in full dress uniform. Her father beamed as he walked her down the aisle of the quaint chapel. He handed her over into Matthew's care and took his seat beside her mother as she dabbed her eyes with a lace handkerchief. Agnes smiled into those sky-blue eyes of the man she adored and promised to love, honour and obey. They adjourned to the officers' mess for their wedding meal, where her father welcomed Matthew into their family and toasted the bride and groom. It was a wonderful day, one which Agnes treasured as she said goodbye to her new husband a week later when he set sail for the Cape and the province of British Natal.

Chapter 28

Charles, 1878

Southampton was buzzing with activity. The might of the British army was in their final preparations to ship to South Africa. As Charles marched a platoon across the main square, he noticed some members of the medical corps huddled together, working on a dummy of some sort. Even from the far side of the square, he could recognise that stance. The niggle of familiarity changed to disbelief. It couldn't be. But it was. Charles couldn't believe his eyes.

"James? Is that you?"

The medic stopped what he was doing and turned to face him. He had regrown his beard into a straggly mop that hadn't seen a comb in weeks. His hair was longer, swept back from his forehead in waves of burnt orange. James smiled. That slow lazy smile that Charles remembered. The two men stared at one another, their hands outstretched for a handshake that neither wanted to end. They circled, summing each other up, grinning like Cheshire cats until Charles remembered the silence and the loss of contact.

"What are you doing here? Did you get my letters?" Charles said. "Why didn't you reply?"

"It is a very long story, Charles. It is so good to see you."

Charles was suddenly aware of the men watching them and unspoken questions that hung in the air. He called his sergeant and instructed him to continue with the platoon across the square to the mess hall.

"Well? I'm listening."

James looked at the group of medics who all as one were obviously earwigging while pretending to compare notes.

"Later, Charles. I am going to be here for another few days. I will meet with you later, and we can catch up, okay?"

James saluted Lieutenant Best and winked as he withdrew his hand before returning to his group. Charles stared after him, his emotions racing from anger to relief. James Langton was alive and well and in the British army.

Later that evening, Charles sat out on the boundary of the billet, on a low stone wall and stared skyward. It was ink-black and littered with stars. As he picked out the Milky Way and the Plough, he was startled by the slap of a hand on his shoulder.

"Lieutenant Best. How are you, sir?"

Charles scowled and jumped to his feet to face James, ignoring his outstretched hand.

"Why didn't you reply to any of my letters?"

"I'm sorry, Charles, truly I am. I just couldn't. I was so upset, so unsure of myself or who I was. I couldn't be around you. I couldn't be around anyone. I just needed some time to figure out what I wanted."

Charles looked at James, more than a little puzzled. "And you joined the military?"

James laughed. "Okay, okay, maybe I'm still not sure what I want to do. But one decision I have made is that I am never going back to Greenore. I dropped out of Trinity; you probably already know that. I just couldn't do it."

"So, how did you end up here, in a uniform, as a medic?"

"I still love medicine. I might not have wanted to finish medical school, but I was still drawn to it. A couple of months after I dropped out, I met an old college friend one day in Dublin. He was a few years ahead of me in medical school, but he qualified and went to St Thomas' in London, then became a military surgeon. I was curious, so I went back with him, and he introduced me to Netley, and here I am."

"You should have contacted me. You could have answered my letters. I thought you were dead, you know. We all did."

Charles could hear the rebuke in the tone of his voice but carried on regardless. He was quite annoyed James had turned up again out of the blue, apparently happy enough and without a thought for the distress his absence may have caused those who cared for him. He was more than a little hurt James had made no effort to let him know he was okay.

"I am sorry. Look," James waved a dog-eared letter at him, "I even wrote to you, but I couldn't send it."

"Too little, too late."

Charles shrugged, and an uneasy silence fell between them. A nudge in the ribs threatened to push Charles over the low wall.

"What's happening at home anyway? Tell me about your parents, about Amanda."

Charles felt his temper rise.

"What do you care? My parents thought very highly of you."

"And I am sorry. I wrote to your mother, but..."

The hairs on the back of Charles's neck frizzled, and two red spots flashed on his cheeks.

"How good of you," Charles sneered. "Was that before or after she died?"

James gasped; his eyes wide, obvious disbelief written across his face. Charles watched in horror as he flopped down onto the low wall and sank his head between his knees. Then, he heard the sob, loud in the silence of the night. A dejected James shook his head, his long fingers covering his face.

"Are you trying to tell me you didn't know?"

"No… no, of course not. How? When?"

Flummoxed, Charles's anger disappeared, banished by James's obvious anguish. But he was surprised James hadn't heard. It had been in all the local papers and the subject of discussion around the dinner tables of most society families. The death of Colonel Best had been quite shocking: a moment of carelessness during a grouse shoot by a man who had handled guns before he could handle a knife and fork. Lady Best had died some months later. The society rumour mill suggested a broken heart, and Charles did nothing to dissuade them. They wouldn't understand a woman of his mother's social standing contracting tuberculosis. His mother had always believed charity begins at home. Her visits to households throughout the estate with food and medicines were, in her eyes, part of her duty as the Lady of the manor. She could have sent the kitchen maids or any of the footmen, but no matter how much his father, or Charles himself, had argued with her, she insisted it was her duty. After her husband's untimely death and with Charles away, she redoubled her charitable endeavours.

"Your father too?" Horror stalked James's face.

Charles stared at James, his anger reigniting, burning his cheeks. With clenched fists he paced to within two inches from James's face.

"I was there for you, James, when your grandmother died. I went straight to your side. Where were you when I needed you?"

"I am so sorry."

Charles took a step backwards as James rose and enveloped

him. His body stiffened, and he tried to push James away, but James clung to him. Charles tried to punch James, struggling to free himself but James held on tighter. He felt James's strength engulf him, and he relented. The pain of his parents' passing revisited him, sweeping away his anger and replacing it with grief. He felt James's tears on his collar and felt his chest heave against his. Charles felt his legs go weak, and he collapsed to the ground, blinking away hot, silent tears before they could emerge. He felt James fold against him, sobbing, and he held him, cradling him as he wept, his shoulders heaving. Finally, James pulled away and put his hands firmly on Charles's broad shoulders.

"I am so sorry. I had such respect for your parents." He sniffed. "I cared so much for them..."

Charles's anger was gone, replaced by a sense of relief that James was finally back in his life. He had been so worried and had imagined all sorts of scenarios. Not once had it occurred to him James would end up in Southampton, let alone in the medical corp.

They sat on the low wall in silence, both men deep in thoughts of Colonel and Lady Best. Charles took his wallet from his breast pocket and slipped out the photograph of Amanda he kept tucked away in the centre. He handed it to James as tenderly as if he was handing over a piece of delicate porcelain.

"She said yes."

Charles laughed as James slapped him on the shoulder, his other hand outstretched to receive the oval photo into the palm of his hand.

"She looks as amazing as always. So, when is the big day?"

"Not until I get back. I've been posted to British Natal. We leave next week."

"That's where I'm going," James interrupted him.

They stared at each other in amazement. Charles couldn't believe it. No word from James in over a year, and now they were both in the military and sailing on the same ship to the same continent.

Chapter 29

Charles, 1879

CHARLES BEST MARVELLED AT THE AFRICAN SUNSET. HE nudged James, dozing beside him and startled him into action.

"What, what is it?" James jumped and then peered into the gathering darkness. Charles nearly laughed out loud at his friend's reaction.

"Stop, nothing is happening. I just didn't want you to miss that sunset. Look."

Both men watched in silence as the crimson sun dipped below the horizon.

"Spectacular," Charles said as he lay back, his hands behind his head and his rifle on the sleeping mat beside him. "I could get to like this country, James. There are no grey days here, rain from dawn to dusk and damp seeping into your bones. No sir, just sunshine, heat and magnificent sunsets."

"I've seen better sunsets over Carlingford Lough on a summer's evening, and so have you. And as for the rain, sure you can't beat that earthy smell of light rain on freshly cut grass, or the gentle lap of the lough as it licks the shore." James stared into the darkness; pictures of Ireland so vivid in his head he could almost taste the rain.

Charles grinned.

"If I didn't know you better, I'd say you were homesick."

James threw the book he was holding at Charles, who ducked, laughing as the book hit the ground. A clamour of voices in the darkness of the billet behind them shushed them into silence, and they sniggered as Charles threw the book back at James. Both rolled away, play-fighting like they did when they were kids, on the lawns of Charles's family home.

The guttural rumble and the splat of phlegm hitting the sun-baked clay alerted them to the presence of Private Jones. He was standing to the side of the building, watching them, a scowl on his hawk-like features. Jones spat again in their direction before retreating inside the billet. Charles scrambled to his feet frantically, beating the evidence of his play-acting from his uniform, his face reddening even in the darkness. He muttered to himself, purposely ignoring eye contact with James, who lay where he fell, watching him with those expressive eyes that reminded him of the clouds above Carlingford Lough. Charles stood ramrod straight, silent now, and brooding. He heard James sigh but kept his back to him while every nerve-ending in his body called out to him like some ancient Greek siren. He felt rather than heard James stand up, dust himself down and take his place beside him.

"We're not kids anymore. I have my family's reputation to protect," he whispered.

"I know, Charles, I know."

Charles glanced at James, who was staring out into the black night. His eyes hooded, his medical bag at his side, the fiery sunset reflecting off his auburn locks. James's jaw was set in a manner Charles was familiar with. It sparked a distant memory of them as boys on the shores of Carlingford Lough admiring a sunset, not unlike the one they were looking at now.

"Do you think George could have stood here? Admired an

African sunset or extolled the virtues of the Irish landscape to whoever he shared the post with?" Charles said.

"Doubt it. Your brother was an officer, a professional. You and I, what are we doing here? Neither of us was cut out for this military life," James said.

Not for the first time, Charles wondered what had possessed him to follow his dead brother's footsteps in the military. George had been a career soldier, well-respected, feared even, a chip off the old block. They were both Sandhurst graduates, but he could never fill his brother's shoes.

"I thought it would make my father happy. Stupid, eh?"

Charles felt James pat his shoulder and stepped away, out of reach. Whatever this was, this frisson between them, it had to stop. He could sense the men talking about them. Hear their whispers when they thought he was out of earshot. It had started when James arrived at the outpost to replace a medic who was ill. Charles had been so happy to see a friendly face, someone from home, who knew him, who cared about him, that he didn't stop to think how the men would judge how close he was to James. He had thrown his arms around his friend in reckless abandonment. They talked and laughed and walked and caught up on old times. And then he heard the whispers. He was surprised at first, shocked even. He had been friends with James since their first day in boarding school, and he certainly never thought about James in that way. He was betrothed to Amanda and besotted by her. James was his friend. No more.

The post was temporary, near the town of Ulundi, and the offensive was well underway. All the men were aware of the massive defeat at Isandlwana earlier that year. One thousand three hundred soldiers were killed, and thousands injured at the hands of the Zulus. The tide appeared to be turning with the defeat of the Zulus in Kambula the previous month, but the men were wary. Tales of the Zulus' brutality and fearlessness spread around the campfires every evening. None of them had been in Isandlwana on that fateful night. Nor had they been in Rorke's Drift the following night, but they had all heard the stories.

"I wish I were home, James. Imagine trekking the Mourne Mountains when the summer flowers line the trails. I can nearly smell the sea, the freshness, the cool breeze. Do you remember the great fun we had at the annual cricket match and fête over the years? Amanda in her white dress and her ribbons. Vincent and the tennis tournaments. I would give anything to be back in County Down for that."

"But then you would miss that spectacular sunset you woke me to see."

Charles laughed as he stared off into the distance.

The sound of footsteps behind them brought them both back to reality.

"Sir."

Charles turned and returned a salute to the private in front of him.

"Captain Higgins wants to see you, sir."

"Thank you, Private Jones."

Charles had to make a conscious effort not to show his contempt for Private Jones on his face. Although he was younger than either Charles or James, his demeanour made him appear older. He was a miserable little man, mean-spirited and nasty to his fellow soldiers. Charles had cause to reprimand him on numerous occasions for his behaviour. He hated bullies and firmly believed they had no place in the military. He also suspected Private Jones was a thief, but he had no proof yet, although he was determined to catch him out. Charles knew Jones would slip up at some stage, so he was content to wait. Catch him in the act. He dispatched Private

Jones and, when he turned away, gave a mock salute to James and a wry smile before making his way towards the centre of the camp.

Chapter 30

James

What a day, James thought as he helped carry the next injured soldier into the makeshift hospital. The battle was raging, and the list of dead and wounded was multiplying at an alarming rate. He wondered aloud why he ever got involved in the military. For the first time, he compared his day with his father's practice on that wild peninsula, and longed to see it one more time, something he never thought would happen. It would be nightfall soon, and his shift would end, like the others, with a bed if he was lucky and a snatched couple of hours before tending to the injured to the best of his ability. The lucky ones were sent to the field hospitals. He had been in one in Ladysmith a few weeks ago. The Nightingale nurses were doing an excellent job even though most of the men didn't agree with them being there. They argued that war was no place for a woman, which amused James, for he had always believed women were the stronger sex, but who was he to argue.

Perhaps it was those thoughts roaming around his head that made him careless, but his shoulder exploded with pain as the bullet passed through it. He stumbled and fell on top of the body, the blood warm on its red coat. He slithered as he tried to find his footing and his hands slipped as he pushed himself away. The pain in his shoulder burnt, and he recoiled then stopped, stunned as he recognised the jawline. The world around him felt like it had gone into slow motion and the noise of the battlefield disappeared into the distance. He felt for a pulse and found a weak one. He turned him over and gasped as he saw the gaping wound in his side. Charles gave James a weak smile, his eyes half-closed and raised his hand to James's face.

"I knew you would come for me. Look after Amanda for me."

"I will not. You are going to do that for yourself."

James called for help, and another two medics came running with a stretcher before James blacked out from the pain in his shoulder. He woke as they entered the field hospital and called out for Charles, who lay silent on the stretcher beside him. A nurse arranged for Charles to be placed in an alcove on the side of the hospital while James was sent directly to a doctor to treat the gunshot wound in his shoulder. James protested, but blood loss left him weak, and he blacked out again. When he gained consciousness, his wound had been treated, and the pain had lessened. He felt groggy and weak, but then the memory of Charles's face hit him like a flash of lightning. He struggled to sit up, staring frantically around him.

"Charles." He didn't recognise his own voice as he called for his friend.

The nurse looked across from where she was treating another soldier and smiled at him.

"Welcome back, Sergeant. Your friend is in a different room. Give me a moment, and I will bring you to him."

James wouldn't leave Charles's side. He knew it was hopeless but couldn't admit it to himself or anyone else. Charles drifted in and out of consciousness while James chattered to him constantly. He talked about the estate, about the tenants, about their favourite day of the year, the annual cricket match and the garden fête. James chattered while Charles got weaker and weaker. His blood loss was too great, the damage to his organs too much. The heir to the Glassdrumman Estate, Charles Best, died with his best friend James tending to him, in a tent outside the town of Ulundi under an African sky.

Chapter 31

Agnes, 1879

THE REPORTS OF WHAT HAPPENED WERE SLOW TO FILTER through to England. Agnes was on the wards when the matron called her aside.

"Agnes, you must prepare yourself. There have been major casualties in Natal. A battle with the natives, Zulus I believe they are called, savages, in my opinion."

She sniffed her disapproval as if that would stop the Zulu warriors in their tracks.

"There are many casualties, so Doctor Williams's expertise will be badly needed."

Agnes went back to work and immersed herself in her patients, pushing Matthew to the back of her thoughts. Every so often, thoughts of Matthew and the situation he was in overcame her. She took a moment to breathe, say a short prayer for his safety, then she moved on, back to her patients and her calling in life. The papers were full of it. There was total shock at the defeat of the British army by the Zulus, with differing reports of the number of dead and injured, ranging from five hundred to thirteen hundred dead. The headlines read *The Zulu War – Defeat of the British* and *Heavy Casualties on Both Sides.*

A few days later, when she was summoned to the matron's office, she wasn't surprised. She somehow knew Matthew was dead before Matron could get the words out. She heard the platitudes, the words of sympathy and accepted the leave she was issued with. Agnes had never heard of Isandlwana, neither had her parents, but that was where Matthew had died. By then, the papers were full of the victory of Rorke's Drift, of how one hundred and fifty men held off an attack by about three to four thousand Zulu warriors. There was little printed about the previous day's events at Isandlwana when over one thousand three hundred British soldiers had died at the hands of the Zulus.

Agnes went to visit Matthew's mother to tell her the dreadful news. She sat and cried with her as she mourned her only son. Her parents called to pay their respects and brought Agnes home to grieve in her mother's arms. There was no funeral for Matthew. They had no corpse to bury, for Matthew's earthly body lay buried in a mass grave along with his fellow soldiers in South Africa. His commanding officer advised there would be a memorial service at a later date, but Agnes cared little. She accepted the love and attention lavished on her by her mother and did not give any thought to her future, living only in the present. Dressed in widow's garb, for the first time in her life, she felt unsure of herself. She had always wanted to be a nurse and had never given any credence to the possibility of marriage. Yet here she was, a widow at just eighteen years of age and any ambition to follow in the footsteps of her idol, Florence Nightingale, a distant memory.

Each morning she stared at herself in the mirror unable to recognise the black-clad woman who stood in front of her. She didn't recognise herself, but she didn't know who else she should be. Matthew was gone. Agnes couldn't think about the person she was before. Her enthusiasm for life, for caring for others, was swallowed whole by the widow's garb she was expected to wear. She felt lost and totally alone.

It was her friends who reminded her of who she was meant to be. Emma, Yvonne and Mary arrived at her parents' home, unannounced, just two weeks later to tell her their latest news, news they were sure Agnes would want to hear.

"Matron is forming a group of volunteers, nurses, to travel to the Cape," Emma said.

"We are all going. We are needed out there. Our soldiers have suffered massive defeats, and the list of injured is growing," Yvonne told her.

Agnes looked from one to the other, their enthusiasm slowly seeping into her pores, lifting the fog she had been living in since the days of Matthew's death.

"We are to travel on the *Dublin Castle* ship out of London, arriving in Cape Town in August. Will you come with us?" Mary said, her face eager as she pleaded. "You are the best with open wounds, you know that."

Emma took her hand, her eyes piercing into Agnes's. "We can make a real difference, Agnes. It is what we were trained for."

The women filled her in, leaving out one crucial detail, the fact they had already given her name to Matron, who had accepted it gratefully and given the women permission to visit Agnes and get her on board. It didn't take much persuasion. The news shook Agnes out of her stupor, and she knew what she had to do. She was meant to be on that ship. This was her calling. She was sure of it.

Chapter 32

Agnes

AGNES'S PARENTS WERE HORRIFIED. HER SISTER APOPLECTIC.

"You can't go to Africa. You're a widow, mourning your husband," Bernadette said. "It's preposterous."

"You're not going," her father blustered. "I forbid it."

"Hush now, Father," her mother intervened. "Don't upset yourself. Let's discuss this rationally."

"There's nothing to discuss as far as I'm concerned," Bernadette said. Twin spots of anger burned her already rosy cheeks. "What would people say? She's only a widow five minutes and she's gallivanting off to another country."

"Now, Bernadette," her mother interjected. "It certainly could not be described as gallivanting. Your sister is a nurse. She's trained to look after soldiers."

"But Africa. They don't call it the dark continent for nothing you know." Her father paced the room, then stopped in front of Agnes. "Seriously, Agnes. I supported you when you said you wanted to be a Nightingale nurse. I supported you when you moved to Southampton. In fairness, I was thrilled when you married Matthew. What happened to him was a tragedy. A good man like that, cut down in his youth.

But you can't compound that injustice by putting your own life at risk."

"I have to, Father," Agnes said. "Can't you see that? It's what I am trained to do. Matthew would never expect me to forego my training. If he were still alive, he would write to me asking me to meet him there."

"But he's not alive. Who would look after you? Who would keep you safe?"

"I will, Father. I'm not travelling alone. My friends are travelling with me. We're taking over field hospitals, helping soldiers like Matthew."

The argument continued long into the night. Agnes refused to budge. Her father pleaded. Her sister argued but in the end her mother used her calming influence.

"Agnes is a trained nurse. If, by following her calling, she saves a life, or holds a man's hand in his final hours, then she will have balanced out the injustice of Matthew's early demise. Let her go, Father. Be proud of our daughter."

Mr Rickman could never say no to his wife and his daughters. He reluctantly gave his blessing although Bernadette still fumed, annoyed at being overruled.

The Nightingale nurses didn't have long to prepare. Within a week, the women set sail from London. The crossing was very rough. Most of the passengers suffered from seasickness and were glad to see land. Agnes was lucky to have found her sea legs early in the journey and spent her time administering to those who remained ill. The ship was bringing replacements, men and equipment, to the colony of Natal. Despite the massive losses suffered at the hands of the Zulus, spirits were high.

Agnes stood on deck watching the shoreline as they drew close, wondering if somehow, she would feel closer to Matthew once she set foot on the dark continent he had died in. It had only been months since she had seen him, but his face was already a blur, his scent a distant memory. She had his photograph, the one taken on their wedding day. It was of the two of them, Matthew in full formal uniform with a happy smile plastered over his handsome face as he stared into the camera. Agnes on his arm, staring into the eyes of her new husband. It brought a smile to her face, but she had the feeling of a friend lost, not a lover, a companion, not a husband. She couldn't dismiss the thought that perhaps she hadn't loved him enough. That idea made her sad because he deserved so much more than that.

Chapter 33

Agnes

THEY DISEMBARKED IN CAPE TOWN AND BEGAN THEIR JOURNEY to the colony of Natal. Agnes was surprised at the attitude of some of the high-ranking officers who treated them as little more than a nuisance, one colonel suggesting they would have been better staying at home. Their matron, Mrs Deeble, was a war widow and a formidable woman who ignored the attitude of the men, intent on her mission. She accepted gratefully the assistance of the owner of the Castle Line shipping company, who volunteered to arrange transportation to their final destinations. They were to be split between the various hospitals. Mrs Deeble sent Mary and Yvonne to the capital, St Pietermaritzburg, while Emma and Agnes were dispatched to Ladysmith in the northern part of the colony.

Agnes was amazed at the scenery. The Drakensberg and Biggarsberg mountain ranges were on either side of the town, providing a striking backdrop. The hospital was basic but clean. On their arrival, they were introduced to the nurses from the community of St Michaels and All Angels who had ran the hospital for the previous six months. They quickly reorganised with the meagre provisions they had. The hospital had been set up in a Dutch Reformation church augmented by some large tents. Agnes and Emma came equipped with the latest supplies from Netley. They quickly restocked the cabinets and took over the running of the one hundred and fifty-bed hospital. The patients were suffering from fever and dysentery, as well as open wounds from daggers and gunshots. While the scenery outside had impressed them, the carnage inside the hospital did not. They worked around the clock, saving those they could and praying for those they couldn't. After each battle they were overwhelmed by fresh patients, but they persevered, treating all patients with the same expertise and compassion, native or British, even Zulu. The women fell into bed each night, exhausted. They woke each morning to repeat the same relay of bathing and treating these young men, for invariably, they were young men. Agnes felt older than her years as she held their hands and listened to their stories. Some had left wives and sweethearts behind in England and Ireland, others spoke of their mothers. She wondered if someone had held Matthew's hand as he died.

Agnes wondered who had devised the separation of officers and enlisted men in the hospital. Not that it made any difference to her. She treated all her patients with the same compassion. But, one particularly long day, when she started to ask Emma about one of their patients, she struggled to describe him. It was as if all the faces had blended into one generic person. Agnes was horrified.

"Emma, if I lose compassion for those we treat, how can I call myself a nurse?"

"You are tired. You have too much compassion for these men. We all have. But look around you. This is hard. This is the most difficult situation we have ever been in. You haven't had a single day off in weeks. We need a break."

The two women arranged for their day off together and took some time out to explore the area. Ladysmith was too far away from the fighting to be dangerous, but the commanding officer of the base did give them a stern lecture about where to go and where to avoid. They set out for a walk along the banks of the Klip River, admiring flora and fauna, so different from anything they had seen back in London. They inhaled that fresh earthy smell only wild grass imparts mingled with the musky scents of wild flowers that sprouted along the riverbank. The sound of the river inflow trickling over large stones had a calming effect on them both. For just a moment, Agnes felt homesick as she felt herself transported to the bottom of her garden at home. A tributary of the Thames flowed past as it wound its way to the river and out to sea. As children, she and her sister had often stood on the small footbridge and raced small thin sticks purporting to be boats to the next bend in the stream. The water was clear and shallow, with a rocky bottom that hid minnows and the occasional frog.

"When I get home, I am going to hug my sister. I don't think I have thought kindly of her in months, and she was a great big sister to me." Agnes told Emma about their stick boats and their adventures catching minnows.

"You are lucky. I don't have anyone. You women are my sisters. My whole life is wrapped up in my career at Netley," Emma said in a low voice. Agnes took her friend's hand. Emma's parents had both died only months apart some years earlier. Emma was alone in the world, brought up by a guardian who controlled her trust fund. She had nursed both her parents in their final days, which is how she discovered her calling.

"And a wonderful sister you are."

The two women strolled back to Ladysmith hospital, arm in arm, relaxed and content after a day out of the wards and away from the stench of death and disease. They made a promise to each other they would get away from the hospital for a few hours at least once a week. The walks became a regular feature. They ventured slightly further each week, sometimes bringing a small picnic etched out of their meagre rations. They spread a blanket on the grassy bank and ate, savouring the rush of the clear water as it raced past and the hum of insects flitting through the wild flowers.

They became accustomed to the blazing heat of the African sun, shielded themselves with wide floppy hats, and acquired the skill of using fans to flick away the more aggressive bugs attracted to their porcelain skin. The commanding officer had warned them of the dangers of wild animals, particularly the wild dogs. He insisted they bring his favourite walking stick with them to be used as a weapon if the need arose. It had a Malacca wood shaft, polished to a mirrored shine. The unit crest was engraved on the silver collar, on top of which sat a polished ebony grip. Each week before they set out, he offered the stick and each week, they accepted and strode out, armed with their talisman.

"We should name it Artemis. After the Greek goddess."

"The protector of maidens." Agnes laughed. "Not sure how the colonel would feel about that."

They checked back with the colonel each week and returned their talisman with thanks. As the months passed, they became acclimatised to the heat and humidity but sometimes longed for the coolness of the English summer rain.

Refreshed after a day off, Agnes started work with renewed vigour. A new batch of patients arrived each week, suffering from various fevers and conditions. Agnes got to know them all by their first names and shared in their small victories and setbacks, always encouraging them with a smile and a gentle touch. Their trip was coming to an end, with only three weeks before they travelled to Cape Town to get the boat back to Southampton. Agnes was looking forward to getting home. Her parents and sister wrote regular letters to her, weekly missives telling her about the weather and their social lives and their mundane everyday events. Agnes treasured them. She ached for summer rain and English tea, creamy butter and hot crumpets, a hot bath and clean sheets, the chill of an autumn breeze and the sharp bite of winter frost. She had no regrets about her time in Africa. It was what she was trained to do, what she was born to be, but she felt the need for some home time, some downtime, some time to devote purely to her little pleasures. She folded the latest letter and put it in the bottom of her trunk with the others. Pulling her apron over her sheath dress, she straightened her shoulders and made her way to the wards.

Agnes started on the officers' ward. It was laid out with six beds on each side, and she approached the first bed on the right. Captain Hornbill was recovering nicely and due to be sent back to the unit later that day. She went on with her rounds until she got to the last bed in the right-hand corner and gasped. The bed was newly occupied by a woman. The white skin of her bare back was gleaming with sweat, and her hair was matted and of an indeterminate colour. Agnes wondered if one of the nurses were ill and touched her shoulder to gently wake her. She gasped again as the figure turned and she realised her new patient was a man. His face was flushed, beads of sweat poured from his forehead. His coarse beard showed shades of ginger and grey and was wet and straggly, his moustache unkempt, but what struck her most was the sorrow in his lake-grey eyes. She could see the scars on his shoulder from an old gunshot wound, the scar still angry and puckered. *Bad workmanship,* she thought to herself. He was delirious, and she began treating him, sponging him down and feeding him drips of water, purified and as cool as she could make it. She made him comfortable then continued her rounds, going back to him as often as she could manage throughout the day.

Over the next few days, she paid special attention to James

Langton. Like many of her patients, he suffered from dysentery, but he was already weakened by the gunshot wound he had sustained. He was barely conscious, and he mumbled in his stupor, sometimes calling out, sometimes weeping. Agnes kept a close eye on him and, when her day off arrived, pleaded with Emma to adjourn for another day, afraid to leave him.

"What is it about him?" Emma asked.

"I don't know. I just feel some sort of affinity to James. A responsibility, if that makes sense. He is different from the other men. And I need to make sure he pulls through this."

Emma sniffed, her usual response when she didn't agree with something, but when Agnes pleaded with her, she acquiesced and put in an extra shift herself. Agnes returned to nursing James but made a special effort to pay more attention to her other patients. After Emma's comments, she became acutely aware she may have inadvertently neglected their care in favour of James.

By the end of the week, his fever had broken. His eyes still haunted Agnes, but his general appearance improved with the benefit of water and soap. She fed him watery soup and biscuits and walked him to the latrine. His body hung on his frame like a deflated balloon, and she wondered if he would ever make a full recovery. She reluctantly left him to walk with Emma on her next day off.

"There is a sorrow in him, Emma. A sorrow reflected in his eyes."

Emma linked her friend's arm as they walked. She also felt the sorrow in the young man but reminded Agnes that many of their patients had been through the hell of battle and disease. That they had lost friends and colleagues and had killed other men in battle.

"Each of them is fighting their own demons, Agnes. Every patient who goes through that hospital has their own story."

The two women walked on in silence, each lost in their

thoughts, as the water rushed past, ruffling the long rushes at the bank. Suddenly, an anteater made an unannounced appearance twenty feet in front of them. The two women stopped to watch, fascinated as he hoovered up an army of black dots and then disappeared into the riverbank. They looked at each other and burst out laughing.

"What an experience this has been. I know it has been difficult. My mother would faint if she saw where I am sleeping, but… how do you describe that sky, the mountains, the landscape?"

"The sun. How could any English person understand the heat of that sun?"

The women laughed and turned to head back to the base hospital, refreshed and ready for their last week under the African sun.

Chapter 34

Agnes

Agnes checked the list of patients they were bringing back to England and was relieved to see James Langton's name. She went straight to the ward to give him the good news and found him lying on his side, his back to the room. Once again, she was struck by his form. His smooth pale skin was striking against the vibrant auburn of his hair which curled down to his shoulders. He was sleeping, his eyes closed, his hands joined and cupped under his left cheek. She felt his brow and nodded to herself, happy with the normal temperature and left him to sleep while she returned to her other patients. They were packing up their patients in two days and starting the journey to the port. They would be back in Southampton within a month where convalescence could begin in earnest. Agnes reckoned some good old-fashioned stews and bread would soon put meat on their bones, particularly James. She could practically taste fresh bread smothered in creamy butter as she envisioned their first meal back in the Royal Victoria Hospital in Netley.

Agnes and Emma barely got time to speak during their journey to the port. They were bringing eighty men, ill and injured, from Ladysmith Hospital. Every moment was consumed with making sure they survived the journey. Once they had their patients on board and settled in their sick-bay, they went on deck and breathed a sigh of relief. Mary and Yvonne had arrived earlier with more ill and injured men from the capital, and the women met on deck. It was late afternoon, and the view from their vantage point silenced them all. Agnes stared at the tableau in front of her. Table Mountain rose in the background, towering over the sprawling city while the sun danced off the waves, sending shards of light skywards.

"The sea looks like a ship has shed its cargo of diamonds, and they are floating on the surface of the waves, trying to get back to their base on the far side of the mountain." Agnes pointed aft and was rewarded with peals of laughter from her friends.

"Fanciful notions, Agnes." Emma hugged her friend.

"Whatever about diamonds trying to get back to Kimberley, I am dying to get back to England. Africa, you have been wonderful, but it is time to go home."

They stayed on deck until after nightfall, all amazed at how quickly Table Mountain disappeared from view on the horizon. They swapped stories of hardships and triumphs until the chill in the air drove them to their bunks for their first night at sea.

The journey lasted over three weeks and was a much calmer voyage than their outgoing trip. Agnes was glad of that. Their patients would not have survived bad seasickness. The rhythmic lull of the waves rocked her to a good night's sleep every time but she was relieved to see the English coastline.

Chapter 35

James, 1880

James looked around him. The hospital wards at Netley were large and well laid out. Dysentery had left him weak, but grief had left him bereft. How could he explain that to the doctors who attended him? He felt like he was in a deep hole, and he couldn't claw his way back out. When he was totally honest with himself, he acknowledged he didn't want to get better. All he wanted to do was lie here with his eyes closed and wait for death to take him. He wished he had died in Africa with Charles, for he had no wish to live in England. No desire to return to his occupation as a medic. That had been ill-thought out. To jump from medical school in Dublin to a medic in the British army was the stupidest thing he had ever done.

When he signed up initially, he had given them Charles Best as his next of kin. He had even concocted an elaborate story of how Charles was his half-brother, how Colonel and Lady Best had adopted him while he was in boarding school. Then, when he made his soldier's will before they shipped out, he had named Charles as his beneficiary in the event of his death. He had no idea that Charles had done the same. When the legal officer approached him and told him Charles had bequeathed him his personal wealth, he buried his head under his blankets and cried for days. Under inheritance rules Glassdrumman Hall and its vast estate went to a distant cousin of the Best family, who lived in the north of England and had never set foot in Ireland, let alone the Glassdrumman Estate. James wept for Charles, for his plans to marry Amanda, and his ambitions for his beloved Glassdrumman Hall.

James couldn't get out from under this cloak of despair. Thoughts of Charles haunted him. In his dreams, Charles walked beside him, laughing and joking. He could smell the earthy scent that surrounded him, feel the granite path under his feet as they traversed the Mourne Mountains. In his dreams, he felt happy, alive, and then, when he woke, came the crushing realisation he would never see Charles again.

He couldn't spare a thought for Amanda. She figured briefly somewhere in the back of his mind, but he dismissed her. She was young, beautiful and talented. There was a myriad of suitors waiting in the wings to take Charles's place. She wrote to him shortly after he came to Netley. She had met someone, someone who wanted to marry her. It was as if she were asking his permission for her to move on. He wrote a short reply, two brief lines wishing her the best. A week later, she arrived to visit him in the hospital. The thought of talking to Amanda about Charles made him feel ill. He did not want to share his grief with anyone, let alone the woman Charles was pledged to marry. It was a short visit. James had nothing to say no matter how much Amanda tried to induce him into the conversation. Before she left, she gave him the promise ring Charles had given her.

"I can't keep it now, James. You understand, don't you? It wouldn't be fair on my fiancé to keep a promise ring from another man. I did love him."

James could only nod, unable to speak, for fear of emotion

spilling out of him in great black waves. He watched as she waved goodbye then sank under the bedclothes to wallow in his misery. Amanda had found someone to comfort her. Who would comfort him? Waves of despair washed over him, and he felt himself drowning.

It was Agnes who slowly brought him around. Every day she spoon-fed him soup like he was a small child. Every evening, she spoke gently to him while she bathed him. She put him in a wheelchair, covered his emaciated frame with a blanket, and walked him around the grounds. She told him all about Matthew and how he had been killed in Africa. James remained silent. He couldn't speak to her. At first, he didn't even listen, but gradually he heard her, and eventually, his thoughts became less dark, less wrapped up in death and his own despair. James found himself looking forward to seeing her, to hearing her voice instead of the voices inside his head. Eventually, he started to sleep through the night, dreamless sleep that refreshed him for the first time since Charles had died in his arms.

"I won't be here for a few days, James. My father is ill, and I must travel to London to see him. My friend Emma is going to look after you."

James was alarmed. He hadn't cared who looked after him for a long time or if anyone had even bothered. But he had become accustomed to Agnes, her chat and her gentle touch. He looked at her, and his mouth started to form the words, but nothing came out. He couldn't speak. James wanted to tell her he was sorry about her father; he wanted to wish her a safe journey; he wanted to tell her to hurry back. But his voice wouldn't work. He could see Agnes watching him, willing him to talk to her, but he froze. It was no use. Closing his eyes tight against the disappointment in her face, he pulled the sheets up to his neck, hoping she would disappear. Everyone he ever cared about had gone away. His grandmother, Charles, what did it matter?

Chapter 36

James

Every day James listened out for Agnes's voice but every day he was disappointed. Gradually he could feel dark fingers clutch his soul and start to slowly drag him under again. Then on day twenty, he heard her.

"Good morning, James. I'm back."

He looked out from under the covers, half afraid he had summoned her voice out of his imagination. But there she was, smiling at him, such a warm smile that he felt himself smile back. It had been so long since he had smiled, he could feel the muscles in his face contracting in what he knew was more of a grimace, but it must have pleased Agnes.

"Oh, it is good to see you too, James."

She got his wheelchair, wrapped him up warmly before setting off on a walk around the grounds. Agnes parked the wheelchair under an ancient oak tree, and they sat in companionable silence until Agnes broke the quietness.

"My father died. He was a good man, who will be sorely missed. My poor mother is distraught, but my sister and her husband are looking after her now. It was such a sad time."

James listened to Agnes as she told her story and felt her

sorrow. He reached out and patted her hand where it lay in her lap. Agnes placed her hand over James's.

"Thank you for listening."

They quickly fell back into their old routine. Every evening, Agnes would bundle James up and walk him around the grounds. On the occasional Sunday Agnes bundled James into her carriage and brought him further afield. Gradually James could feel the dark chains inside him breaking, and a lightness that he cherished entered his soul. It took him some time to start talking again, but it was to Agnes when he did. James haltingly started to tell her about his younger days at boarding school and his holidays in Glassdrumman Hall with his best friend Charles. Agnes, in turn, told him all about Matthew and her life as a nurse.

"I always wanted to be a nurse. I had visions of myself as the Lady with the Lamp, but it's not what I imagined. I should never have married Matthew. I didn't love him enough. I feel so bad for him, that he died in Africa, and what makes it worse is it was a relief for me. Knowing that I never have to live as a wife was a blessing for me. How bad does that make me?"

"Agnes, there is no badness in you, only good. He loved you so much he asked you to marry him. You made him happy. Matthew died happy in the knowledge that he had married the woman he loved."

"Thank you. I don't know if I believe that but thank you for saying it."

Armed with the support and friendship offered by Agnes, James slowly started to heal. He confided in her how he felt about Charles. How much he had loved him and how much he missed him. He confided in her about his days in Dublin and about his despair after his grandmother died. But he stopped short of talking about his sister. Through it all, Agnes listened with a ready ear and no reproaches.

"James Langton died in Africa. I don't know who I am, but I can never be the same James Langton again."

"So, you need to figure out who you are now. Think about what you want to do. Where you want to live. You can have a fresh start."

James considered for a moment before nodding his head.

"Yes. Who wouldn't want a fresh start, an opportunity to start over and make a new life for oneself." He grinned as the thought struck him. "Although if I could start over, I would prefer to be a woman. I have always thought they were the stronger sex. I have always associated better with women than men."

"So why don't you?"

James snorted. "Don't be ridiculous. How could I?"

Agnes laughed at his reaction. "You're right. Who would want to live under the restraints placed on women? If anything, it should be the other way around. I sometimes wondered about the possibility of living as a man. But… I must say, while I may not be attracted to men, I certainly did not want to be one. I am quite comfortable in my skin, happy to be a widow. That title gives me a certain freedom to live a life independent of men."

"You have it all figured out."

"What will you do with your life?"

"I have no idea. I have no one."

That night, as he lay in bed, he replayed that conversation over and over in his head. Agnes's questions were pertinent. They set him thinking. He finally came to the realisation that he felt, deep down in his bones, he was meant to be a woman. Emotionally, logically, every fibre in his being screamed at him that he was a female, but the outer trappings of his body were male. He realised he had struggled with his sexuality all his life. He had only admitted it to himself when he finally got to wear women's clothing in Dublin as part of the drama society. It was the first time he had felt truly at home in his skin. His grandmother had known. She had realised when he was a small boy. So had Ellen, their housekeeper. Both tried to influence him, make him more masculine, more manly. Their tactics had worked for a little while, but he was never the man they wanted him to be. It wasn't in his nature.

When he was a young boy, he used to think he had somehow absorbed parts of Jane into his being so she too could have a life. Fanciful, yes, but maybe it was just wishful thinking on his part. He loved his sister and despite how hard he'd tried to share his life with her, she had no life, no joy, no hopes and dreams. He believed that if he carried her in his heart and mind, then she'd live through him: that the empty shell she presented, was just that, a façade for the world she inhabited in her mind, shaped by the thoughts he shared with her on some level. An interaction that no one else could comprehend.

He slept fitfully, images of Charles interacting with Jane's serene silent smiles, flickering through his dreams.

Chapter 37

James

The next day on their usual walk, James mentioned his sister to Agnes.

"What about Jane? What happened to her?"

James looked at Agnes. He trusted her completely, but he wasn't sure if he was ready to talk about that year. That fateful year, when his life had fallen apart. When he found out she was dead, he was devastated. He still thought he should have known somehow, should have felt the shift in his universe, that this other part of him was no longer on this earth. The memory of that day haunted him.

"Several weeks after Grandmama died, it hit me, that my sister and I were the last remaining members of my mother's family. I couldn't face going back to college. Honestly, Agnes, I felt like I was sinking in this swamp, getting deeper and deeper into depression."

James hesitated. Agnes took his hand. "Go on, James, I'm listening."

"I decided to visit my sister, to try and explain to her what had happened to Grandmama. When I arrived, the house was in darkness. I went straight to the parlour expecting to see the fire lit and the lamps throwing a welcoming glow. Instead, the parlour was empty and cold. There was a smattering of dust covering every surface. I could smell cooking from the kitchen, so I went in search of Ellen. The kitchen was empty, but the stove was recently lit, and a pot was simmering on top of it, yet all the shelves were bare. Panic started to rise in my throat as I ran from room to room, calling for Ellen, like some sort of lunatic."

James exhaled. "I could hear movement in my father's office, so I opened the door. I can still see his face. It was all mottled, a dark, wine colour, his words were slurred as he slumped over the desk in his office, an empty bottle of whiskey lying sideways on the floor beside him. He tried to sit up mumbling at me to whist. Then he said Ellen was gone. I was totally puzzled. Ellen was the one constant in that house. She had been there the night we were born, and she had been there every night since. I couldn't understand where she could have gone to. 'Gone back to wherever she came from. No need for the likes of her here, interfering old biddy', he said. So, I asked him, 'But what about Jane?'."

James exhaled, haunted by the events of that night. Agnes waited, holding his hand in silent encouragement until he could speak again.

"My father stood, wavering from side to side, only keeping his balance by holding on to the desk, and shouted at me, 'Jane's dead'."

Agnes gripped his hand. "Oh, James, how awful for you."

"I will never forget that second; I felt my breath leave my body as if he had punched me in the ribs. My limbs turned to jelly. I couldn't believe it. It felt like the air around him expanded, peppered with whiskey-fuelled rage emanating from him in waves. Then I heard a door open in the hallway behind me. I felt relieved when I saw Ellen, thinking she could explain everything; that it was all a mistake, but it wasn't. Ellen took my arm and led me into the parlour where she told me what happened. Jane died in her sleep the night my father returned to the Cooley Peninsula after Grandmama's funeral. Influenza. The moment she said it I knew it was true. I felt her absence, a gaping hole in my heart."

Agnes put her arms around James, hugging him tightly until he was ready to continue.

"Ellen made excuses for Father. Said he was distraught; that he'd lost his mind. He threw Ellen out. Said he didn't need her anymore, that the only reason she was still there was to look after Jane. Ellen said she had written to me asking me to come home. I felt so guilty, there was a pile of correspondence sitting on the sideboard in Grandmama's house, waiting for my attention, but I'd ignored it. I was so caught up in my grief for Grandmama I ignored everything."

"You weren't to know, James."

"I should have known; I should have felt the shift in the universe when Jane died. Two sides of the same coin. That's what I told Jane, every chance I got."

"You couldn't have known, James. Your father should have sent you a telegram."

James snorted. "It gets worse. Ellen moved into the stable boy's cottage and still tried to look after my father. She even tried to explain his behaviour. She swore he had lost his mind. Said he hadn't left the office since that night. She left food, and sometimes he would eat it, but most times, he'd just swear at her to get out and leave him alone. Ellen openly wept as she told me everything that happened."

James's voice trembled as the words tumbled out of him. Once he made the decision to tell Agnes what happened, he couldn't stop talking.

"Ellen kept Jane's pendant for me. The match to the one I wore around my neck, up until that day."

The memory brought fresh tears to James's eyes and a

stabbing pain in his heart. He felt Agnes's arm around his shoulder and took in her scent as she leaned into him and kissed his cheek, wiping away his tears.

"Hush, James."

"Jane is dead," James whispered through his tears. "He didn't even give her a proper burial. Our father buried her himself. He took a shovel in the dead of night and buried Jane beside our mother. No gravedigger, no church service. He didn't even file the paperwork. And he didn't tell me. She was dead and buried before I found out."

James looked up at Agnes as his tears fell, and a fresh wave of pain engulfed him.

"My poor boy."

"How could I not have known, Agnes. We were so close. I was her life. How did I not know? How did I not feel her leaving this earth?"

Agnes held James as he cried. They stayed for over an hour, hidden by trees in the walkway. Agnes wrapped around James as she stroked his hair. James was comforted by her warm embrace, and gradually, his pain subsided.

The following evening after their walk, they stopped in the same spot. Agnes knelt in front of James.

"James, do you remember the discussion we had yesterday?"

"How could I forget it. Thank you for listening to me, Agnes. You are the only other person I have spoken to about Jane, other than Charles, of course."

Agnes stared at him as if debating what she should say next. She tapped her index finger against her chin as she stared into James's intense grey eyes.

"I was thinking about what you said. Hear me out."

Agnes paused and took James's hand in hers.

"James Langton could die here at the Royal Victoria Hospital in Netley. He could die from his underlying injuries sustained in the war, injuries he never recovered from. His sister Jane could move to Manchester or Belfast or some city where she is not known, and she could start a new life for herself."

"What are you talking about?" James pulled away from her, his mouth open, his eyes burrowing into her soul.

"You said it yourself, if you could reinvent yourself, you would be a woman. Why not be Jane? Give Jane the life you always wanted for her."

James carried the thought further. "Her father may have been a drunk, but her brother left her well provided for."

They stared at each other, eyes wide, thoughts racing. James felt the first stirring of something like hope for his future. It was as if a tiny piece of the boulder that contained his grief had been chipped away. Somehow, thanks to Agnes, there was a glimmer of daylight squeezing through into the darkness of his soul. Years later, he recognised that day as the turning point, the moment he decided his sister would live on through him.

Chapter 38

James, 1881

THE PAPERWORK DEEMING JAMES LANGTON DEAD FROM INJURIES sustained during the Anglo-Zulu War were easily enough to obtain after some initial planning. Agnes put James into a wheelchair every evening and brought him around the grounds. They talked over every aspect of their plan, picking holes where they could and looking at it from every angle. They eventually decided James would have an accident at the nearby cliffs. For their plan to work, James would have to establish a routine of going outside every day and eventually going unaccompanied. Agnes always brought him out for walks, but he would have to be alone to stage the accident. If the accident happened while Agnes was with him, it would only throw unwanted attention on her and on how the accident happened. If it was known he was alone, then what happened to him would be a mystery and a matter of guesswork, which suited their purposes. Agnes obtained a one-year lease on a small cottage some miles away under an assumed name. It was compact and remote, perfect for their plans.

James started going out for prolonged periods of time in his wheelchair unaided. Arriving back, his mood was jubilant, invigorated, and the medical staff praised the new James. The risk-taker, the forward thinker who took back control of his life, despite his injuries. He took short walks around the hospital grounds building up his wasted leg muscles. The doctors were delighted with his progress. Agnes sang his praises to the other patients, extolling James as a model patient, one who aided his recovery with fresh air and exercise.

They waited until the weather obliged with a rainy, miserable day with poor visibility – a day when the damp drizzle forced even the most stalwart indoors. Emma was on duty with Agnes and two other nurses. The wards were busy but became busier still for Emma when Agnes became ill with a tummy bug, leaving her to manage their ward alone.

Shortly after lunch, James donned a raincoat and hat and set out on his meanders.

"I won't be long today, Emma, it's a bit wet and cold, but I don't want to miss even one day's exercise. I'll bring the chair with me and alternate between sitting in it and pushing it," James said.

"Are you sure? I'd prefer it if someone went with you in that weather. But I can't spare anyone at the minute." Emma looked worried. "Oh, I suppose it will be all right. Just be careful. The wind is picking up out there. I'd say we are in for a stormy night."

Emma waved at James and turned back to her new patient, only admitted that day and very poorly, worries about James relegated to the bottom of her list.

Agnes felt terrible about keeping Emma in the dark about her intentions, but no one could know if their plan were to work. Mid-afternoon, she slipped out of her room and hurried to her carriage. She waited for James on a side road at the rear of the hospital. James climbed into the carriage as Agnes folded the hospital wheelchair into the back. Within minutes they were on their way. They headed out the coast road to the path that James had frequented every day for the past month. The pathway was deserted. At 3pm on a wet and windy day, it was not the safest place to be.

"Not a sinner," James said as he scanned the horizon.

Agnes got the wheelchair, and with one last look around, she pushed it and watched as it veered off the path and over the cliff into the sea. The rest of the journey only took forty minutes. They prayed that no one had noticed them. Agnes had left the cottage prepared for them. She helped James inside and lit the fire and the lamps.

"It's cosy, James," she said with a smile.

"It's Jane now. James died this afternoon."

Agnes shivered as the significance of what they had done threatened to overwhelm her.

"I just hope we get away with it," she said.

"You need to get back. You need to be in bed when Emma gets home."

Agnes hurried back, stripped out of her damp clothes and into night-time attire. She no longer needed to fake a stomach bug. Her stomach was doing backflips, and a thin layer of sweat settled on her forehead and stayed there regardless of how many times she wiped it away. James would be missed soon, and Emma would come looking for her. Unless Emma had already been home before she got back from the cottage, which meant her plan would fail. Emma would want to know where she was, why she wasn't at home. Agnes's mind raced with endless what-ifs. She was sitting in bed pretending to read a book, doing her best swan impersonation, when Emma arrived less than an hour later, calling from the hallway. The door burst open, and Emma rushed into the room.

"Is James with you? Have you seen him?"

Agnes sat up in the bed, conscious of her heart skipping a beat and hoping Emma could not see how distressed she was.

"James… why would James be here?"

"He's missing. I was hoping against hope he decided to call on you."

Emma sat on the side of the bed and took Agnes's hand. Agnes stared at her friend, hoping her face was registering the correct amount of surprise and worry. Now that Emma was sitting beside her, she didn't know how she was going to keep up the lie. How could she lie to her best friend? But what choice did she have? She couldn't tell her, couldn't tell anyone. A voice inside her head reminded her that this was Jane's chance at life. It wasn't her secret to tell. Conflicted, she sat staring at Emma as she told her how James was in great form and how busy the ward was, but she had begun to worry when James didn't arrive back at dinner time.

"It's dark now, Agnes. Where could he be?"

"Poor James." Agnes got out of bed. "I must go look for him."

"But, Agnes, you're unwell."

"I feel much better now. Besides, how can I rest while James is missing?"

Emma waited while Agnes got dressed, and the two friends went back to the hospital to raise the alarm. Other than checking the hospital and the grounds, there wasn't much that could be done that night apart from organising a search team for the morning. The search for James Langton commenced at first light. The following day, a wheelchair was found washed up on a beach at low tide. The markings on the undercarriage were traced back to the Royal Victoria Hospital at Netley and, in particular, to Ward 2. Searches continued for several days, but James Langton's body was never recovered. Agnes joined in the searches and continued with her duties in the hospital. James was declared dead. Marks in the ground beside the cliff path showed where the wheelchair had swerved and went over the cliff. It was concluded that a gust of wind must have taken control of the chair, and James, in his weakened state, was unable to prevent it from tumbling over the cliff and into the sea.

Agnes was overcome by grief for the patient she had cared so much for. Emma did what she could to support her friend when she confided in her how much she had loved James.

"I can't do it anymore, Emma. I must get away. To lose Matthew was bad enough, but now James. I have no heart for nursing anymore."

"Take a break, Agnes. Go home to your mother. Spend some time away from here. I know how fond you were of James. You did everything you could for him. His final days were better because of your care. There was nothing more you could have done."

Agnes took some time off and travelled to London. Her mother was a shadow of her former self, still grieving for her husband and a source of concern for Agnes and her sister. Agnes decided not to burden Bernadette with her problems when their mother was in such a delicate state, so she said nothing to her about her dilemma. During those few days in the arms of her family, Agnes did consider her future. She had realised quite some time earlier that she was in love with James. However, to all intents and purposes, James was dead. Now she had to consider was she in love with Jane? Or would she forever grieve for James, just as Jane grieved for Charles? It was a vicious circle, and she debated long and hard over whether she should get caught up in it. In the end, Agnes felt drawn to Jane like a moth to a flame. She had to be part of her life. And if that meant they would be friends for the rest of their days, then so be it. Friendship was the better part of marriage. She had decided that long ago. She had married Matthew, who had loved her dearly, but she knew now her feelings for him could not have been true love but companionship. She weighed up continuing her life as a widow, nursing these poor soldiers, against starting a new life in tandem with her best friend. Two widows helping each other through their grief. For Jane was now a widow. Agnes saw to that.

When she was still at Netley, she gathered up the belongings of James Langton to hand over to the authorities. Amongst his papers, she planted a marriage certificate. The certificate recorded the marriage of Charles Best and Jane Langton in Dublin shortly before Charles set sail for Africa. It had been easy enough to forge the names onto an old marriage certificate stored amongst paperwork left behind at Netley by former patients, army veterans of numerous wars. It was a conversation with Jane that had prompted her. They had been talking about Jane's clothing. She had borrowed clothing from Agnes, all black.

"I feel like a widow. I miss Charles so much. I did love him, Agnes. I grieve for him every day."

Agnes sympathised with her. She had worn black for a time after Matthew died, but she had never felt like a widow. But, when she thought about it, she felt more of a widow now after James's supposed accidental death.

Jane was strangely touched when Agnes told her what she had done.

"I never considered anything like this. Now I can legally live as the widow of Charles Best. I cannot thank you enough, Agnes."

Agnes felt a surge of pride and smiled at Jane. She could do this. She was ready and willing to start a new chapter in her life in tandem with this woman.

Chapter 39

Jane

During the year in the cottage, Jane developed her sense of style. She worked out which type of clothing suited her, how to wear her hair, how she walked, how she talked. Every morning she bound her male appendages tightly and donned the clothing of the woman she wanted to be. Her tastes in clothing hadn't changed since the days in Dublin, and she quickly discovered she was much the same size as Agnes. Jane favoured dark greens but insisted on wearing Agnes's black widow's garb in memory of Charles.

Jane spent most days and nights alone, becoming the woman she wanted to be. Agnes continued to work in the hospital. They had planned she would hand in her notice in time for the end of the lease and, in the meantime, work out where they would live.

It took them some time to decide on where to settle. Agnes and Jane debated the merits of losing themselves in the bustling metropolis of London. Agnes was against it, citing her large and intricate family was heavily involved in the commercial interests in the city. Jane discarded living in Dublin. Too many memories of James's hellion days in

Trinity College and his grandmother's home, which he had sold in the months after her death anyway. Dublin was too small a city to get lost in, the social circles too tight. They were sure to meet people who knew the Langton and Cantwell families.

After much debate, they decided on Belfast. It was a thriving town, growing rapidly and with a large migrant population. People flowed into the city searching for work in the linen industry, the shipyards, and the engineering works. They could find somewhere to live, anonymously amid the teeming masses. Their search started shortly after James had transitioned into Jane. Their finances were the first hurdle. In his grief after his sister's untimely passing, the Langton inheritance had depleted, squandered by James. Charles had left his personal wealth to James which then passed on to Jane. It was enough to get them set up but not enough to sustain them until the end of their days.

"We need to supplement our income," Agnes said. "It's a pity you didn't inherit the estate as well."

"I'm happy Charles's widow cannot inherit Glassdrumman Hall. In the first instance, I spent so much of my youth there I would be recognised. If not by the tenants, certainly by the staff. I love Glassdrumman Hall, but it was James who loved it there. It is no place for Jane."

"You are right, of course." Agnes hung her head. "That was thoughtless of me."

Jane leaned over and patted Agnes's hand.

"You could never be accused of being thoughtless. Thanks to you we still have my inheritance. It will be perfectly adequate for us to buy a large house and perhaps open a boarding home for young ladies to supplement our income. Belfast it is. It will be a clean slate for us both."

Agnes nodded and returned Jane's smile. Jane felt a new sense of purpose. It was good to finally feel alive again after such a long time under the dark cloud of grief. She would make Charles proud of her.

Jane wrote to estate agents in Belfast requesting details of any properties that might be suitable for their use. The following month, they received a reply, and both pored over the brochure. It was an old house, in need of some attention, but both Jane and Agnes could see the potential. The area was perfect, and the owner was willing to negotiate on price for a quick sale. Agnes was due some furlough from the hospital, so the next day, she applied for her vacation and booked two tickets for the next sailing from Southampton to Belfast. Jane was suddenly nervous. It was one thing being Jane in the cottage, but this would be her first outing, and she wondered if she was ready.

"Of course you are. Look at you. The first time I saw you, I thought you were a woman. You are even more so now. Look in the mirror. Who do you see?"

Agnes turned Jane towards the mirror which hung over the fireplace and watched Jane's reflection as she stared at herself. Jane smiled: a slow realisation of a smile, an acknowledgement that Agnes was right. She turned to Agnes and kissed her, a slow, tender kiss that felt right. They both turned back to the mirror, smiling, calmly elated at the revelation of that first kiss.

The women travelled the short journey to Southampton and boarded the ship to Belfast the following week. Agnes had booked a double cabin for them below deck, which was perfectly adequate for their needs. They stood on deck to watch the ship leave port. It was mainly businessmen on board, some families, and most hugged the rails on a lovely sunny day.

"Beautiful day, ladies."

The man beside them doffed his hat and introduced himself.

"Henry Kinsella, at your service. Are you travelling far?"

"No, we are disembarking in Belfast. I believe the ship is

travelling on to America." Agnes held out her hand. "I'm Mrs Williams, very pleased to meet you, sir, and this is my friend Mrs Best."

They chatted for a while, incidental chat about travelling and Belfast, a subject about which he was quite knowledgeable.

"They call it Linenopolis, a term I am deeply grateful for, as I earn my living from selling our Belfast linen all over the world. I am returning to Belfast with orders that will keep our mill busy next year."

Mr Kinsella was charming and entertaining. Jane watched him as he interacted with the other passengers. He reminded her of Rev. Turner, the principal of the Dundalk Educational Institute in both age and attitude, and she felt at ease in his company. During dinner on the second day, she found the courage to speak to him. She had been practising for months to speak in a higher tone and no longer had to think about it on this voyage. But still, using her voice for the first time in company unnerved her. She kept her replies short and to the point, answering only what was asked of her. She fancied Mr Kinsella must have found her quite shy and retiring, and she couldn't contain the smile that thought brought.

The three-day journey ended on a cold frosty morning in Belfast. The port was busy, and Mr Kinsella very kindly offered them the use of his carriage, which was waiting for him on the quayside. They accepted his offer gratefully and were transported to the offices of the waiting estate agent. Jane watched with interest at the passing landscape. The town straddled the River Lagan with Black Mountain in the distance, watching over the sprawl. Before long, the estate agent had transported them to the viewing.

The moment their carriage entered the road, Jane knew it was the one. It was such a beautiful house. An imposing red-brick building in Rosetta Park, a cul-de-sac with eight large houses each side leading up to their house, like sentinels guarding an entrance to the main building. Set back from the road with a sweeping gravel driveway, the double front door was accessed from six granite steps.

It looked sad somehow, run-down and shabby like an elderly lady down on her luck. Jane had seen the potential though, and so had Agnes. They had said nothing as the estate agent brought them from room to room, but Jane could sense Agnes's rising excitement, could see her own thoughts mirrored in Agnes's eyes.

"Well, ladies, I shall leave you to discuss it. It does require major renovation work, but it is solid. I'll wait for you in the carriage."

They stood outside the front door looking up at the double entrance. Jane turned to Agnes, whose expression mirrored her own.

"Agnes, it is perfect. There is plenty of room to take in at least twelve boarders and still have private quarters for us. The attic rooms are perfect for staff. It's exactly what we are looking for."

The purchase went through very quickly. The former resident, an elderly widow, had passed on some months earlier. Her heir, a middle-aged, harassed father of four daughters of marriageable age, was anxious to liquidate his inheritance to pay for the dowries he anticipated being liable for during the next London season. His débutante daughters had expensive tastes, a trait they had inherited from their mother, a former débutante and follower of the royal court. He accepted Jane's first offer and instructed his solicitors to close the deal as soon as possible.

Agnes planned her goodbyes at Netley. She knew she would find it hard to say farewell to Emma and dreaded telling her she was leaving.

"Oh, Agnes, I knew you were unhappy, but Belfast. Why?"

"I can't nurse anymore, Emma. My heart isn't in it. This

governess position is perfect for me. Since my father died, my mother doesn't seem to care, and as for my sister, well, she is so busy with her family, she won't even miss me."

Emma pleaded and begged and shed tears, leaving Agnes with nagging guilt, but she couldn't tell her the truth. She couldn't tell anyone. This was her secret, hers and James or rather, Jane, and Agnes couldn't divulge it to anyone, not even Emma. So, she left Netley with cards and good wishes from the staff and patients and a letter from Emma she knew she would treasure forever. A few days later, they finished out their lease on the cottage, packed their belongings and set sail for Belfast.

Act 4

Chapter 40

Agnes

JANE AND AGNES TOOK ON THE RENOVATIONS WITH A CLEAR vision of what they were trying to achieve. Their builder shared their vision, a local man named Eric, recommended to them by the estate agent. He had a flair for restoration and an enthusiastic attitude. He pored over their plans and added details they had never considered. It took six months of hard work, but the two women were delighted with the end result.

The brass knocker sparkled against the mahogany doors. The Best family crest etched into the glass panel above, dared strangers to knock at their peril. The large hallway showcased the staircase they had restored, which wound down from the upper floors, its banisters gleaming from decades of gloved hands and beeswax. To the right was the large drawing room with an Italian marble fireplace and deep couches, the windows overlooking the rose garden draped with golden damask.

Further down the hall, the door opened onto a polished mahogany table, which could comfortably seat sixteen diners in front of the French doors, which overlooked the extensive gardens to the rear of the house. The kitchen and scullery were adjoining the dining room, with the staff dining room on the other side but on a much smaller scale. A corridor led to the staff bedrooms while Mrs Best and Mrs Williams's private rooms were tucked discreetly to the side of the house.

Agnes's favourite rooms were the kitchen and the private parlour. She shopped for each piece of kitchen equipment personally and worked with Eric to design a working kitchen that was functional and practical. She paced out the garden and planned each element. She planned flowerbeds and lawns to the front of the house and the functional kitchen garden to the rear. There was a herb garden, a sizeable vegetable area and a sun-scorched back wall where she planned to train fruit trees and berries. She employed a boy to do the hard labour and oversaw the next stage every day. They had already decided Agnes would take on the role of housekeeper while Jane would look after the young women boarders.

Jane and Agnes thought long and hard about the name and, in the end, decided to name it after Jane's grandmother's house in Dublin. Riverdale House was christened midway through 1883, with their first young woman lodger settling in shortly afterwards. She was the niece of one of the tradesmen who'd worked on the house. He approached them one day and asked if they would consider taking her. She was his sister's daughter, a young single girl from a country area who had found work in one of the larger mills. She was quickly followed by several more girls, all young and eager for work. Good accommodation was difficult to find in the rapidly expanding town. Belfast grew into a city within a very short time period, and Riverdale House expanded with it. By the end of the year, they had full occupancy and a waiting list of young women eager to avail of the excellent lodgings of Riverdale House.

Mary-Jane O'Brien was nineteen when she first came to the house. Her aunt had told her about Mrs Best's lodging. Her parents had travelled from their country village of Annalong to meet with Mrs Best and check out their daughter's living arrangements. Mary-Jane was a beauty, with flowing red hair and a creamy complexion. A good conversationalist, she fitted in quite quickly with the other lodgers, who appreciated her calm and friendly manner. So, when her young man called to the house and asked permission to court her, Mrs Best was most impressed. Charlie was a handsome man, tall, with a shock of dark hair and expressive eyes. Before long, Charlie was accompanying Mary-Jane on her monthly trip home to visit her parents. Mrs Best wasn't surprised when Charlie proposed, but she was surprised by her parents' reaction and his.

"Although I shouldn't be surprised, Agnes. That type of thinking is endemic in this country."

They were sitting in their private parlour for their evening tea and chat, a habit which became a tradition. Jane and Agnes had worked together on choosing the furniture for their room, and each had brought something of themselves to it. They both felt at ease in that room and treasured their quiet time there.

"Religion certainly plays a huge role in life in Belfast. Although, I have to say I never really considered it when I lived in London."

"And it's not as if there is a huge difference in their religions. They're both Christian. But the reality is that religion does matter in Ireland. The Protestants are mainly descended from Scottish and English settlers, while the Catholics are mainly descended from native Irish. I might add that the nationalists, mainly Catholic, are campaigning for Home Rule for Ireland. At the same time, there is a large cohort, particularly in this corner of the country, who detest the idea. Who knows where it might lead but, in the meantime, what can we do to help Mary-Jane?"

Jane Best shook her head and sighed. She never considered

religion to be important. Her father was an atheist who cared little for religion or politics. What little religious training she had received was banished from her mind in South Africa. She no longer cared for God or religion but was careful to keep her views impartial during conversations with her young lodgers. Jane believed in the inner good of people. Perhaps there was a mystic being who was a force for good, but in her experience, that goodness was sadly lacking when she needed it most. She knew Agnes felt differently and had witnessed her friend say a silent prayer of thanks when life was good to them and a prayer for help when it wasn't. Jane felt a pang of jealousy on those occasions. She felt the absence of faith deeply and envied Agnes that comfort.

"I will speak to Mary-Jane and Charlie tomorrow. I think maybe if they marry in a registry office and have separate small ceremonies at a later date in their respective churches, it may solve some of their parents' issues."

The following week Jane reported back to Agnes.

"The wedding is on. The parents are finally on board, with some persuasion, I might add, but at last, they can set a date."

"We should offer to cater a wedding lunch for them," Agnes said. "We could set up the dining room with the best china and linen. It would be a great wedding present for Mary-Jane."

Mary-Jane was delighted with the offer when Mrs Best put it to her, but she wasn't so happy when she returned from her next visit home.

"My father was furious, Mrs Best. He has never spoken to me in that way before. He was so angry."

Mrs Best listened to her and pondered what she had to say.

"Why Mary-Jane, the solution is simple," said Mrs Best. "Your father is quite right. It is his duty to pay for his daughter's wedding. However, it does make sense to have the meal here in Belfast. So why don't you ask your parents to come and see me? We can host the meal here, but your father can provide the supplies. The only item I must insist on supplying is the wedding cake. Mrs Williams is already planning the ingredients and the design. She is very excited about it."

The wedding was an enormous success. The cake was a triumph for Mrs Williams. The dining-room table was adorned with the finest Belfast linen and the best china and silverware. Mary-Jane's parents provided the best of lamb and fresh salmon, vegetables from their own fields and home-made cheese and chutneys. Charlie's parents were so impressed they practically forgot that their new daughter-in-law was a Catholic.

Chapter 41

Agnes, 1900

THE TURN OF THE CENTURY WAS CELEBRATED QUIETLY IN Riverdale House. Agnes attended Sunday services at the local church on the last day of the old century and returned home in a contemplative mood. Her bonnet restricted her peripheral vision and muffled the sounds around her as she strolled along, lost in her thoughts. As she walked the final yards, she relished the view of her home, resplendent at the end of the avenue. The solid brasses on the front door glinted in the weak winter sunshine, the imposing granite steps leading up to the black doors glistened with frost that refused to melt. She felt the warm glow of contentment envelop her. It had been the best decision of her life to move to Belfast with Jane. She was happy. A widow for the past twenty-one years, she didn't mourn Matthew. She realised now that she hadn't loved him. She had loved the idea of him. He was kind and sweet and was good to his mother. He had been going off to war, and she wanted him to be happy, but it would never have worked out between them. She didn't love him the way she loved Jane. Jane was the love of her life.

The moment she laid eyes on her in that hospital in Africa,

she had fallen for her. Agnes knew straight away James was not like other men. She felt a kindred spirit in him, recognised his feminine spirit. Agnes sometimes wondered what type of person that made her. She had always been different. Different to her sister: different from the other women in the Nightingales. While others dreamed of meeting the man of their dreams and living happily ever after in wedded bliss, Agnes dreamed of attaining the status and reputation of her heroine, Florence Nightingale. Men never entered her dreams.

Matthew had been the one exception. Even then, their ambitions were to travel, to set up a community hospital in poor countries, to work together as husband and wife, doctor and nurse. Children never entered her head. At times she felt guilty that she had been untruthful in some way to Matthew. It was Jane who put her mind at rest where Matthew was concerned. Agnes was also grateful that the one good thing to come out of their marriage was the respectability that widowhood bestowed on her. It allowed her the freedom to live her life without the societal pressures single women must endure, not just to marry, but to marry well.

Although in the deepest corners of her mind, she was married. Agnes felt as if she was betrothed to Jane with bonds more potent than any church could impose on them. She wasn't stupid. Agnes knew public displays of affection between them would ostracise them forever. But living as they did, as two widows, allowed them the opportunity to spend the rest of their lives together.

The fact Jane was once a man named James did not alter in any way how Agnes felt about her. In her mind, James and Jane were the same person, two sides of the same coin. With Agnes's help and support, Jane had grown into an accomplished, compassionate woman. Agnes was proud to call Jane her friend and in the privacy of their rooms at night, her partner and lover.

As for the physical side of lovemaking, she thought she put that behind her when Matthew died. She didn't know whether it was inexperience on both their parts or whether they were not compatible but at the time she did not care for it, seeing it as her husband's right and her duty as his wife. The first time he tried to enter her, it had hurt, and she had bled afterwards. She had been expecting that but presumed it would be more pleasurable the next time. It wasn't. Matthew appeared to enjoy it, though, and she took some comfort knowing that she had sent him off to war happy and content. When Matthew died, all thoughts of lovemaking died with him. It wasn't until years later that her sexual desires were awakened. One winter's night, Jane had slipped into her bed, and they had kissed and cuddled. The next night, when Jane made love to her, Agnes experienced intense sexual pleasure. Jane became James in their bed but with a tenderness that only a woman knows how to give. To Agnes, it was as natural as the sun in the sky and leaves on the trees. Two people who loved each other, expressing that love for each other.

Agnes wondered what the twentieth century would bring for them both. Was there a brave new world out there, just waiting for them? Riverdale House was now at full capacity. The women who lodged with them were from all over the country. Belfast was still proliferating and attracting people in their thousands to live and work there. The gardens she had so carefully planned and nurtured were flourishing and had provided them with fresh vegetables all through the autumn and well into winter. The winter sprouts were gradually being harvested, and the last of the potatoes had been lifted. The berries had made the most delicious jams and chutneys she had ever produced.

When they bought the house, the first person they had hired was a cook. Denise was an older woman, well experienced and happy to share her extensive knowledge.

Agnes discovered a previously unknown flair for cooking and spent every spare minute with Denise learning everything she could. It was not something she had been taught as a child. If anything, it was quite the opposite. She had been taught how to hold the silver spoon, not how to use it.

When Denise died two years later, Jane and Agnes discussed hiring another cook, but Agnes told Jane there was no need. Agnes was not only perfectly capable of running the kitchen but surprised herself by wanting to do it and do it well. They took on a young girl to help in the kitchen and a lad to help with the labouring in the gardens. The arrangement suited everyone.

Agnes rounded the corner of the house on her way to the back door. The area to the left side of the house was laid out in an ornamental lawn. She mused about expanding her vegetable area and wondered if that could be an ideal spot, although she would need to consider hedging or planting of some sort to shield the vegetable area from the roadway. The driveway followed the outline of the house from that side, past the back door and on around the far side. It was wide enough to facilitate a horse and cart to deliver fuel and supplies to the back door. She lifted the latch and entered the back hallway. A closet just inside the doorway held outer clothing, hats, coats and boots, and she slipped off her bonnet and heavy winter coat. The heat from the stove spread throughout this part of the house, and it was always warm, even on the coldest of winter nights. The stock she had prepared earlier was simmering away on the stove, and she breathed in the heavenly scent. It was time to start dinner preparations.

"Ah, good, you're back."

Jane's warm smile reinforced Agnes's sense of contentment with her life, and she returned the welcome.

"Tea?"

"I have a pot ready on the table for you," Jane said, turning back into the kitchen. "I thought you might like a hot drink on a frosty morning like this one."

Agnes decided all was good with the world. What more could a woman want, she thought, a lovely home, a rewarding occupation and a true friend to share it all with. The secret to happiness is recognising the true value of companionship.

Chapter 42

Jane, 1907

A SHARP FROST SETTLED EARLY OVER THE CITY STREETS AND both women felt its pinch as they walked home from the Women's Institute. Despite her gloves, Jane's hands felt numb.

"A nice cup of tea is in order, Jane," Agnes said as she hung her wool coat in the cupboard. Both women were partial to a cup of Earl Grey at this time of the evening. The day's work completed, their young lodgers retired for the night, it was their time to relax. The monthly Women's Institute meeting went well. As a group they were preparing for the strike. Numerous families would need their support.

Jane removed the long pin which fastened her hat securely and placed both along with her gloves on the shelf above the coat hooks. She rubbed her hands together trying to get some heat into them.

"Dear me, it's a cold one tonight," Jane said. "I thought we would be over the worst of the cold weather at this stage."

"Hopefully it will be warmer by the time the strike happens. By the looks of it, there's no avoiding it."

"Tommy's brother spoke very well tonight on behalf of the

workers. I think our ladies were quite moved by what he had to say."

"He did. Very inspiring I must say. I believe Mr Larkin is quite an impressive orator. He certainly must have something special to be able to unite both sections of this community."

"Who would ever have believed it? Catholic and Protestant workers uniting for the common good. It's quite an achievement."

Agnes poured the boiling water into the waiting teapot, covered it with the knitted cosy and set it on the tray. Jane followed her into the corridor leading to their private parlour. They had a lot to think about. The workers in the Belfast docks were on the brink of a strike never heard of before. They were led by Liverpool born James Larkin who arrived in Belfast in January to encourage dock workers to join the National Union of Dock Labourers. He succeeded, where many had failed. For the first time in centuries Catholic and Protestant workers had a common goal. They were about to call a national strike for union recognition. Women's groups, like the one Agnes and Jane attended, prepared to help families who may need financial support and otherwise during the strike.

"I must say, Agnes, I am in awe of people like James Larkin. It is quite a gift to be able to motivate men, to gain their trust and respect in such a manner."

"Let's just pray the strike comes to a successful and quick conclusion. If it drags on, too many women and children will suffer the consequences."

"Why is it always the women and children? Why can't those in a position of power share some of the pain? After all, if they paid a fair wage with decent working hours there would be no need for a strike."

"Jane, dear, in an ideal world, men would gain adequate reward for their labour, but nothing in this world is ideal.

Workers have always struggled. I was going to say always will, but I sincerely pray that is not the case."

"You and your prayers. I wish I had your faith. In God as well as in humanity."

"Someday I will convert you, my dear. I know you struggle when we finish each meeting with a prayer, although tonight I thought you managed quite well. I swear I may have even seen your lips moving."

"Agnes Williams, I do declare. You should have had those inquisitive eyes of yours firmly shut like a good Christian woman. All the others did, especially the pious ones, the women, who pray to God to help those less fortunate, yet shy away from doing anything about it."

"Try not to be so judgemental. Every woman there has their own cross to bear. We don't know what goes on in the lives of others."

"That is so typical of you. You always see the best in others. You're right of course. I am very quick to judge people. I should follow your example. I do try. When it comes to your faith, I really do try but I just can't seem to put all my trust in a God who would allow the type of conflict we saw in South Africa, the horror of that war lives with me."

"With me too, but it was man that perpetrated that evil, not God."

"Mmm, maybe."

The two women sipped their tea in silence, each wrapped up in their own thoughts of God and man. An hour later, Jane knocked on Agnes's door, more as a signal she was on her way in, than a request to enter. She knew Agnes was expecting her. Tonight, they needed each other, wanted to make each other feel loved and respected. They were all too aware their relationship would be vilified if any of their acquaintances or indeed their staff found out the truth. Jane and Agnes loved each other. They were best friends, confidantes and most importantly, lovers. They maintained their separate bedrooms but rarely slept apart.

The strike went on for months. Every evening the young women boarders discussed the latest news around the dining-room table. Each week brought fresh news. Non-union workers at Sirocco Engineering works walked out demanding wage increases. On Queen's Quay, coal merchant Samuel Kelly dismissed union members from his workforce, the others went out on strike. He and other major employers, such as Thomas Gallagher, brought in blackleg workers. Tensions ran high in the city, but the workers were united in their aim. Better working conditions for everyone.

"Mr Larkin said Gallagher is an obscene scoundrel," Ruth told the women around the table. "There were massive cheers for that one, I can tell you."

Ruth worked in Gallagher's tobacco company. The previous evening, they had staged a walk-out. One thousand women walked out of their place of employment in a display of solidarity with seven women who had been sacked for attending a meeting held by James Larkin.

"Will you all go out on strike?" Jane asked.

"I wish we could," Ruth said. "But we're not in a trade union. And no union would take us on now. It's the men the unions are supporting at the minute. But it is so wrong. The mayor even has RIC and troops protecting those blackleg workers. It's disgraceful."

"Mr Gallagher is blaming socialism of course," Vera said. "Instead of blaming his own policies, indeed his own greed. If he paid better wages, provided decent working conditions, none of this would have happened."

July brought further chaos. Workplaces all over the city closed due to strike action. Every day up to ten thousand strikers rallied outside the Custom House. The union demands remained constant, union recognition, wage increases and better working conditions. The employers were equally intransient, refusing to grant any concessions. There was a strong police and military presence protecting the blackleg workers brought in to keep the wheels of industry turning.

"Sid said it was unbelievable," Tommy said, in between mouthfuls of mutton stew. "Shipyard confetti, they called it."

"Shipyard confetti?"

"Rivets, nut, bolts, anything they could find to use as a weapon. They ended up having to move the blackleg workers to a ship moored in the harbour, for their own safety."

"Good enough for them," Mary said. "Taking work from our men."

Mary's comment brought raised eyebrows from Agnes, for Mary's bone-lazy husband hadn't worked in a decade, preferring to spend his days drinking ale.

"There's a march organised for the 26th of July. From the Shankill Road to City Hall. Everyone is going, Catholic, Protestant and no religion at all. There'll be pipe bands and marchers from every walk of life."

"I think I might just attend that," Mrs Williams said. "Perhaps Mrs Best will go too."

It was an amazing experience, one hundred thousand workers united in the march in support of the strike. By the time they arrived at City Hall the numbers had doubled.

"I have never seen anything like the solidarity outside City Hall today in all the twenty-five years we have lived in this city."

"It was something else to behold, Jane. If we could harness the energy in that crowd today, we could make this world a much better place."

"We?" Jane raised her eyebrows. "Once again, I am amazed at your faith in humanity."

"Always the cynic, Jane."

Only a few short months later Jane's cynicism was proved correct.

"This city will never change."

"It's such a pity," Agnes said. "There was so much optimism in the spring. Now, here we are, facing into the autumn with the strikers defeated and both communities at each other's throats again."

"At least there's harmony in this household," Jane said. "We must be mindful of the workers who lost their jobs. Their families will need our support."

Many of the more militant strikers were not reinstated after the strike. To make matters worse they were blacklisted, unable to find work to support their families. Through their volunteer work with the Women's Institute Jane and Agnes were acutely aware of the families. Some were in dire straits. Luckily the linen mills were always looking for women. Having the mothers in paid employment while the men stayed home went against the ingrained beliefs of some people, but others accepted their new reality. Charities such as the one Agnes and Jane were involved in took up the slack, helping families with food and essentials.

Chapter 43

Jane, 1912

THE CHAT AROUND THE DINING-ROOM TABLE WAS ALL ABOUT Home Rule. Mrs Best preferred to keep conversation clear of politics, but in Belfast in 1912, it was impossible. Home Rule for Ireland was on the way.

"My father says it's a travesty. That Home Rule means Rome Rule. We would be overrun with Catholic priests telling us what to do."

"That is just scaremongering. In this corner of the country, unionists have stirred up anti-Home Rule feelings. Of course, we have all heard the saying, *Home Rule means Rome Rule,* but it doesn't have to be that way. The people of this corner of the island will be represented in the parliament. It doesn't matter where it sits."

"Rubbish, they will prioritise agriculture ahead of industry, and Belfast will be the loser."

"Ladies, please. If the well-intentioned men who sit in Westminster cannot agree on Home Rule, then I doubt if we will agree around this table."

"In the mill today, I heard Mr Carson is asking for all men to sign a Solemn Covenant, swearing opposition to Home

Rule. And..." Betty paused and looked around the table. "For all women to sign a declaration giving their support."

"That's the first time in my lifetime that we women have been asked for our opinion."

Mrs Best couldn't contain her smile at the last remark. It was a fact she was all too familiar with, the constraints placed upon women in society outweighed any advantages.

"Yes, but only to support the men. The unionist leadership are opposed to women's suffrage. They have made that clear."

"If they were truly in favour of women, they would have asked everyone to sign the same covenant, not a separate one for women."

"Ladies, there has been much debate about extending the vote to women, but it will never happen, not in our lifetime anyway. Both sides of the Home Rule argument are totally against it. It is the only thing both Mr Carson and Mr Redmond agree on."

Mrs Best listened with interest to her young ladies debating the ongoing situation in relation to women's suffrage and Home Rule for Ireland. Like most of her young ladies, she had read the literature compiled by the Irish suffragette movement and was aware of the intricacies of the situation. Mrs Williams was a close follower of the suffragette movement both in Ireland and in England. Later that evening, over tea in their private parlour, Mrs Best recounted the conversation around the dinner table earlier that evening.

"All this talk of defending the union by any means is dangerous talk, Jane. God knows where it could lead. This organisation, the Ulster Volunteers, you've seen them. Many of them are veterans of the Boer War, former soldiers of the Empire. They will not give up easily."

"That is true, Agnes. There is a real threat of civil war in this country. They are extremely organised. They march past the avenue down the main road to the city every evening. I don't know why, maybe a show of strength? Who knows, but the rumour is the Nationalists have formed their own army in response. Who would ever have believed it would come to this?"

As the date for the signing of the Ulster Covenant and Declaration grew closer, tensions rose across the city. Cocooned behind the robust front doors of Riverdale House, Jane and Agnes felt safe and secure, but their daily forage into the city brought stories of further unrest. Mr Carson and his followers organised a series of meetings around the city to reach as many of the population as they could.

"Will you sign the declaration, Jane?" Agnes asked one evening.

Jane looked at Agnes, as surprise at being asked registered with her for a second.

"No. I think it is best if I stay clear. I have never seen such division before. Even in this house, our young ladies are divided in their opinion. I try to guide them, to advise on how compromise is usually the best course of action in most difficulties, but several of them are entrenched in their viewpoint and refuse to hear anyone else's opinion."

"Answer me this, Jane. Do you really believe everyone should compromise their position, even if they know in their heart that their course of action is the correct one?"

"Yes, I do, Agnes." Jane dropped her needlework in her lap and looked at her. "Human nature being what it is, we will never agree on every aspect on how we should live our lives. Everyone has different opinions, formed by their upbringing, by the trials and tribulations they deal with every day. First, read what Mr Carson has to say on why Home Rule would be a disaster for Ireland. Then, read what Mr Redmond has to say on how Home Rule is the only way forward for Ireland. The real truth of the matter is somewhere in between, and compromise is the only way to get there."

Jane wasn't surprised when she read about the number of people who had signed the Ulster Covenant.

"Over five hundred thousand men and women have signed. It says here that one man signed his name in blood." Jane sighed as she read the front page.

They retired to their parlour early. It had been a long week. Tensions were running high inside and outside Riverdale House. Jane felt like the city was sitting on a tinder keg, just waiting on the fuse to explode and devour them all in a flood of sectarian hatred. Riverdale House was a refuge for her inhabitants in the middle of it all.

"I was looking around me as I walked home earlier from the butchers. I think every one of our neighbours signed. I saw several of them heading into Ballynafeigh Orange Hall on Ulster Day. That's what they are calling it, you know."

"All we can do is hope and pray that a solution can be found before we descend into the chaos a civil war would bring. We need to think about stockpiling anything we can, just in case. Like oil for the lamps, firewood, sugar and flour."

"I have already started, Jane. Like you said, just in case, but let's hope and pray it doesn't come to that."

"I look at Riverdale House as our refuge, a place of safety and comfort for ourselves and our young lodgers."

"And so it is, and so it will remain. We have worked long and hard to establish this house. No matter how things turn out, people will always need a place to live. It wasn't pure luck that got us here. It was hard work, which will stand to us in the long run."

Jane smiled at Agnes. She had gained a little weight over the years. She couldn't be called fat, not by any stretch of the imagination, nor could she be described as matronly. She was tall for a woman and big-boned as her grandmama used to say. When they had first met, she had reminded her of a gangly youth not yet grown into their body, but now in her fifties, she had matured into a fine-looking woman with enough flesh in the right places to be curvy and womanly. She didn't realise she was staring until Agnes spoke.

"What is it? Have I spilt something on myself?"

Agnes put down her knitting and scanned over her dress.

Jane laughed. "Why, not at all. I was just thinking of how much we have been through together. You're right. We have worked hard. Life is good, no matter what is going on outside our front door."

Jane smiled at Agnes. Where would she be without her? Agnes was the glue that held her together, her anchor in life. The best friend anyone could ask for.

Chapter 44

Jane, 1914

"We are at war."

Mrs Best read the headline from the newspaper and felt her heart drop to her polished black boots. There was an excited murmur around the table as her young ladies digested the latest news. Mrs Best excused herself and hurried to the kitchen to tell Mrs Williams.

Mrs Williams took the paper from Mrs Best's hands and scanned the headlines. Mrs Best watched her friend as she took in the details and recognised the anguish which washed over her face in waves as memories of an earlier war sprang into the present. Agnes blessed herself, uncharacteristic for her, but this day was not the average day.

"The papers say it will be over by Christmas."

"I hope and pray they are right, Jane. I really do."

Agnes looked around the table at Tommy, the young labourer, who was finishing his meal by mopping up the juices with a chunk of bread. Tommy was happy in his work in Riverdale House but that didn't mean he wouldn't enlist. She knew his brother would. Sid worked in the shipyards until the national strike some years ago. He became prominent in the union, but when the strike was broken, he struggled for work. He was branded a troublemaker. Every day he went to the docks and stood in line, hoping to be called for a day's work. Most days he returned home, broken and angry. He had a family too, two mouths to feed as well as himself and his wife. She worked in the linen mills, and Tommy's mother helped with the children. Ever since Agnes had heard the story, bread and leftover stews had found their way to Sid's home, sent by Agnes and delivered by Tommy. Mrs Best encouraged Mrs Williams to send what they could. She had vivid memories of food baskets leaving the kitchen in the Cooley Peninsula bound for local families. She often thought they were the only happy memories of her childhood.

The months rolled into one another, and Christmas came and went with no sign of an end to the war. Agnes had been correct. Sid was one of the first to enlist and one of the first to die. Tommy was devastated by the death of his brother and worried for his sister-in-law and her children. It didn't stop him enlisting though. Mrs Williams begged him to wait but he wouldn't. In his absence she sent a food basket daily to Sid's widow, hoping to alleviate the family's suffering in some small way. Every evening when they retired to their private parlour Agnes took out her knitting basket. She began knitting socks and scarves for the soldiers in France. Her output was prolific, and every month or so, a new letter would arrive from some poor soul who was thankful for the warmth of a scarf or the relief of knitted socks on trench-wet feet.

As the war entered yet another year, food shortage became an everyday fact of life. Agnes was careful in her shopping and an excellent cook. Jane marvelled at the meals she turned out of her kitchen with the most basic ingredients. Every evening she said grace before meals with their boarders. Several of their boarders had boyfriends and friends fighting in France and Belgium, and they ended every meal with a prayer for the end of the Great War.

"The papers are calling it the war to end all wars," Vera said.

"Well, I wish it would end soon. I haven't had a letter from Bernard in over four weeks now." Susan stared forlornly at the hall table where any post for the boarders was left. Every single day Mrs Best checked the list of dead and injured. Her sigh of relief when she didn't know anyone on it personally was heartfelt. Then guilt hit her, and she said a prayer for those women who wailed at the sight of their loved one's name on the list.

The following day Mrs Best was relieved to see a letter addressed to Susan and waited with bated breath for Susan to return from work. Susan ripped open the letter, read it line by line with a huge smile on her face, and then disappeared upstairs to read it again. Over dinner that evening, she confessed to the others that Bernard had proposed. He was due some leave in the autumn, and he had asked her to marry him before he went back to France.

"What do you think, ladies?"

"Yes."

"Of course, yes."

"You have to say yes."

The clamour was enough to convince anyone. The boarders were all in favour. Even Miriam, the suffragette and confirmed spinster, was caught up in the romance of it. Susan bloomed as she listened to the other women. Mrs Best smiled. It was so apparent Susan never had any intention of saying no. Her happiness was infectious.

The happy mood in Riverdale House was disrupted by the news of the rebellion in Dublin that Easter. The constant bad news from the war was hard enough but reading about troops being sent to Dublin to fight their own people was a source of consternation for most of the young women and sparked debate around the dinner table for quite some time. When news filtered through about the executions of the ring leaders, the house became divided. Some of the young women declared it was time Ireland became independent from Britain and that the rebels had been correct in their actions. Others declared they had been traitors to their country, not patriots. After one very heated argument, Mrs Best banned the topic from the dinner table for the sake of peace within Riverdale House.

The summer was marred by the ongoing horrors at the Somme, which made for sombre reading in the papers. To Mrs Best, it felt like every street in Belfast had suffered a death or injury.

Mrs Best was arranging flowers from her garden into vases on the dining-room table when she heard her name being called. Miriam stood in the hall, her arm around Susan. She was standing there, her face completely white as if she had seen a ghost and her mouth was opening and closing like a goldfish.

"What is it, Susan? Tell me, what is it?" Mrs Best put her arms around Susan's shoulders and looked over at Miriam, who shrugged her ignorance.

"He's de…"

Susan started to cry as her body crumpled onto the floor. Mrs Best went with her, trying to hold on to her.

"Bernard. My Bernard is dead."

Susan shook as sobs racked her body. Mrs Best wrapped her arms around her and rocked her back and forwards.

"Oh, my poor girl."

They stayed there, on the parquet flooring, while Susan sobbed, and Mrs Best comforted her. Miriam wrung her hands and brushed away silent tears as Susan's anguish echoed around the house. Eventually, Mrs Best rose and led Susan to the parlour. Mrs Williams followed with hot sweet tea and helped get Susan comfortable on the couch. They left her there while they organised the evening meal for the other boarders.

"My heart breaks for that poor girl."

"As if the bloodshed wasn't bad enough. It says in the papers that nearly sixty thousand men were killed on the first day at the Somme." Miriam put down the paper and looked around at the other women at the table. "How is that even possible? All those lives lost. It just beggars belief."

"I have no idea, Miriam. This so-called war to end all wars is decimating our menfolk. There doesn't seem to be an end to it. I have never witnessed anything like this before. All we can do is pray for an end to it," Mrs Best said.

She had no appetite for food that evening. Susan's distress had put an end to that. She excused herself and went through to the kitchen where Mrs Williams had put together a dinner tray for Susan. Mrs Best carried it to the parlour.

"Oh, Mrs Best, thank you, but I couldn't eat. I just couldn't." Susan cried fresh tears.

"I will leave it with you, Susan. Just try a little bite."

After the evening meal was over, the other boarders retired to the parlour to join Susan. Mrs Best listened in at the door and felt a sense of pride in the manner in which her young women spoke to the grief-stricken Susan. She sighed at the realisation that Susan's grief was replicated in homes across the country. Jane shook her head and returned to the dining room to help Helen clear off the remnants of the evening meal.

Agnes and Jane sat in their private parlour that evening, both subdued and lost in their own thoughts. Jane relived the day Charles had died from his wounds in South Africa and the intense grief that followed. Agnes remembered Matthew and wondered if he had lived would they have children now, who themselves would be fighting in France or some far-off distant land for king and country.

Chapter 45

Agnes

"Those poor unfortunates, Jane. How much longer can this go on?"

Agnes shook her head, not expecting an answer. Her needles clicked furiously as if mirroring her inward anger at the fate of her young pen pals, young men at the front, now in their fourth year away from friends and family.

"How can those in power allow this to continue? So many lives lost, so many families destroyed, and for what? There soon will be no men left to fight."

Agnes put down her needles and pinched her nose between her eyes. Jane handed her a cup of tea and a sympathetic pat on the shoulder.

"I know, Agnes, I know. It is a dreadful state of affairs."

Agnes took a sip of the hot tea and lifted the letter she had been reading.

"Listen, Jane, listen to what Tommy has written: *I fear for my life, every hour of every day. The crackle and whistle of the howitzer is in my head, every hour of every day. I even hear it in my head in the dark of night when all around me is silent. I do not know how much more of this I can endure*. I cannot bear it. What those men are going through is unbelievable. Every letter brings a different horror, stories of death and mud and vermin. Oh, Jane, the stories about the vermin, of wounded men being bitten, of dead bodies still lying where they fell and rats feasting on them. All in full view of the living. We both saw the war in South Africa, but it was nothing like this. Nothing on this earth has ever been as bad as this."

Agnes's hands shook as she folded the letters and slipped them into the pocket of her basket. She lifted her needles. The motion of sorting the wool and counting the plain and purl stitches helped to soothe her angst. Agnes was knitting yet another scarf and hat for the soldiers at the front. She had taught the boarders to knit, and every week they sent off another parcel, filled with colourful scarves and warm gloves. Agnes looked at it as her contribution to the war effort. That and her garden filled with vegetables and herbs. The food shortages that the longevity of the war had brought had little effect on Riverdale House, thanks to her green fingers and enviable cooking skills. But tonight, she couldn't shake off her anger and despair. The latest batch of letters had been full of horror, and she had memorised every line. Her needles fell silent as she thought of Matthew. That had been a different war, but it had also been bloody and needless.

"Sometimes, I wonder about Matthew. If he died alone." Agnes looked across at Jane. "Do you think he had someone with him to hold his hand, to give him strength in his final moments?"

"We will never know for sure, Agnes, but you should content yourself with the knowledge that he couldn't have suffered. Death was instant to everyone at Isandlwana. The Zulus made sure of that. It was a cruel war. Having said that, I genuinely believe every war is cruel. Every war is needless. Surely there must be a better way."

"There has to be. We have too many old men in power, old

men willing to sacrifice our youth. It is time to put an end to such nonsense."

Chapter 46

Jane, 1918

THE WAR TO END ALL WARS ENDED EVENTUALLY, AND celebrations spilt out into the streets. Agnes and Jane stood, side by side, watching their young women boarders sing and dance with friends and neighbours. The war was finally over, and the men would be coming home. Jane wondered if the young women had considered the difference that would make to their lives, particularly Una and Nora. Both young women worked in the post office, sorting the thousands of letters and parcels that flowed between Ireland and France. Those jobs would go to men when they returned. Another eight of their boarders worked in various linen mills. They no longer made tablecloths and bedding but had converted to the war effort making linen coverings used by the Royal Flying Corps. When Agnes and Jane retired to their private parlour that evening, they celebrated the end of the war with a nip of whiskey in their tea.

"Thank the Lord that it is finally over." Agnes raised her cup to Jane.

"Thank God is right. We can finally look forward to a peaceful Christmas."

For the next few weeks, the conversation around the dinner table was filled with joyful talk of homecomings peppered with sadness over friends and loved ones lost forever. An election was called for December, and Jane was shocked to find out she could vote in a General Election for the very first time.

"How times have changed, ladies. All men over the age of twenty-one now have a vote. Those men who came back from war, who never had a voice before, now have a say in who runs our government. And for the first time, some women have a voice."

"But Mrs Best, we don't have the vote. Why should we not have a voice?" Una had been given notice that day, her position as sorter given to a man who had returned from France.

Vera spoke out, "Because we are women, Una. I know it might not seem fair, but men have always been the providers, and women cared for everyone in the home. That is just the way it is. We don't have the education, the knowledge to make the right decisions. That is a man's prerogative. They gave the vote to women over the age of thirty who owned property because they reckoned at least they would have an education behind them."

Nora laughed out loud, followed by several of the other boarders.

Mrs Best held her hand up to silence the laughter.

"Everyone is entitled to their opinion, ladies. For the first time ever, I have the right to vote in the upcoming election, and I intend to use my vote to support those who support women. I have no doubt whatsoever that in years to come, the right to vote will be extended to all women, but until that day, I will do my duty by using my vote wisely."

The room erupted with a round of applause and a rousing chorus of "For she's a jolly good fellow" much to the amusement of Mrs Williams, who came to the door to find out what all the noise was about.

The election was a landslide for Sinn Fein with 73 seats out of 105, but the Unionist parties retained their control in the northern part of Ireland with 26 seats. Mrs Best wasn't surprised. Neither was Mrs Williams. What did surprise them was the election of a woman.

"Well, I never thought I would see the day a woman would be elected to parliament. Countess Constance Markievicz is the first woman ever elected to Westminster."

"It is amazing, Agnes. A woman MP. This is only the start. You mark my words, before we know it; half of the House of Commons will consist of females."

Agnes laughed. "I don't know about that, Jane, but yes, it is a start."

The following morning two places were empty at the breakfast table. Nora and Una shared a room at the back of the house, and both were usually very punctual. Una was last to the table and looked pale and sweaty.

"Mrs Best, Nora is feeling poorly. She looks quite frightful..." Una sat down abruptly, clutching her stomach. "I have the most dreadful stomach pain."

Mrs Best led her upstairs back to her room and gasped when she saw Nora tangled up in her bedclothes, damp with sweat. Her skin was clammy yet hot to the touch. Mrs Best helped Una to bed and went back downstairs to fetch Mrs Williams. They both had heard the stories of the nasty flu that was sweeping the city, and Mrs Best feared the worst. Mrs Williams sprang into action. She stripped Nora's bedding and got her comfortable again before opening the bedroom window. After organising chicken broth and lemon tea laced with whiskey for both girls, she ordered everyone to stay away from their room. That night she made face masks for every member of the household and left strict instructions they were always to be worn.

Both girls became violently ill very quickly. Mrs Williams had never seen anything like it before. When their skin took on a blueish tinge, and their mouths and eyes discoloured, she finally understood the rumours she had heard of the "black death" or "Spanish flu." The doctor was called, but there was nothing he could do. Nora died within forty-eight hours of contracting the illness, coughing up blood and mucus as her immune system fought the virus. Fear gripped Una as she watched her friend choke and die, and she cried out for help. She held on to Mrs Williams with fear in her eyes as she coughed and spluttered until her last laboured breath. Finally, Mrs Williams closed her eyes and pulled the sodden sheets over her prone body.

That night Agnes wept as she prayed while Jane sat holding her hand. The young women boarders' families had been notified. Unfortunately, they never got the chance to say their goodbyes. The Spanish flu had struck so quickly and so violently, there had been no time. Riverdale House sank into mourning and remained in mourning through Christmas and into the New Year.

"We had such hopes for Christmas and the New Year, such anticipation of a life free from war and death." Agnes sat in her armchair, a woollen shawl around her shoulders.

Jane handed her a cup of tea before settling into her own chair. The dying embers of the fire threw out shadows into the corners of the room. Agnes sat in the semi-darkness, unusual for her, as Agnes's hands were always busy. If she wasn't knitting, she was mending or sometimes reading a book, but her hands were never empty.

"Are you all right, Agnes?"

"I am as good as I can be. It has been such an awful time, and I fear for our future. I fear for this country. Ireland is facing war with England, and I don't know how much more war we can take."

"Whatever happens, we still have Riverdale House. We will continue to make it a haven for our young women and for ourselves. Let the world rage around us. We will remain safe behind our front door, in our little piece of the country."

Chapter 47

Agnes

Agnes welcomed Tommy back from the war with open arms. His job was waiting on him and he settled back in quite quickly. At times he needed to be alone. Agnes heard the stories. Men who returned from the war, marked by the violence, violated by the horrors they witnessed. Tommy was better than most. Agnes could read his moods. She recognised the signs when the moroseness crept up on him. At those times she assigned him chores that took him away from the others. Menial chores that required little thought but kept his hands busy until his normal persona returned.

Today, Tommy was in right form, regaling them all with a story about his nephews and their recent attempts to help Tommy in the kitchen garden. Mrs Williams had been happy to see them. She whipped up some soda farls, hot from the griddle and dripping with creamy butter, to fill their bellies before returning to their widowed mother. They were eating dinner and listening to Tommy amidst laughter and debate, but Mrs Williams kept a watchful eye on Katie. Katie fidgeted with her napkin, dabbing her mouth, then smoothing it out again over her lap. She took a small bite of food, then dabbed again, shifting in her seat. She cleared her throat.

"Mrs Williams..."

"What is it, Katie?"

Katie cleared her throat again.

"I am due my Sunday off this weekend. Would it be possible to finish early on Saturday? I want to travel home to see my mother."

"But of course."

"Thank you, Mrs Williams."

Mrs Williams watched as Katie dropped her eyes to her plate, her cheeks flushed, her fingers once again fidgeting with her napkin. She knew instinctively Katie was in trouble, but she had no idea what kind of trouble. A glance in Helen's direction gave no clue. Helen concentrated on her plate, pointedly avoiding eye contact with anyone else. She dismissed her doubts for the time being.

Agnes voiced her concerns to Jane later that evening.

"If she doesn't tell us, how can we help her?" Jane implored Agnes.

"I'm not sure. I could be wrong. What if I am wrong and we ask her if she is expecting, and she isn't. How embarrassing. How insulting."

"Have you met her young man?" Jane asked.

"Yes, Peter seems to be a nice fellow. He was polite, well-mannered, like I said, a nice fellow. He's working in the shipyards, although I do not know precisely what he does."

"And you don't think Helen knows anything?"

"No. I don't think Katie has confided in anyone. But what if I am wrong and there is nothing to be confided? Maybe Katie is just homesick." Agnes looked at her friend. "Maybe she is going home to tell her mother."

"That could well be. We may just wait and see how she is when she gets back on Sunday evening."

The two women sat in quiet contemplation, sipping tea from their bone china cups. Jane picked up her needlework. She loved this hour in the evening when the young women had retired, the work of the house was complete, and Agnes joined her in their private parlour. They talked about everything and nothing, from sourcing new bed linen to which vegetables were in season, the intimate lives of their boarders, to the workings of the government of the day. Sometimes they just sat, each wrapped up in their thoughts. Jane loved needlework; it was as if her long nimble fingers were designed for it. Agnes preferred knitting, and the clatter of her needles was sometimes the only sound in their parlour until they both retired for the night.

"Louise will be delighted with this. It is so lovely."

Jane ran her hand over the soft white blanket Agnes was finishing off with a pink satin ribbon. It was part of a baby layette for one of their former boarders. Louise had left the year previous. She had met her beau in the mill where she had worked as a spinner, and he was a sorter. They had settled in the city and were blessed with a baby girl. Agnes had started the layette months earlier. As soon as it was finished, Agnes and Jane planned to visit Louise and her baby. They had lost count of the number of young women who had lodged in Riverdale House over the years. They were always happy to see them move on to marriage or sometimes just move home to look after elderly parents. They even had women who had boarded with them in their youth, sending their daughters into their care.

The next morning Mrs Best fixed her hat and left Riverdale House through the back hall, her shopping list securely in her basket. Mrs Williams hummed as she kneaded the bread for the evening meal.

"Mrs Williams, can I speak to you?"

Katie stood in the doorway, wringing her hands together.

Mrs Williams noted the pale face and dark circles around her eyes.

"Yes, of course, Katie, I was about to pour a cup of tea. Can I get you one?"

Katie gratefully accepted and sat in the chair indicated by Mrs Williams.

Mrs Williams placed a cup of strong tea in front of her and a plate of shortbread biscuits, pale yellow and sparkling with sugar. It was the mid-morning lull in the kitchen, not yet time for the midday staff meal and not yet time to prepare for the evening meal. Mrs Williams took the seat next to Katie and lifted her teacup. The strong woody aroma refreshed her before she even took a sip.

Katie held her hands in her lap. Her shoulders slumped forward, and her head hung low on her chest. A silent tear dropped off the end of her chin. Mrs Williams sighed.

"Come on, Katie, nothing is that bad. Spit it out."

Katie started to sob in earnest as she accepted the handkerchief offered. Mrs Williams sipped her tea and waited for the tears to subside.

"I'm expecting," Katie whispered between sobs.

"I see," Mrs Williams said, putting her arm around Katie's shoulders. "You're expecting a baby. You are not ill, not dying. You are expecting a new life."

Katie looked up at her, her mouth open in astonishment. She dried her eyes and blew her nose, still looking at Mrs Williams, who went back to sipping her tea.

"Drink your tea. That's a good girl. A grand cup of tea that is. It'll make you feel better. Have some shortbread. It was an excellent batch. So nice and crumbly, you can taste the butter. I'll give you the recipe."

Katie remained seated, mouth open, unable or unwilling to speak. Mrs Williams wasn't sure which. She continued to talk, describing in detail her method for baking the best shortbread.

Katie listened; her head cocked to one side. She shook her head and lifted her hand to signal Mrs Williams to stop.

"Mrs Williams, I'm expecting a baby. That's why I'm getting married."

Mrs Williams patted her hand. "I know, dear. But it's not the end of the world. It's a new life. That is always good news. You are not the first, and you won't be the last girl that has found herself in that position."

Katie stifled a sob and took a deep breath.

"I just didn't think it would be me. I don't know if I want to marry Peter."

"Ah." Mrs Williams patted Katie's hand. "Now, that my dear, is a different matter altogether. Talk to me. Do you not care for Peter?"

"I do. He's a good man. But I'm scared. What if…" Katie's voice broke into sobs.

"There, there." Mrs Williams patted her hand and replaced the sodden handkerchief, "What if what? What if he turns out to be exactly what you know he is, a good man?"

Katie's sobs gradually subsided once again.

"What if he's not, though? What if he is mean-tempered? How would I know? I'm seventeen. What do I know about men?"

Mrs Williams sighed and took Katie's hand in hers.

"Now, Katie, you have been stepping out with Peter for over a year now. Has he always treated you with respect? Has he always been kind?" Mrs Williams quizzed Katie, who nodded her agreement. "Well then. Chances are, if he is kind and respectful now, he will continue to be good to you. You are scared. That's not surprising. But you must think about what is best for you and best for that precious baby you are carrying. If you don't marry Peter, where would you go? What would you do?"

"My mother said I must marry Peter. She will not take me

in unless I marry him. She has offered for us to live with her for a while until we get sorted."

"Well, that's good. At least you will have a place to live." Mrs Williams smiled at Katie; a reassuring smile designed to ease her fears. Katie's red-rimmed eyes studied her hands in her lap, twisting the handkerchief.

"Will you and Mrs Best still come to the wedding?"

"Of course we will, my dear. Why would we not?" Mrs Williams gave Katie a quick hug. "We will be honoured to watch you wed your young man. Provided that is what you want. You need to make that decision now. Don't string that young man along. If you are certain you don't want to marry Peter, you need to speak out now."

"Oh, I am so confused. I love Peter. Honest, I do. I would have been over the moon if he had asked me to marry him before I found out I was expecting. I just can't help feeling he only asked me to marry him because of the baby… and I'm afraid, in time, he will blame me for trapping him in some way."

"Oh, my dear girl. Peter loves you. He has told you that. He wants to marry you. If you love him, marry him."

"Everyone will know that he only married me because of the baby."

"No one has to know that you are expecting. Say nothing. When the time comes, you can say the baby came early. People will suspect, but they won't know for sure. And believe me when I tell you, you are not the first girl to find herself in this position, and you will not be the last. Now I must get on with the cooking, and you, my girl, have work to do. We will talk again tomorrow, okay?"

Katie nodded her agreement, a faint smile on her lips as she hurried away to throw cold water on her face before returning to her chores.

Chapter 48

Agnes

Later that night, Agnes related the whole conversation to Jane.

"Katie is expecting," Agnes said as she poured the tea, adding milk and sugar.

"Well, we did suspect that. It was obvious when she got back from that weekend with her mother, with the reading of the banns at church arranged, a date set, and so soon. So, what now?" Jane accepted the cup gratefully.

"She is two months gone. She told her mother, who insisted the wedding be arranged as soon as possible. The poor girl is a bit confused. But what choice does she have, Jane? Let's face it. What choice does any girl have who finds herself in her position?"

"You have met her young man?"

"I have. He is a good fella. She does love him, and he treats her with respect. I think he will make a good husband."

"Well then. We must help Katie dispel any doubts. It would be different if her young man was of bad character, like some we have come across over the years," Jane said. "Did you read the letter we got from Teresa? It has worked out well for her, thankfully."

Jane sat in silence as Agnes read aloud the two-page letter from their former boarder. Teresa had lived with them for three years. She was a lovely young woman, but she had fallen for a scoundrel, who abandoned her when she became pregnant.

"Little Wilfred is five. Oh my, how the time has flown," Agnes commented as her eyes skimmed the pages. "What do you think about this new suitor?"

"We shall wait and see. I think Teresa has learned to be a better judge of character. It was a good choice to move her to your sister's friends in England. They do still believe she lost her husband during the war?"

"Yes, they do. Teresa has perfected her image as a young widow. My sister wrote to me only last week and mentioned how it was time for Teresa to move on, that she had grieved long enough for her husband."

"That's good to hear. Maybe this suitor is the one for her, and she will have her happy ending," Jane said with a smile. Teresa had been a favourite. A smart girl who deserved a second chance, in Jane Best's opinion. When that scoundrel abandoned her, Teresa had been devastated. She told her family of her predicament, but her father threw her out in the street after beating her and told her never to return, despite her mother's protestations. Her mother had to sneak out of the house under the guise of helping a neighbour through childbirth. She brought Teresa to Mrs Best and begged for her help.

"I know I've said it before, but I don't understand men like Teresa's father. How can you bring your daughter up to adulthood, then abandon her in her hour of need? What God does that serve? She still hasn't heard from him, but at least her mother keeps in touch with her."

"Thankfully, not all men are like that." Agnes folded the letter and placed it back on the bureau. "Teresa's suitor seems to be a good sort. She appears to be happy."

"That she does, and her mother approves. Who knows, maybe in time, her father will soften his stance and get to know his grandson. Stupid man." Jane shook her head. "The folly of male pride when it comes to their wives and daughters."

Chapter 49

June, 1922

"Can I have a quick word, Mrs Best?"

"Of course, come in." Mrs Best signalled to Sarah to join them at the kitchen table. It was unusual for their lodgers to venture into the kitchen, but Sarah was the exception as she had been with them for nearly ten years. Mrs Williams poured a cup of tea and placed it in front of her.

"There's a girl in work. Iris Seoin. She's a tiny, frail little thing with an appetite like a bird. I've got to know her quite well…" Sarah hesitated. "Would she be able to move in here at the weekend?"

"Is she a friend of yours, Sarah?" Mrs Best asked.

"Yes. I know she's not on your waiting list, but she is badly stuck."

"Where is she living at the minute?"

"She lives with her grandfather and well… it's not a good situation."

"I see." Mrs Best and Mrs Williams exchanged glances.

"Ask your friend to come and talk to us. Tomorrow evening, after work?" Mrs Best said. "Would that suit you, Mrs Williams?"

"Perfect. We can have a quick chat before dinner."

The next evening Sarah arrived home from work with Iris in tow. They joined Mrs Best and Mrs Williams in the parlour. Sarah was right, she was a tiny girl, no more than eighteen years old yet wise beyond her years. She answered their questions with yes or no, no embellishment yet Mrs Best could sense fear in her. She knew instinctively Mrs Williams felt the same way.

"Why don't you stay for dinner, Iris," Mrs Best said. "Meet the other girls."

"I'd like that." Mrs Best had to strain to hear her reply.

"That's settled then," Sarah said. "Come up to my room and get washed before dinner."

"I will get back to the kitchen or there will be no dinner," Mrs Williams said.

The next day Sarah accompanied Iris to her home to collect her few meagre belongings. She settled in well with the other girls, despite her shyness. Mrs Best tried to include her in the conversation around the dinner table but Iris invariably blushed and stuttered, uncomfortable with the attention.

A few weeks after her arrival, Sarah and Iris were the only guests for dinner on a Saturday evening. All the other young women had returned to their homes to visit family. Mrs Best was glad of the opportunity to talk to Iris openly. Having Sarah there put Iris at ease somewhat. Sarah had told her something of what Iris was going through, leaving Mrs Best to ponder whether to broach the subject or not. She didn't need to.

Iris's pale cheeks coloured. "Mrs Best, can I talk to you?"

"Of course, dear. Why don't I get us some fresh tea. I find conversation is always better with a nice cup of tea."

Mrs Best asked Mrs Williams to send a fresh pot of tea and returned to sit beside Iris.

"Now, my dear. What's on your mind?"

"It's my grandfather. He wants me to go home but I can't, Mrs Best, I just can't."

Iris started to cry, silent tears that ran down her pale cheeks. Despite the best efforts of Mrs Williams over the past few weeks, Iris still looked malnourished. Mrs Best handed her a fresh handkerchief and waited patiently for Iris to continue.

"It's not natural, Mrs Best. I thought it was. I didn't know any different."

"Whatever do you mean, Iris?" Mrs Best asked gently as if she were talking to a small child. Iris cried as she talked, silent sobs that racked her childlike body as she told them how her grandfather had crept into her bed at night and had done so since she reached puberty.

"There was one time I got in the family way, and he took care of it. Brought me to this woman, and she hurt me. She put this thing inside me, and I bled, for weeks…"

Mrs Best put her arm around Iris's shoulder. She could feel her bones through her skin, deep sobs coming from the depth of her being.

"It wasn't your fault, Iris. Your grandfather is at fault. Not you. You can stay here for as long as you want. You don't ever have to go back there."

"What will I do, Mrs Best? I can never marry. What man will ever look at me?"

"That's a different discussion altogether, Iris. Let's take one step at a time. You need to rest now. Recover from your ordeal. Everything will look better when you have put some distance between what you have been through and where you are now."

Sarah brought Iris upstairs to their room, still sobbing from her ordeal. Mrs Best retired to her private parlour to talk to Agnes about everything Iris told her.

"We must protect that poor child," Agnes said. "That man will never touch her again."

"I agree with you, Agnes," Jane said. "That poor girl has

been through so much at the hands of that evil man. If I ever get my hands on him, I swear I will not be responsible for my actions."

Mrs Best didn't have to wait long. Some weeks later Iris arrived home from work in a distressed state.

"What is it, Iris? What's wrong?"

"It's him. He followed me home from work." Iris cowered at the foot of the stairs.

Mrs Best rushed towards the front door.

"He's gone, for now anyway," Iris said. "What will I do?" Her voice rose an octave.

"Hush now, my dear." Mrs Best rubbed Iris's arm. "I'll talk to Mrs Williams. We'll figure something out."

It was Agnes Williams who came up with the idea of meeting Mr Jones.

"Meet him, Jane. Face to face. Tell him in no uncertain terms Iris is staying in Riverdale House. She's over eighteen. He can't force her to leave if she doesn't want to."

Neither woman realised that meeting Iris's grandfather would change their lives forever.

Act 5

Chapter 50

Agnes, 1922

Agnes wrung her hands together, unable to fully comprehend what Jane was telling her. Iris's evil grandfather turned out to be someone they knew. More importantly someone who knew them. Someone who met them during that crucial time in their lives. Forty years ago, the former Private Drake Jones was an evil twisted individual. Judging by their latest dealings with him, age had twisted him even further.

How could this happen at this stage of their lives? Despair dragged her into a dark place. Was it some elaborate plot by the gods to clash their past with their present, a punishment of sorts for their wrongdoings? Her logic questioned that. Any wrongdoings they committed forty years ago were way down the chain of right and wrong. She wasn't a bad person, neither was Jane. Agnes attended church services regularly. Both Agnes and Jane obeyed the ten commandments. They didn't kill Jane Best. She was already dead. If anything, James gave his sister life when he took on her persona. Charles Best loved that person enough to leave him his personal wealth. James and Jane were always the same person.

Agnes knew that their relationship was unconventional, but

she refused to believe there was anything bad in it. How could something that brought them both so much joy be viewed as bad by anyone. In their community they were perceived as good Christian women who went out of their way to be kind, to be charitable to those around them. Agnes trained as a Nightingale nurse. Jane as a medic in the military corp. Both had put that training to the test in South Africa. Their partners both lost their lives in South Africa but that's also where they found each other. A rebirth of something wonderful after all that death.

Riverdale House was something to be proud of. Agnes only had to think about the young women who had lived under their roof over the past forty years. Women they had helped, encouraged, educated. Those women kept in touch. Some sent their daughters to Riverdale House, knowing Agnes and Jane would look after them.

That hateful man, Drake Jones, was threatening everything they had built together. The longer she thought about it, the more her initial despair turned to anger. He might have recognised Jane that day, but he didn't see Agnes.

"I remember him in South Africa," Agnes told Jane. "He was a liar and a thief. I caught him, stealing from the dead. I reported him to the commanding officer, but he made me out to be the liar. The commander didn't believe me. He dismissed me as some hysterical woman."

"How awful for you."

"It was just before we sailed home. The commander told me I was making trouble for his soldiers. He actually said women shouldn't be in a war zone."

Jane embraced Agnes. They stood like that together, each seeking comfort from the other. Breaking away from Agnes's embrace, Jane recounted everything Drake Jones had said. Agnes sat, her eyes never leaving her friend.

"He said he wants twenty pounds on the last Friday of the

month, or he will talk." Jane continued to pace while Agnes sat, her face closed.

"Well, he is not getting anything from us." Agnes pulled her friend down to the couch beside her. "Do you hear me, Jane, nothing, not a farthing. Pay him once, and there will be no end to it."

"What else can we do?"

"We stop him. We avenge Iris and all the other women he has denigrated for you can be sure, Iris wasn't the only one."

Anger made Agnes plan to kill the man. She put her Christian beliefs to one side deciding she would make her peace with her Lord afterwards. Drake Jones didn't deserve mercy. He ruined everything he touched and had to be stopped.

The next day Agnes called Tommy to the side of the house.

"We have a leak somewhere and we need to find it before I put in that ornamental fountain I'm planning." She brought Tommy to the exact spot. "Dig down about four feet deep and six feet long."

"But there couldn't be any water pipes over here," Tommy argued.

"There is, Tommy. I remember when we bought the house first, there was a bathhouse on this spot. The ground is permanently damp here. There must be a leak."

Still grumbling Tommy started to dig while Mrs Williams went back inside to her kitchen. He didn't find any pipes or any evidence of leaking water and told Mrs Williams as much over the dinner table that evening.

"Oh dear." Mrs Williams tutted. "But at least you have the ground dug out to put in the fountain. Thank you."

Mollified, Tommy wolfed down the extra portion of dumplings Mrs Williams put in his stew. On the last Friday of the month Jane and Agnes were prepared. Agnes arranged to have the girls go into town with a list designed to keep them away from the house for hours. She arranged for Tommy to go to Annalong to buy the stone she wanted for the patio. All the lodgers were out at work. Mary was given the day off. The only occupants of Riverdale House were Agnes and Jane. Both women knew exactly what they needed to do.

Drake Jones arrived at the back door at exactly eight o'clock. Agnes waited in the hall cupboard, in her bare feet wearing only her petticoat. She had left the back door slightly ajar with the heavy flat iron attached to a rope sitting on top of the door jamb. As expected, Mr Drake Jones pushed open the door. The flat iron swung from its resting place and hit him directly between his two beady eyes. He fell to his knees initially then fell forward onto the covered tiles. Agnes Williams stepped forward, her marble rolling pin held high. She hit him on the back of the head timed to each stroke of the clock. There was no doubt whatsoever. Drake Jones was dead.

The two women disposed of his body and cleaned away the evidence of their crime. By the time the girls returned, Riverdale House was spotless, all evil despatched from its environs. Agnes and Jane continued with their normal duties. Tranquillity had been restored to Riverdale House. At least that's what Agnes told herself.

Chapter 51

Jane, 1922

Mrs Best smoothed her hair as she checked her reflection in the hall mirror. She was surprised to see she looked the same. In her head, she thought somehow the evil deed she had committed would appear on her face, darkening her eyes, dragging her skin downwards into a point at her chin. She looked closer. James's grey eyes stared back at her as if telling her she had done the right thing. Stuff and nonsense, she shook her head to dispel the notion and smoothed her hair again even though it was velvet smooth.

Guilt gnawed away at her insides, and she felt her stomach heave as an image of Drake Jones flashed in front of her eyes. It was the same image that haunted her dreams at night. Those rheumy eyes stared at her accusingly, with one bony finger pointing at her as if to say, *it was you*. Then, his head collapsing into a mess of blood and tissue. She sensed movement behind her and turned away from the mirror to watch Iris descend the staircase.

"Good morning, Iris."

Iris smiled, her head to one side, looking out from under her eyelashes. At first, Mrs Best had thought Iris's shyness was caused by her grandfather's bullying, but now she wasn't sure. She had overheard two of her other ladies discussing it as they sat on the lawn the previous Sunday. Both believed Iris wasn't shy at all and that she had a devious streak. An image of her weasel of a grandfather came into her head, and she wondered whether Iris inherited his nature. Mrs Best dismissed the thought. The poor girl had suffered enough at the hands of that monster. Iris was shy, unsure of herself; her confidence eroded after years of bullying and undue attention from a grandfather she hated.

Mrs Best drew herself up to full height, exhaled and swept into the dining room to supervise breakfast. Breakfast was a simple fare and quickly eaten, the only meal taken in Riverdale House where silence was actively encouraged. Mrs Williams signalled to Mrs Best to join her in the hallway to the kitchen.

"There is a man at the door by the name of Seoin. He says he is Iris's brother and needs to speak to her," Mrs Williams said, her hand on Mrs Best's arm, her eyes conveying a command for calm into her soul. "Will you fetch Iris and bring her to the back door?"

Shock registered on Mrs Best's features, quickly replaced by her usual composure aided by a gentle squeeze from Mrs Williams. Mrs Best took a deep breath and nodded. She turned back to the dining room and called Iris just as she was about to leave the room. Mrs Best led her to the hallway where a man stood, cap in hand, with a shock of black hair and a fresh complexion. Iris's face broke into a delighted smile.

"Fred, what are you doing here?"

Mrs Best left them talking and retreated into the kitchen to join Mrs Williams. They both heard the click of the back door shutting and the rustle of Iris's skirts as she went back to the dining room. The women exchanged glances, both unsure of what to do next, but were saved from making any decisions by Iris's voice calling Mrs Best. Both women went into the dining room where Iris sat, her hands folded in her lap and her fear written all over her face.

"He is missing," she whispered. "No one has seen him in nearly a week. Fred has no idea where he could be."

Mrs Best felt her heart skip a beat.

"Who, my dear, who is missing?"

"Grandfather."

"Oh my." Mrs Best sat down beside Iris. "Is that something he would do? I mean to disappear for a few days."

"No. Grandfather is a man of routine, a military man. Fred was away with work. He works on the railway. When he returned on Friday, he presumed grandfather was out at one of his charities, but he didn't come home that night or yesterday. His bed still has not been slept in this morning, and Fred is worried. I have told Fred to go around to his usual haunts. Maybe he has been needed in one of them and decided to stay there rather than at home alone."

"I'm sure that is the case," Mrs Best said, looking over Iris's head to Mrs Williams for guidance.

"Maybe your grandfather decided to go away for a while. Visit old army comrades?" Mrs Williams said.

"I don't think so, he would have let Fred know." Iris looked up, her eyes glistening with tears.

Mrs Best took Iris's hand. "Maybe he meant to but didn't get a chance. You said yourself he is a military man. Men like that have strong bonds. If someone he knew was in trouble, he would go to him, and he knew you had no intentions of going back to him, and your brother was away working, so there was nothing to hold him."

"Do you think so?"

"Yes, I think it is a distinct possibility," Mrs Best said.

"Part of me hopes his badness has caught up with him, and he has come to a bad end," Iris sobbed. "What kind of person does that make me?"

"Hush now, Iris. That is perfectly natural, but it is not the Christian way. Try not to think like that. It is not good for you."

"I'm glad he's gone. I hope he got his comeuppance," Iris said, her head held high for the first time since Mrs Best had met her. Her eyes glittered. "I know I should be Christian and pray for his safe return, but I can't, I won't." She shook her head in a gesture of defiance. "I can never forgive him for what he did to me. He ruined my life. He put a baby in me and paid someone to take it out of me. I nearly died, not that he cared. Then, the day the bleeding stopped, he was back in my bed, using me. What man will have me now? He has ruined me… I hope he is dead."

Iris's diatribe ended in a sob. Mrs Best covered Iris's shaking hands with her firm yet gentle grasp.

"I understand, Iris, really, I do, but I would advise caution. You cannot use language like that to anyone else in this house or outside it, for that matter. Other people wouldn't understand. They don't know the man like you do, like we do."

"Oh, of course, Mrs Best. Truly I would never consider speaking my mind to anyone. Only you and Sarah know what that vile man did to me. Even my brother has no idea, and I have no desire to tell him. No, my secret remains just that, a terrible secret I will have to bear for as long as I live. I will never forgive him. Good riddance to him. I just hope and pray he never comes back."

Iris dabbed her eyes with her handkerchief and thanked Mrs Best profusely. She made her way upstairs to fetch her coat and returned quickly. Hurrying from the house, already late for work, she turned to wave at Mrs Best on the front step. Mrs Best waved back, a lump stuck in her throat and her arms like lead. She closed the heavy door and leaned against it for support, her legs suddenly as weak as a newborn calf.

"Agnes."

Mrs Williams, still seated at the breakfast table deep in thought, was startled out of her reverie and ran to her friend. The two women met in the middle of the hall and embraced, each drawing strength from the other. The sound of the girls descending the attic stairs broke them apart. Mrs Best fussed with the lace trim on her collar while Mrs Williams hurried back to her kitchen. The daily business of Riverdale House resumed.

Chapter 52

Jane

THAT EVENING MRS BEST FELT LIKE COLD, CLAMMY HANDS were massaging her heart as she waited for Iris's return from work. She kept herself busy and checked in regularly on Mrs Williams. Always grateful for the support of Agnes Williams, today, she thanked God for sending this woman to her. She didn't realise she was staring until she noticed Agnes's raised eyebrow. Mrs Best smiled and made her way out of the kitchen and into the dining room to prepare the room for the evening meal. Her young ladies were starting to arrive back from work. The house groaned and creaked as they made their way to their rooms, changing clothing, washing away the scents of the day and preparing for their evening meal. When they assembled around the dining-room table, Mrs Best noted the empty chair where Iris usually sat.

Sarah spoke first. "Iris won't be here for dinner this evening, Mrs Best. She has gone to meet her brother. I believe she has told you her grandfather is missing."

"Yes, she did mention it."

"Poor girl doesn't know what to think. But, let's face it, she made it obvious she couldn't stand the man but for him to go missing like that, well…"

Mrs Best had to make a conscious effort to keep her composure. Her mind replayed every interaction she'd had with Drake Jones while all around her, the conversation concentrated on his disappearance. Gradually the words impinged on her consciousness.

"Spends all his time helping those less fortunate."

"I hope he hasn't come to a bad end."

"The destitute of this city owes him a debt of gratitude."

Mrs Best was surprised that several women knew him or knew of him and was shocked to hear only good things said about him. She tapped her glass with her knife, the high-pitched cling shutting down the rising murmur of heated conversation.

"Excuse me, ladies. Are you sure we are talking about the same man?" Mrs Best asked, "Mr Jones was an ex-soldier, small thin man, in his sixties."

It was Anne who spoke first.

"Why yes, Mrs Best. Mr Jones is well-known in the city for his charitable work. He works to help those less fortunate." Anne lowered her voice to a whisper. "But some wonder if he has come to a bad end because of that."

Mrs Best listened attentively, conscious of her heart pounding in her throat and nervous sweat running down her back. She raised a glass of water to her lips and drank, relishing the coolness of the glass against her fingers. Her hands shook as she placed the glass back on the table. Her young ladies were painting a vastly different picture of Mr Jones than the one she had in her head. She swore to discuss it with Agnes later and make inquiries about the man's character.

That evening Jane Best was relieved to close the door on her own parlour. She pulled the pins out of her hair and shook her silver-streaked mane down over her shoulders. Then, as she slumped into her much loved armchair, she exhaled deeply. She dreaded telling Agnes what she now knew about Drake Jones, but she need not have worried.

"From what I have heard today, the entire city of Belfast has a completely different opinion of Drake Jones than we do. Since he was reported as missing, there has been so much talk about his good works, but somehow, I struggle to believe it. We both know it doesn't ring true with the Drake Jones we knew," Agnes said.

They compared stories as they sipped their tea. Drake Jones may have been a perverted sneak and a blackmailer in their eyes, but to others, he was a good person. A man who brought up his grandchildren on his own, a man who spent hours every day helping the destitute of the city.

"The man I heard our ladies speak about this evening bears no resemblance to the man I know to be Drake Jones. The soldier was an odious man, foul-mouthed and vindictive. And yes, that was forty years ago, and he may have changed, but how is that possible when we know what he did to Iris?" Jane Best leaned forward as she spoke.

Agnes sighed. "People are strange. Think about it. Drake Jones showed one persona of his character to us, but he could be another person entirely in other parts of his life. We, of all people, should recognise that fact."

Jane wrapped her arms around herself and rocked in her chair. Her skin felt clammy, and her heart was fluttering in her throat. Her thoughts were twirling around her head. What had she done? What had she done to Agnes, her best friend in the world, her only friend? A sob escaped her lips, and Agnes knelt in front of her, her arms outstretched.

"Don't fret. What's done is done. We can't change the past. We just have to live with it. Drake Jones was an evil man. He may have done good things in the city, but even the worst people can do good sometimes. That pathetic excuse for a man was evil. He would have destroyed us and everything we have worked for."

"I know what you are saying is true. We both know how evil Drake Jones was. What type of man would do that to his own grandchild? How can a man be so cruel to his own flesh and blood and yet supposedly help those who are not his kith and kin?"

"I don't know, Jane. I don't understand it. Mind you, nor do I want to. That vile man may have hoodwinked certain members of society, but his evil deeds will eventually come to the fore. I cannot believe the good things I heard about him today. It just doesn't tally with the man we know him to be. It warrants further investigation."

"Oh, be careful. I know you are right. But how do we find out the truth about him? More importantly, how do we let the police know how evil he was without betraying the trust of the innocent?" Jane shook her head.

"Or worse still, we don't want to lead the police to Riverdale House, to us."

Chapter 53

Agnes

Agnes sat at the scrubbed kitchen table and hung her head in her calloused hands. The waft of bleach she had scrubbed the sink with earlier assaulted her nostrils. She took a sip from the hot sweet tea in front of her and listened to the sounds of her beloved Riverdale House as it settled around her. The huge Aga, the kitchen's focal point, hissed and groaned as the logs within its belly crackled and pushed heat into the ovens in preparation for the baking Agnes intended to get to before lunch. The bread rose in the warming pan, but she still had an hour to spare before it required kneading into shape. Upstairs, the floorboards creaked, as Helen and Katie moved from room to room, cleaning and tidying up after the boarders. The small kitchen window rattled as the wind started to rise, signalling the approach of a winter storm. Agnes had sent Tommy outside earlier to dig out the last of the potatoes. Not before time, she thought, best get them out of the ground and into storage before the winter sets in.

Agnes tried to focus on the daily chores, ticking off in her head the bread she would bake and the meal she would prepare, but her guilt ate away at her. She couldn't think straight. In the evening, when she was with Jane, she could reason it out in her head that Drake Jones was an evil man who got what was coming to him. Still, sometimes in the mornings, when the bustle of the kitchen had subsided after breakfast and the preparation had yet to begin for the evening meal, she found herself with time for a cup of tea and some internal reflection.

She was a Nightingale nurse, a trained professional. Her calling had been to heal the sick, help those in need, and nurture life. Yet she had killed a man, beat him to death. Yes, he was evil. Yes, he had done terrible things to Iris, and God knows who else, but his deeds didn't give her the right to play Judge, Jury and Executioner.

Agnes didn't class herself as overly religious. She had been brought up as a Christian to follow the ten commandments. *Thou shall not kill.* As a child, every night before she climbed into bed, she knelt and said her prayers, herself and her sister, side by side under their mother's supervision. In those days, her prayers were simple. She prayed to keep her family safe. She gave prayers of thanks for everything they had in life. Now in her twilight years, she was praying again with renewed vigour, only this time for forgiveness.

Where once she had given thanks for bringing Jane to her, now she prayed for forgiveness for taking that man's life. Even in her pleas to God for forgiveness, she felt conflicted for she knew in her heart that she would do it again without hesitation. Drake Jones was evil personified. He'd threatened to expose everything she and Jane had worked for. When they made the decision, forty years ago, to move to Belfast, she thought that part of their life was behind them forever. They had worked hard in Riverdale House, lavished care and attention to every detail. Agnes loved her life. She enjoyed the cooking and planning and the nurturing of these young women they catered for, but she especially loved the evenings when the day's work was done, and she and Jane retired to their private parlour. That time spent together was precious to her.

Agnes wasn't a bad person. She knew that. Up until the day Drake Jones came back into their lives, her good deeds far exceeded any evil thoughts. She was a pen pal to hundreds of soldiers during the war. Agnes fed families in the locality and clothed many more. Her stomach churned as the image of Drake Jones's battered body crept into her consciousness, and she shook her head to try and dispel it. He was evil, she told herself. He got what he deserved. Agnes heard the back door open and Tommy's cheerful whistle as he came into the kitchen, laden down with a basket of muddy potatoes.

"Where should I put this, Mrs Williams?"

Agnes's thoughts were momentarily interrupted by her daily chores. She had meals to prepare, young women to feed, a house to run. And what a house it was. Riverdale House. Her home. Jane's home. A home from home for all their young women boarders. The only home Tommy had ever known. A revered place in the memories of countless young women. The day loomed in front of her, one task at a time, starting with the potatoes.

Chapter 54

Jane

THE KNOCK ON THE FRONT DOOR ECHOED DOWN THE HALL AND into the dining room, where Mrs Best was busy clearing the table after the late weekend lunch. She wasn't expecting any visitors at three o'clock on a Saturday afternoon. Several of the young women were in the parlour, and more were preparing to travel home to various destinations around the city and further afield to visit family. Leaving Helen to finish clearing the dining table, Mrs Best excused herself and went to answer the door as two more loud knocks hurried her steps. She checked her appearance in the mirror and made her way to the large oak doors.

It was a stormy afternoon with twilight threatening an early arrival. Mrs Best struggled to hold the door as the snarling winds threatened to wrench it out of her hands. Two men in dark suits stood, badges open for inspection, their hats in their other hand. A fierce wind howled through the open door with a whoosh sending sodden leaves and twigs across the polished floor.

"Stand in out of the rain." Mrs Best ushered the two

detectives inside. "Miserable day, officers. How can I help you?"

The larger of the two offered his hand with a respectful nod.

"Afternoon, Mrs Best. I'm Detective O'Neill. This is my colleague Detective Smith."

Mrs Best nodded as she studied their badges, confirming their identity.

"Sorry for disturbing your afternoon, Mrs Best. We are investigating the disappearance of Mr Drake Jones. Can you confirm that his granddaughter, Iris Seoin, is boarding in this house?"

"Yes, detective, that is correct." Mrs Best nodded with a smile. "But Iris has already left today. I believe she has gone to assist her brother in the search for their grandfather."

"Yes, we are aware of that. But we would like to have a word with you, just some general background information."

"I see. Of course, if I can help in any way... but where are my manners? Can I offer you gentleman some tea?"

Mrs Best led the men into the dining room and went in search of Mrs Williams.

"The police are here. I've put them in the dining room for now. They have questions about Drake Jones," Mrs Best said as she rearranged the lace ruffle at her throat. Mrs Williams glanced up from her baking bowl, traces of flour on her cheek. She stopped what she was doing and moved to the sink to wash her hands.

"I will get Helen to bring through some tea. We expected this at some stage. Iris lives here, after all. Do you want me to join you?"

"No, it's fine. I can handle it."

Mrs Best returned to her guests, followed by Helen.

Detective O'Neill was standing at the window peering out at

the windswept garden. His overcoat glistened with raindrops, his dark hair flattened to his head by the hat he had removed when he entered the house and which he now held between two fingers. The younger man, Detective Smith, stood with his back to the fire, a fine mist of steam rose from his shoulders as his sodden overcoat met the heat of the fire. He was engrossed in his notebook, which he held with damp fingers that looked a peculiar shade of blue.

"Helen, can you take these gentlemen's coats and hats and bring them through to the drying room?" Mrs Best said before she sat at the table and invited the detectives to do likewise. Helen curtsied as she took their outer clothing and excused herself.

"Now, gentlemen, how can I be of assistance?"

Detective O'Neill nodded at his companion to start.

"Has Mr Drake Jones been a frequent visitor to Riverdale House?"

Mrs Best considered his question. The thought struck her that it was possible someone had seen him on the avenue, and she thought it better to be vague with her responses.

"No, I can't say he was a frequent visitor. He came here to speak to me about Iris taking lodgings with us. That would have been late June. Generally, my lodgers go home to visit family. It would be unusual for family to visit them here."

Detective Smith scribbled in his notebook while Detective O'Neill nodded.

"So, Mr Jones did not visit his granddaughter here?" Detective O'Neill asked.

"Well, no, not as such. I did meet Mr Jones one day at the end of the driveway. It would have been… possibly the end of September," Mrs Best mused. "It was a very blustery day, and he startled me. I dropped my basket, spilling the contents."

Mrs Best laughed, her hand up to the lace ruffles at her throat. The detectives smiled, more politely than with any sense of the humour at the situation.

"I presumed he had walked Iris back to the house that day. He did not call to visit her as such. He may have accompanied her to my home at other times, but I'm afraid I am unaware of any other occasions. Iris may be able to give you more information on that."

Detective O'Neill nodded. "And you don't recall seeing him at any other time?"

"No, Detective."

"Can you tell us more about…"

A knock on the door interrupted the detective. The door opened and Helen appeared with the tea trolley. Mrs Best thanked her and poured strong, hot tea from a white china pot with a steady hand and a regal smile.

"Now, Detective, what more can I tell you?" Mrs Best asked the detective.

"Iris. Can you tell us about her?"

"Certainly, Detective, if I can. She hasn't been with us for very long. She appears to be quite shy and reserved. I can't say she has made any particular friend amongst my other lodgers, but she may yet. As I said, she is quite reserved."

Detective O'Neill checked his notebook.

The scratch of ink on paper was the only sound as Mrs Best lifted her cup to her lips. She took a sip and replaced her cup with a clink.

"More tea, gentlemen?" Mrs Best rose to attend to the tea trolley. She felt a slight tremble in her hands and a chill down her back as cold sweat gathered between her shoulder bones.

"No, thank you, Mrs Best," Detective O'Neill said. "We have taken up enough of your time. Unless you have any other questions, Detective Smith?"

"Just a quick question, Mrs Best. What did she tell you about her grandfather?"

"As I said, Iris is quite reserved and hasn't been with us for very long. When her brother called to tell her that her grandfather was missing, she was upset, naturally, but I'm afraid there's not much more I can tell you."

"Thank you, Mrs Best. That's all for now. We will be in touch."

Mrs Best rang the bell for Helen to bring the detectives their outer coats and then accompanied the gentlemen to the front door and closed it softly behind them. She could feel cold sweat running down her back and caught sight of herself in the mirror. Her face was white as if she had just seen a ghost. She pinched her cheeks, smoothed down her skirt over her hips, took a deep breath and sailed into the dining room, outwardly composed and prepared to organise the room for dinner that evening.

Chapter 55

Jane

Mrs Williams signalled to Mrs Best from the dining-room door. The ladies were just finishing their evening meal with leisurely chats over cups of tea. Mrs Best excused herself from the table and followed Mrs Williams to the kitchen.

"It's Fred, Iris's brother. He wants to talk to Iris, but he wants us with him. He says he has some disturbing news."

Mrs Best felt her heart miss a beat and the flutter of panic in her throat. Her hand automatically adjusted the white lace trim around her neck while she took a moment to compose herself.

"Bring him to the front parlour and ask Helen to bring the tea trolley. I will fetch Iris."

Mrs Best took a deep breath before she sailed back into the dining room and went straight over to Iris, who was sitting alone and appeared to be lost in her own thoughts.

"Ladies, I need to use the front parlour this evening. I hope you don't mind confining yourselves to this room?"

A murmur of approval rippled around the room. On weeknights, most of the young women adjourned to their rooms after dinner to prepare for the early start the following morning and had no use for the parlour. Iris remained seated, her eyes unseeing, and Mrs Best touched her shoulder. Iris's head jerked upwards.

"Oh, sorry, Mrs Best, I was miles away."

"Iris, would you care to accompany me to the parlour? You have a visitor."

Mrs Best led Iris to the parlour where Fred stood in front of the Italian marble fireplace, the rim of his hat clenched in his hands.

"Fred, what is it?"

Iris's eyes darted from Fred to Mrs Best.

The door opened, and Mrs Williams wheeled in the tea trolley. She bade everyone sit as she served hot tea with milk and sugar. Only when they all were seated did anyone speak.

Mrs Best looked directly at Fred and in her most gentle voice said, "Now, Fred, do tell us what this is about?"

Fred was reticent at first, his eyes downcast and his shoulders hunched forward. He lifted his head, cleared his throat and mumbled, "It seems Grandfather is not the type of man we thought he was."

Mrs Best placed her hand on Iris's, which were joined in her lap and visibly shaking.

"Whatever do you mean, Fred?"

Fred's voice shook as the words tumbled from his mouth, slowly at first, then in a rush, one after the other, as if he had to say everything in one go or lose his resolve forever. The constabulary had been in contact and had filled him in on some of the finer details of Drake Jones's private life. The home their grandfather had told them was to house unfortunate women who had fallen on tough times was actually a brothel, and Drake Jones was the owner. The charitable work he was renowned for throughout the city was not even a charity but a front for his illegal activities.

"And worst of all, Iris. Our mother…"

Mrs Best exchanged worried glances with Mrs Williams; both unintentionally leaned forward as Fred hesitated. He rose and paced the floor in front of the fireplace, wringing his hands and averting his eyes from the three women seated in front of him.

"The women there, in that place… They said he bedded his own daughter. They said…"

Fred's voice trickled into a whisper. Mrs Williams rose from her seat and led him to a chair while Mrs Best kept Iris's hands covered with hers.

"They said he is our father."

The shock and horror on Fred's face was mirrored in Iris's as a heavy silence engulfed the room. Iris buried her face in her hands and rocked back and forth. Mrs Best felt a swell of anger engulf her and stick in her throat, rendering her speechless. Mrs Williams took Fred's hand.

"We don't know if that is true or not. Only your mother can confirm or deny that claim. It could be just conjecture from those women…"

"She said our mother had confided in her, that she died of shame."

Fred's words were barely a whisper. Mrs Williams looked over at Mrs Best, her eyes pleading with her to say something. Mrs Best cleared her throat and stood up, smoothing down her skirt.

"The constabulary has now confirmed what we already suspected. Drake Jones was an evil man who did evil things. This news is indeed shocking, and you need some time to consider it, but please also consider you had no part in this. Either of you."

Fred sat dumbstruck. His head hung between his knees as if afraid to look at the women in the room. Iris continued to stare at her brother, her eyes wide and her mouth hanging open as if words were trying to find their way from her brain to her mouth but failing miserably. She reminded Mrs Best of the shell-shocked hollows of men who returned from the Great War and hung around the legion halls staring aimlessly into space.

"Iris, listen to me." Mrs Best squeezed Iris's hands. "You will never know if this is true or not. People in pain are often pushed to inflict pain on others as if by doing so, they reduce their own. That story cannot be proved."

Iris opened and closed her mouth and nodded at Mrs Best.

"He said… he said she died in childbirth. He said our dad worked in the shipyards, that he died in an accident when I was only a baby."

"He lied," Fred said. "The police have confirmed it. There is no record of our mother ever marrying."

"But we carry our father's name…"

"We don't. Seoin is Gaelic for Jones."

"Grandfather didn't speak Gaelic."

Mrs Best interjected, "But he was a Connaught Ranger. They mainly spoke Gaelic. He would have heard it then."

"How could he? I knew he was evil, but this…" Iris struggled to find the right words. "Although it makes sense though, doesn't it? Look at what he did to me."

"What do you mean?" Fred rose to his feet, a look of bewilderment on his face, then knelt in front of his sister. "What did he do?"

Mrs Best had to strain to hear the question.

Iris started to cry, big heartfelt sobs that started in her stomach and engulfed her. Fred put his arms around her and hugged her close. He patted her back and looked towards Mrs Best, his face twisted with worry at his sister's obvious distress.

"Tell me, please. What is it? What is wrong with my sister?"

Mrs Best hesitated for a moment. It wasn't her secret to tell but Iris nodded, her eyes pleading with her.

"Please, Mrs Best, tell him. I can't," she said, her voice a hoarse whisper.

"What is it?"

Mrs Best wondered just how much she should tell Fred but then decided he needed to know the whole truth. He needed to know the depths of depravity his grandfather was capable of. For both their sakes.

"Your grandfather forced Iris to have intimate relations with him. He made her pregnant at one stage and arranged for that pregnancy to be terminated. When he again forced his way into her bed, she left and came to stay here with us."

The look of worry on Fred's face turned to abject horror. He dropped his hold on his sister and rose to his feet.

"Why didn't you tell me?" He grabbed Iris's arms and shook her, his voice rising several octaves. "Why didn't you tell me?"

Mrs Best intervened and pushed Fred away, who stumbled backwards and was caught by Mrs Williams.

"Let go of her. Can't you see she has been through enough?"

Fred shrugged off Mrs Williams's hold on him and knelt back in front of Iris.

"I didn't know, Iris. You should have told me."

Fred cried as he put his arms around Iris, and the two rocked back and forth, wrapped up in each other's tears.

Mrs Williams signalled to Mrs Best, and they left the room. Mrs Williams hurried to the kitchen to get some glasses while Mrs Best opened the drinks cabinet in the dining room and retrieved a bottle of brandy.

"For medicinal purposes," Mrs Best said.

"If ever brandy was needed, it is now," agreed Mrs Williams.

Chapter 56

Jane

JANE HELD THE SIEVE ABOVE THE BONE CHINA CUP AND POURED strong black tea from the powder-blue teapot. She filled two cups and added one sugar cube to each, using the silver tongs, a gift from one of their former lodgers. Jane handed one cup to Agnes before placing her own on the table beside her armchair. She stirred her tea three times in one direction before tapping the teaspoon on the side of the cup with a satisfying clink. She took a sip and gave a sigh of relief as she savoured the hot, sweet liquid. After an emotional meeting with Iris and her brother, they had retired to their parlour later than usual.

"That poor girl is so confused," Agnes said.

"She is. But you were right to point it out to her. I just hope she gets through this. It is only natural she is upset at her grandfather's disappearance, especially when she is in the company of her brother. It is also only natural she is happy about it too, for who wouldn't find some modicum of relief when your tormentor disappears."

"We must be careful. The temptation is there to tell Iris she need never fear that man again, but we cannot."

"It would ease her mind to know he will never torment her again, but you are right, as always, Agnes."

"Poor Iris. I just hope and pray the passage of time will ease her suffering, and she can put it all behind her."

"At least her brother now knows the truth about his grandfather."

"Yes. It is such a pity Iris didn't confide in her brother at a younger age. But then again, he isn't much older than Iris. He may not have been able to do anything about it."

Both women lapsed into silence as they considered the latest news about Drake Jones. Jane sighed and put down her teacup.

"For the first time, I am glad, and I know I should be ashamed to say this, but I am glad he is gone. I am glad we did what we did. He deserved to die. He was an evil, vile person who destroyed everyone he came in contact with, and I feel no remorse."

"I agree with you, Jane. What a hateful individual. I cannot stop thinking about those poor women he exploited. And as for what he did to his daughter and granddaughter! Whatever happened to his wife?"

"I don't know. I must ask Iris, in a day or two, when she has had a chance to absorb this latest information. For now, we must support her in any way we can. I think we should refrain from letting any of the other young women know about this. We should do all we can to prevent that news from becoming public for Iris's sake."

"Of course. The poor girl has been through enough."

The following evening the chatter over dinner was all about the upcoming church hall dance.

"I got a lovely new dress for the dance on Saturday night."

"Oh, it is lovely. That shade really suits you."

"I have my blue dress with the white collar. I've only worn it once before."

"I am looking forward to it so much. It has been an age since I danced."

"Ladies, if anyone needs any help with your preparations for the church dance, I am sure myself and Mrs Williams can be of assistance."

Iris was silent as the conversation flowed around her and over her head. Mrs Best glanced over and tried to include her from time to time, but Iris neither heard nor understood. She appeared to be lost in her own world and barely touched the food on her plate.

"May I be excused, Mrs Best? I have a slight headache; I think I will retire early."

"Of course, Iris. Perhaps an early night will do you good."

Iris nodded and left the room, barely acknowledging the other women who bade her goodnight. Sarah even offered to go with her, but she declined, stating she preferred to be alone. The solid oak door clicked to a close behind her, and the silence echoed in the room for thirty seconds before the latest rumours erupted around the table.

"Poor Iris. She must be so concerned about her grandfather."

"That's as maybe… but I heard today he wasn't the philanthropist we all thought he was."

"No…"

"Yes… they were saying he was a keeper of a house of ill repute."

The last words were said in a stage whisper as if the speaker was afraid to say the words aloud.

"Whatever do you mean?"

"Well, exactly what I said. That home for destitute women we heard about was just a front. It was actually a disguise for a house of ill repute."

"What does that mean?"

"A house where women sell their bodies for money… to men… you know…"

"No…"

"Aye, and there's worse. There's talk Mr Jones was behind all these gambling dens and that he was involved in extortion."

"Aye, and the talk today was that he came to a bad end. Some say he's at the bottom of the River Lagan with stones in his pockets."

"Do you think Iris knows all this?"

"Sure, how could she not know? Didn't she live with him since she was a baby?"

"I told you I thought there was a sly streak to her."

"No wonder she's been quiet. Didn't want to draw attention to herself."

The sharp tap of a silver spoon against glass silenced the room.

"That is enough, ladies. I will not tolerate idle gossip around this table. Whatever the truth is about Mr Jones, Iris had no part in it. She is as much a victim as those poor women, so I will have no more of that kind of talk around my table."

That evening in their private parlour Jane Best relayed what she had heard to Agnes.

"At least the true nature of the man is widely known," Agnes said.

"Yes, that is true, but my heart goes out to Iris. What can we do to protect her from the gossip of others? They don't know what she has been through at the hands of that man."

"But we can't tell them, Jane. That can never be common knowledge. It would destroy Iris."

Jane sighed. "I know, but that poor girl."

Chapter 57

Agnes

The avenue was dappled with winter light. The trees which lined each side of the road were bare, their branches glistening with a hard frost. Agnes inhaled the sharp freshness and sighed. She usually loved this weather. Christmas was only around the corner, and Riverdale House sparkled with warmth and spirit, the holly wreath on the door a welcome to all. This year she felt sick. Nothing Jane said could free Agnes from the sense of impending doom. They had worked so hard. It had been worth it. It was a beautiful house, a wonderful home. Until now, Agnes thought. The peace and tranquillity that inhabited Riverdale House had been punctured, possibly forever, by the evil presence of Drake Jones. She took one last look back before the cab turned the corner, heading for the port.

The storm the night before had uprooted trees and lifted roof tiles. It had even uprooted the fairy Drake from the top of the fountain. Maybe that was why she felt so uneasy, but there was nothing they could do about it today. It would have to wait until their return. Agnes looked across at Jane, sitting serenely staring into space as if at peace with the world. Although she knew from experience that Jane was the ultimate swan, calm and serene on the surface but underneath paddling furiously to stay afloat.

Smoothing down her skirts Agnes wondered if Jane had noticed how much weight she had lost. Nowadays she was a paler version of her usual self. Hopefully Jane put that down to the stress of the last few months. They were on their way to London. Agnes's sister had died, and she wanted to attend the funeral. Her sister approved grudgingly of Agnes's nursing. Growing up, she was the reserved sister, following a traditional role of marriage and children. It was hard to believe sometimes they were the product of the same mother. However, she was instrumental in helping them start a new life for one of their lodgers. Teresa had fallen foul of a blaggard who had left her pregnant. Agnes brought her to her sister, introducing her as a young widow with a baby who needed a roof over her head and a job as a nanny. Agnes's sister took her in gladly. Teresa worked for her until she met the young man who would become a devoted husband to her.

"I want to pay my respects."

"As do I, Agnes. I will go with you. Mary is perfectly capable of running the house for a few days. I will make the necessary arrangements."

The journey was uneventful and very tiring. London was damp and smoggy. Jane started to cough from the moment they arrived, much to Agnes's amusement.

"I had forgotten how smoggy London gets at this time of year. It creeps into your lungs and chokes like nothing else."

Jane and Agnes arrived at the Rickman house close to midnight on the night before the funeral.

"Gerald inherited my parents' house, and he has kindly offered to accommodate us."

"That is truly kind of him. I must say I am curious to see

the house you were raised in. It must be difficult for you to go back there now in these circumstances."

The thick London fog lingered over the course of the funeral and the next day as they prepared to travel back to Belfast. Both Agnes and Jane were happy to set sail and welcomed the fresher air on the sea. The cold breeze was refreshing after the crippling fog, and Jane breathed in deeply as she scanned the horizon for the first sight of Ireland. They had only been away three days, but it felt like an eternity to her. She missed Riverdale House. She missed Belfast. They had made a home for themselves there, a home she would do anything to protect. The thought struck her that not only had they committed murder to protect their home but that she would do it again and gladly to preserve the life she and Jane led there. She wanted to live out her final days in that house with her companion. She smiled as Jane joined her at the railings.

"Any sign of home yet?"

Jane tucked her arm into Agnes's, and they strolled around the deck, ignoring the biting cold. The sailing was uneventful despite the freezing weather. They docked in the early evening and hailed a cab to Riverdale House. Agnes was looking forward to getting home and sitting down in their parlour with a nice cup of tea. She felt tired after their journey, and she was sure Jane was equally exhausted.

As they rounded the corner onto the avenue, the dark night was illuminated by strong lights, temporarily blinding their cab driver. A police cordon across the road prevented the cab from accessing the house. The two women exchanged horrified glances. What terrible event had occurred during their absence? They alighted quickly. Mrs Best paid the cabby as he dropped their bags on the pavement. Fear gripped Agnes's chest as Tommy ran up to them, his cap in hand.

"I am so glad you're home. There's a body, in our yard, a

body," he said with a quiver in his voice, his eyes as wide as saucers. "They think it might be Iris's grandfather."

The two women again exchanged glances, noting the fear mirrored in each other's eyes.

"Whatever do you mean?" Mrs Best looked from Tommy to Detective O'Neill, who was approaching them from the house, his wide strides covering the distance in seconds.

"Mrs Best. May I have a word, please?"

"Of course, Detective. Shall we go inside, and perhaps you can tell me what is happening here. Tommy, will you bring our bags into the house? Come, Agnes."

Mrs Best led Mrs Williams and the detective inside the door of Riverdale House and into the front parlour. They could hear voices inside until she opened the door. Silence fell like a curtain. Several of their women boarders were seated and had obviously been discussing the ongoing situation. They excused themselves and retreated upstairs, leaving Mrs Best and Mrs Williams alone with Detective O'Neill.

"Can I offer you some tea?" Mrs Williams inquired. "I think myself and Mrs Best may be in need of a strong cup of tea at the minute."

Mrs Williams opened the door, but Helen was already standing there, her hand in mid-air, ready to knock on the door. Helen set off to the kitchen and returned with the fully laden tea trolley within minutes. Mrs Williams poured as Mrs Best removed her outer clothing and sat under the portrait of Colonel and Lady Best. Agnes noticed her friend hold her head to one side, a trait she knew meant her mind was racing ahead, trying to figure out the best course of action.

"Now, Detective, please tell us what is going on?"

"A body has been found on your property. We believe it may be Mr Drake Jones who was reported missing approximately six weeks ago."

The blood drained from Agnes's face. "Oh dear, how shocking."

"Are you okay, dear? You look quite pale."

Mrs Best rang the bell to summon Helen, who she sent to fetch some smelling salts.

"No, no, I'm fine. It's just so much to take in."

"We have only just returned from London where we attended the funeral of my friend's sister, Detective. It has been a very tiring time for her, for both of us."

"Of course, Mrs Best, Mrs Williams, I will not delay you too long. Can I ask a few brief questions to clarify some matters so I can be on my way?"

"Yes, of course, Detective. How can we help you?"

"I believe the flowerbed to the side of your property is a recent addition."

"The flowerbed?" Mrs Williams frowned and stood up, facing the detective. "What on earth has a flowerbed got to do with a body?"

"The body was found in the flowerbed, Mrs Williams."

Mrs Williams sat down again, allowing puzzlement to crease the lines around her eyes.

"In the flowerbed," she repeated. "Mr Jones's body was found in our flowerbed?"

She kept her tone incredulous as she looked at the detective for clarification.

"Yes, Mrs Williams. It seems your employee…" the Detective checked his notes, "Tommy, found the body, or at least found part of it and alerted us."

"Oh, my." Mrs Williams's hand flew to her mouth. "Poor Tommy. I really don't know what to say, Detective."

"Perhaps you could answer some questions for me? The body has been identified as Mr Drake Jones, who, as you know, has been missing for some time. Tommy has told us the flowerbed is a new addition. Is that the case?"

"I see, Detective. I think I can answer that for you. That area was all lawn, but we had to have it dug up to try and trace a leak from the kitchen. I think it may have been October. It certainly wasn't any later than that. Would you agree, Mrs Best?"

"Yes, yes, it was before the winter frosts… definitely October." Mrs Best nodded her agreement. "Detective, are you working on the theory that someone murdered Mr Jones and then disposed of his body in our flowerbed?"

"That is one theory we are considering."

"When was this discovery made?"

"Tommy called us yesterday when he found dogs had unearthed part of what he believed to be a human hand. There was a fountain of some sort that had been toppled by the storm last Friday, exposing bare earth. Tommy found the dogs digging yesterday morning, and as he chased them away, he saw the body part and called us."

"And is the body still there?"

"No, ma'am. It has been moved to the mortuary, but the area is still under investigation. I have already advised your lodgers and staff that no one may leave the city for the time being. The same applies to you two ladies."

"Are you seriously suggesting that we are suspects in your investigation?"

"The body was found on your property, Mrs Best. At this point, we cannot rule anyone out. That includes everyone who lives or works in Riverdale House."

"Oh my." Mrs Williams's voice was barely a whisper.

Mrs Best looked over at Mrs Williams, whose face was now a ghostly white with large dark rings for eye sockets as if she hadn't slept in days. Mrs Best gave her a tight smile.

"I see, Detective. I understand of course. Mrs Williams and I will do anything we can to aid your investigation. I would appreciate it if you could keep us informed of any developments… our boarders are the main concern. The reputation of Riverdale House is at stake here."

"Yes, of course." Detective O'Neill closed his notebook and tipped his hat in the direction of Mrs Williams.

"One more thing, Detective, may I ask if his grandchildren have been informed?"

"Yes, ma'am, they have."

"Poor Iris. I will go to her. She will be upset."

Mrs Best rose from her seat but was halted by the detective's outstretched hand.

"Iris Seoin is helping us with our enquiries."

A shocked silence filled the room. Mrs Williams stared at the detective, unable to process what he had just said.

"Whatever do you mean?" Mrs Best asked.

"Miss Seoin is a person of interest in this investigation. She had a motive to kill her grandfather, and my colleagues are speaking to her in the station."

"That is preposterous, sir." Mrs Best wrung her hands. "That waif of a girl could not have killed a man."

"Probably not, but she may have had an accomplice." The detective placed his butt of a pencil behind his ear. "So, if you will excuse me, ladies, I will get back to the station and see how the questioning is going."

"With your permission, sir, I would like to accompany you. Iris has no legal guardian, no one to look out for her other than the women in this house, and we would like to support her in her hour of need." Mrs Best pulled herself up to her full height and stared directly into the eyes of the detective.

He stuttered. "Of course, ma'am, of course."

Mrs Best pulled on her coat and gloves.

"I will be back as soon as I can, Agnes." She gripped her friend's hands in her own, worried now about the greyness of her complexion. "Promise me you'll get some rest."

"Good luck. Give Iris my regards."

Chapter 58

Jane

Mrs Best and Iris crept into the house in the early hours of the morning. Iris was pale and even more waif-like than she had appeared months earlier. Mrs Best had managed to persuade the police to let Iris go. She had argued they had no reason to hold her other than a faint hope that fear might lead her to confess to a crime she did not commit.

"Thank you, Mrs Best. I don't know what I would have done without you tonight."

"Not at all. We both know you didn't kill your grandfather. The police know that as well. It was utter nonsense for them to question you at all."

"I know I said he deserved to die… but I didn't mean it, well, not really. I'm not sorry he's dead, but that doesn't mean I would kill him."

"I know that, and so do the police. Now, get some rest and stay in bed in the morning. We can talk again tomorrow afternoon."

Mrs Best locked and bolted the heavy front door and stood in the hall watching Iris's dejected frame drag herself up the stairs. Then, tutting to herself, she made her way to her private rooms and let herself into her parlour, where she found Agnes asleep in her chair. The room was cold. Jane lifted the poker and rattled the remaining embers in the grate to throw up their last spark of heat. Agnes stirred and sat upright, fear etched on her face.

"Jane, what's happening? How is Iris?"

"It's okay, Agnes. She is upstairs in bed. All is fine."

Ashen-faced, Agnes stared at Jane.

"That poor girl. What are we to do?"

"We do nothing. We keep our nerve. Now let's get to bed. It has been a long night, and we need our sleep if we are to get through tomorrow."

Jane led Agnes to her room and helped her to bed.

"Goodnight, Agnes. A good night's sleep will help. Everything will look better in the morning."

Jane felt as if her arms were made of lead as she undressed and put on her night robes. She slipped between the covers and listened to Agnes's steady breathing. But, unable to sleep, she stared into the darkness. One side of her felt only anger that the police even considered Iris could be involved in her grandfather's death. But a tiny voice at the back of her head was whispering that it was a good thing. That at least the police weren't looking at her and Agnes. She closed her eyes and dismissed all thoughts by counting sheep. When she eventually slept, it was a fitful slumber, haunted by dreams of Drake Jones and his rheumy eyes amidst black cold clay.

The next morning Agnes looked dreadful. Her grey complexion and bloodshot eyes told Jane all she needed to know. She persuaded Agnes to lie down and get some more sleep, promising she would bring a breakfast tray later. Then, she went straight to the kitchen to instruct Mary to take over the meal preparation and cooking for the day. As she made her way to the dining room, Mrs Best caught sight of herself in the hall mirror and pinched her cheeks to try and force some colour into them. The stress of the last few days was taking its toll on them both, she thought.

In the dining room, the ladies were noticeably quiet at breakfast. They spoke in hushed whispers of inconsequential things, ate quickly and left the room as soon as they finished. When Mrs Best finished clearing away after breakfast, she assigned the girls their daily tasks. She put on her coat and slipped out the back door and around the side of the house. The cold frosty weather had given way to icy rain, which pricked her face like icicles. The flowerbed was now just a muddy hole in the ground. The Drake fairy was cracked in half and lying to one side, muddied and forlorn. Mrs Best sighed and went back inside. She was putting her coat away in the closet when she heard a sob. Tommy was buried at the back of the closet, standing flat against the wall and hidden by a great overcoat, tears running down his face. Mrs Best pulled him out and led him to the kitchen, where Mary fussed around making him tea while Mrs Best gave him her handkerchief.

"Now, now, Tommy. It must have been awful for you."

"It was, Mrs Best, it was. I got such a fright. And now, every time I close my eyes, I think I can see that body. It was awful." Tommy's voice broke down to a whisper, and he shook his head as if trying to shake free the memory. "The dogs were making such a mess. I chased them off. All I was thinking was Mrs Williams would be furious if she saw the state of the place. So, I went to the shed to fetch the shovel, but when I came back, they were there again, fighting over something, and I separated them, put the shovel between them. And… and… then I saw… saw the hand."

Mrs Best sat beside him, patting him on his shoulder, making soothing noises as Mary bustled around the kitchen. After several cups of hot sweet tea, Tommy started to feel better, and Mrs Best left him in Mary's care while she went to check on Mrs Williams. She was still grey and tearful, so Mrs

Best insisted she remain in her room and relax. The rest of the day was taken up by household chores, and before long, darkness had returned. Mrs Best brought Agnes a dinner tray and made her comfortable before returning to the dining room to facilitate the evening meal. The young women boarders were all aware Iris had been brought to the police station. They were also aware she was back in her own bed before they left for work that morning. As they filed into the dining room, there was no sign of Iris, and they all took note of the empty chair.

"Maybe she is embarrassed to face us."

"They must have had some reason to question her," one girl said.

"Well, they were wrong. Iris couldn't possibly have had anything to do with it."

"I heard when they told her his body had been found, she told them she was glad, that she hated him."

"That would explain why they arrested her."

Sarah spoke out. "You don't know the full story, and not one of you has any right to comment, not without the full facts."

"So, what are the full facts, Sarah? Since you seem to know so much, enlighten us."

Mrs Best clapped her hands once, stood and looked at each young woman.

"Ladies, Iris had nothing to do with her grandfather's death. She is, quite understandably, distraught, and I expect you all to treat her with compassion and respect."

Mrs Best left the room and returned ten minutes later with a red-eyed Iris behind her. She took her seat as Mrs Best called for service. Dinner was a muted affair, with each of the young women stealing furtive glances at Iris, who pushed her food around her plate but ate very little. After dinner, she excused herself and fled upstairs to her room. Sarah asked to be excused and followed her but not before throwing a look of pure daggers at the other lodgers.

That evening in their private parlour, Mrs Best recounted the whole conversation to Mrs Williams.

"My heart goes out to that poor girl." Agnes shook her head. "She must be going through her own kind of hell. We know what that vile man did to her. But he was the one who brought her up. And now he has met a violent end."

"It must be so confusing for her. I doubt she knows how to feel. But I have something more important to tell you. The police called this even…"

Jane was stopped by the clatter of Agnes's teaspoon hitting the floor. Agnes's hand was shaking so much Jane had to take the cup from her and place it on the table.

"It's okay, Agnes, honestly. Don't fret."

Jane took Agnes's shaking hand and stroked it gently.

"They came to let Iris know she is no longer a suspect. It transpires the police were aware of his illegal activities. They said he wasn't the pillar of the community he pretended to be. They also said he had been seen in the company of certain unsavoury characters, one of whom ended up in the river."

"What does that mean for us, Jane?"

"I'm not sure. But I know one thing: they are looking elsewhere, which can only be good for us."

Chapter 59

Agnes

Agnes tossed and turned in her bed. She had persuaded Jane to sleep in her own room, pleading a bad cold that she didn't want to pass on to her. It had taken some persuasion, but Jane had eventually agreed but not without tucking Agnes in with a hot toddy and a promise to check in on her first thing in the morning.

Agnes couldn't get the image of Drake Jones out of her head. Every time she closed her eyes, she could hear Iris telling them the things he had done to her. When Agnes managed to shut out that memory, Fred moved into her head and his horror at the thought of Drake Jones being his father. Agnes remembered the blackmail and the anguish Jane had suffered at the idea of her secret going public. She imagined poor fragile little Iris sitting in a police cell accused of killing her tormentor.

It was near dawn, but sleep continued to elude her. She could see no way out for them. If they were discovered, their motive would be revealed. Everything they had worked for in the last forty years would be destroyed, violated even. No one would understand that James was Jane. She had loved James, but she had loved his femininity. He had been born in the wrong body. He only became whole when he became Jane. Agnes had watched the transition, fascinated with Jane's sense of style, her self-worth. Jane Best was who she was born to be.

Agnes had been incredibly happy in Riverdale House. She had been extremely happy living in tandem with Jane Best, her friend and confidante. When the doctor gave Agnes his diagnosis, she agonised over telling Jane. At the time the doctor had told her she had a few months, so she had plenty of time and anyway, this business with Drake Jones was enough for Jane to worry about. Jane had always been a worrier, Agnes thought. But now time was running out. She knew it, could feel her body gradually giving up on her.

And then it struck her. The idea slowly started taking form in her brain. She got out of bed and started pacing up and down the floor. As she paced, her mind jumped from one scenario to another. Agnes knew what she had to do, and for the first time since she had received her diagnosis, she felt a sense of purpose. Pulling on her dressing gown, she tiptoed silently to the parlour and sat at her writing desk. Agnes took out the scented writing paper she favoured and started to write. It took some time to complete both letters, to put into words the message she wanted to convey. There could be no mistakes, no chance of misinterpretation. Her letter had to be crystal clear. Agnes crumpled up several attempts and threw them into the fire. Eventually, she sat back and reread her final letter, happy now with every sentence. Agnes sighed as she folded the letters and propped them up against the back of the desk. She suddenly felt exhausted, like a wave of inertia had entered her head and was making its way slowly down her body, washing over her organs and shutting them down one by one. Only her heart continued to beat. It's thump in her chest and throat, threatening to overcome her completely. Agnes slipped off the chair and, using the wall for support, made her way back to her room and into her bed. She sank underneath the blankets and gave a sigh of relief.

Chapter 60

Jane

The following morning Jane knocked on Agnes's bedroom door. There was no sound from inside, and Jane tapped sharply again, two raps with her knuckles, and called out Agnes's name. Puzzled by the lack of response, she rapped again before slowly turning the door handle. The room was in darkness, and there was a rasping sound from the mound of bedclothes. Jane held up her lamp and hurried to the bed. Agnes was struggling for breath. Her cheeks were ruddy and wet with sweat, and her hands clutched her breast.

"Agnes, what is it?" Fear gripped Jane's heart as she took Agnes's hands in hers. She bent over to hear the words Agnes was trying to form.

"Let me go, Jane. I can't live with…"

Jane tried to shush her.

"Look at me. We can do this. Do you hear me?"

Agnes sat up abruptly, then appeared to collapse into herself. Her eyes were open and staring, but her body became totally limp, like a discarded rag doll. Jane heard a voice screaming and calling Agnes's name without realising the voice was her own. She felt Mary take her by the shoulders and lead her away. She couldn't form a coherent thought. Mary led her to the parlour and poured her a brandy. Jane sat still, trying to make sense of what had happened. Agnes was dead. She had felt the life leave her body, the light dim in her eyes like the last flicker of a spent candle.

The household appeared to be in chaos. The doctor had been called. He examined Agnes superficially, felt for her pulse and pronounced her dead. Jane sat still, one hand to her mouth, the other to her throat, fiddling with the lace on her collar. The doctor prescribed a sedative for Jane, but she refused it.

"Mrs Williams suffered a massive heart attack. There is nothing you could have done for her, nothing any of us could have done. If anything, it was a blessing for her."

"Whatever do you mean?" Jane said.

"I'm assuming Mrs Williams told you she had cancer. She was dying."

Jane stared at the doctor, trying to assimilate what he was telling her. She kept staring at him, but his words barely penetrated the wall of grief surrounding her. Jane felt herself falling, flailing through black space, hands over feet, spiralling out of control until the blackness overtook her. The smelling salts under her nose brought her around, and she struggled to sit upright. Mary was starting to unbutton the neck of her dress. Jane slapped away her hand, then gasped as she took in Agnes's body in front of her and the realisation that Agnes had died hit her again like a knife through her heart. Jane lifted Agnes's hand from the bedspread and felt its coldness. Mary took her gently by the arm and led her away.

"Come, Mrs Best. Let me look after Mrs Williams."

Mrs Best locked herself in her room and got into bed. She couldn't raise the energy to get undressed, so she lay fully clothed under the bedspread and cried. How long she stayed there, she had no idea. All Jane could think about was Agnes.

What would she do without her? How could she continue without her? Agnes had been by her side for over forty years. She didn't know how to live without her, her best friend, the love of her life.

The next few days passed in a blur. Jane let Mary look after the running of the house while she organised the funeral. She wrote to Agnes's nephew in London informing him of her sudden death. Jane shivered as she sealed the envelope that would wind its way across the same body of water they had only crossed two days previously. How suddenly life can change beyond recognition, she thought, as she caught sight of herself in the hall mirror. Jane drew closer and stared at James's eyes, staring into her soul. There was one undeniable fact running around her head. Agnes loved her, the keeper of her secrets, her protector. How could she continue without her? Jane moved closer to the mirror and looked into the depths of James's eyes. A sliver of sunlight bounced off the skylights over the door and highlighted her face. She needed to be more careful. Her chin showed tiny hairs peeping through the skin, and she gasped. Then again, she thought, old women get hairs on their chin. Who would guess her true identity at this stage? Drake Jones is dead. Agnes is dead. Her beloved Charles died long ago. Was there any point in going on?

Chapter 61

Jane

THE FUNERAL WENT SMOOTHLY. JANE WASN'T SURPRISED BY THE volume of people who came to pay their respects to her dearest friend. There were past boarders and their families mixed in with current boarders and their families. Tradespeople mingled with the landed gentry, and ex-soldiers wore examples of Agnes's handiwork with pride and respect. Jane felt joy in Agnes's achievements, and intense gratitude that she had known and loved this woman for so many years.

That evening Jane retired to her private parlour. She hadn't entered it since the night before Agnes had died. She had no reason to. This was the room they sat in every night to unwind after a busy day. It was the room they shared their hopes and dreams in, the place they made their plans for the future, discussed their boarders, sorted out the problems of the day and rejoiced in their small triumphs. Jane had been unable to open the door without Agnes, but tonight she felt Agnes's presence in spirit and turned the handle. Jane smiled as she noticed the small fire, obviously lit earlier by Tommy. He was heartbroken like herself but going through the motions.

Jane stood in the middle of the room and looked around

her. Agnes's armchair was in its usual position, her knitting basket to one side and her writing desk behind it. Two framed photographs were on the wall behind the desk. Jane moved closer to examine them. In her nurse's uniform, a young Agnes with her colleagues and her heroine Florence Nightingale. That photograph was one of Agnes's most treasured belongings. Beside it was a photograph of Agnes and Matthew on their wedding day. They had made a handsome couple. Matthew was in dress uniform, staring straight into the camera with Agnes standing beside him in her gown with her lace veil covering her rich dark hair.

Jane remembered their conversation one evening shortly after they moved into Riverdale House. They were discussing their paths in life, and Jane had commented that if Matthew had lived, Agnes would never have gone to South Africa, and they would never have met. Jane told Agnes if they hadn't met when they did, she would never have had the courage to start her new life. Jane smiled as she remembered how annoyed Agnes became with her.

"You were always Jane. You couldn't be anyone else. If Matthew had lived, we still would have found one another, for you and I are soulmates, more than any man and wife could be, more than any friends can be."

Those words were seared into Jane's mind ever since, and the memory was oddly comforting to her now. She sighed and tentatively sat in Agnes's seat. It rocked gently, and she found herself dozing off, exhausted by the trauma of the past few days. She woke sometime later with the fire starting to die down, lending a gentle glow to the room. It registered with her that Agnes's writing desk was open. She usually kept it closed and only opened it for correspondence or work on the household accounts. Jane noticed the two envelopes propped up on the green inlay. It was Agnes's handwriting that grabbed her attention. She lifted them, wondering when Agnes had left them there. She moved as if in a trance, turning them over in her hands. One was addressed to her. She opened it tentatively.

Dear Jane,

You have been my best friend in this world, and I love you dearly. You know at this stage that I have been ill. I wish things were different, but such is life! If you are reading this, it means the police have not yet caught up with us. I know I should feel remorse for taking the life of another human being, and to some extent, I do. But! And here it is. Drake Jones was an evil man who made the life of his daughter a living hell, destroyed his only granddaughter (or daughter) and has left a terrible legacy. He destroyed the lives of countless others and would have gone on to do more harm if we hadn't stopped him. I have no regrets. I had fears but no regrets. I know scripture teaches us 'Thou shall not kill', but we both know that in war, killing is justified. In this case, the killing was justified. We did not kill a human being; we eliminated an evil monster.

So, I have written a confession. It is worded as a confession to you. Please read it then give it to the police. When that is done, you can move on with your life. I implore you to put all thoughts of Drake Jones behind you. It gives me comfort and joy to know that you will continue in Riverdale House. It is such a wonderful place, full of happy memories of so many young women. Women we helped shape and nurture.

Please think kindly of me when you think of me in the future. I am now and always have been your loyal friend.

Yours faithfully

Agnes

Grief overcame Jane once more. She read both letters over and over again. She felt tears choke her, and then anger bubble up, threatening to unhinge her. As had always been the case, Agnes took charge of the situation and faced the danger they were in, giving no thought to herself. Jane felt bereft, as if her left arm was missing. She asked herself, how could she go on without Agnes by her side? What was the point? Their entire lives were intertwined and had been for forty years. How could she function alone?

Jane read over the confession again. Agnes had thought of everything. But Jane reasoned that just because she had written it down didn't mean she should use it. She didn't want anyone to think badly of Agnes. Jane remembered all those people who had attended the funeral, those who had sent cards and letters. How could she change their opinion of Agnes? Jane put the letter back on the writing desk and closed the lid. She wouldn't use it. She couldn't.

Jane tossed and turned that night. When sleep came, it was filled with visions of Agnes smiling at her, scolding her, telling her to do the right thing. Jane woke the next morning feeling disturbed and out of sorts. She struggled through breakfast and noted the sideways glances of the boarders at her pale cheeks and sunken eyes. Jane made her way to the front parlour and stared at each of the Best family portraits. Staring at Lady Best's regal smile, she remembered the innate goodness that permeated her life. Lady Best had a sense of fairness that she instilled in her son, her beloved Charles. Jane drifted into the hall and stood in front of his portrait. He looked resplendent in his red dress jacket, his sword by his side.

The portrait captured the sparkle in those sapphire eyes she had loved. She thought Charles would have made beautiful children, just not with her. She granted herself the luxury of allowing her mind to wander, to think about what would have happened if he had lived. He would have married Amanda for sure. Blond-haired and blue-eyed children would have roamed the Glassdrumman Estate and undoubtedly led to grandchildren at this stage. The house would be full of life and laughter, and the annual cricket match and fête would attract people from far and near to be part of this wonderful family. But the family name had died with Charles, in that field hospital, under an African sky. The loss of his future made her weep.

She turned away from Charles and stared into the mirror.

If Charles had lived, Jane would not. James would exist as Charles's friend and Amanda's confidant. And then it struck her, what of Agnes? Would they have even met? She would have lost out on all those years of close and true friendship, a friendship not even her beloved Charles could match. For Charles was just that, a memory. Agnes had been an integral part of her life, her constant companion. They had been a team, an unbeatable team but no more. Jane sank to her knees, grief clutching her heart and overwhelming her.

Tears poured down her cheeks, hitting the parquet flooring in great plops. Sobs ripped from her throat, and she covered her face with her hands and wept. She wasn't sure how long she remained there, prostrate in front of the mirror. She only knew that as her tears subsided, she felt a calmness surround her. The sounds of the household chores going on around her upstairs and in the dining room trickled into her consciousness. Jane suddenly felt self-conscious, stupid even. What would the girls think if they could see her prostrate on the floor like a destitute woman with no breeding? Agnes would have been horrified. She scolded herself as she pulled herself upright and looked into the mirror again. Taking out her handkerchief, she dabbed her eyes and blew her nose. Jane made her way to her bedroom and made a cold compress for her eyes. An hour later, she emerged ready to retake charge of the household, determined to make Agnes proud of her.

Chapter 62

Jane

A RAP ON THE FRONT DOOR ECHOED ACROSS THE HALL AND made her start. She pinched her cheeks and smoothed down her skirt, and with a last affectionate nod to Charles's portrait, she turned to answer the door. Detective O'Neill stood there in front of her. Detective Smith was at the bottom step.

Detective O'Neill removed his hat and bowed his head.

"Mrs Best, may I offer my condolences?"

"Thank you, Detective. You know the way, gentlemen." She waved her hand in the general direction of the parlour. She walked across the room to the fireplace and stood facing them, ramrod straight with the letter in her hands. Mrs Best cleared her throat then hesitated. Now that the police had arrived, she was suddenly nervous, but she knew what she had to do.

"Detective, I found this letter in Mrs Williams..." She cleared her throat. "It was in her papers, and I believe you need to read it... it is... it is relevant to your investigation."

"Is there some reason you think so, Mrs Best?"

Detective O'Neill looked curious as he took the letter from her hand and turned it over as if somehow its contents would shout out to him. He scanned the first two paragraphs, stopped, looked at Mrs Best, and blew out a short breath. He lowered himself heavily onto the couch and continued to read.

Dear Jane,

You have been my best friend in this world, and I love you dearly. You know at this stage that I have been ill. I wish things were different, but such is life! If you are reading this letter, I have passed, but I cannot rest in peace until I finally confess my sins. I have tried to tell you what I have done, but I couldn't face you. I couldn't face you thinking less of me knowing what I have done.

I killed Drake Jones. I am so deeply sorry. If I could change the sequence of that day, I would, but I cannot. I have had to live with my guilt and remorse, but I cannot go to my grave with this secret hanging over me.

In my defence, Drake Jones was an evil man. You remember the day he called to Riverdale House intending to force his granddaughter to return with him, and she refused, and we asked him to leave? I recognised him that day as the same Private Jones who served with the Connaught Rangers in British Natal. I was a nurse then, working in Ladysmith Hospital. I know I have mentioned my time in British Natal to you before, but I never mentioned that hateful man. That was forty years ago, and even then, he was mean and spiteful and known to be cruel. I have told you about my husband Matthew and how he died in British Natal, killed by the Zulus in a terrible battle that made all the papers back in England. It was a terrible defeat for the British army. When Private Jones found out that Matthew had been my husband, he took immense pleasure in telling me in graphic detail how Matthew had died and how his body had been desecrated by the Zulus. I complained to his commanding officer, but he dismissed me; told me that if I couldn't handle the detail of the war, then I shouldn't be in a war zone. The other patients weren't so dismissive, and they told him off. But that is just a testament to the meanness of his character. It was much worse than that. I caught him stealing and reported him. He stole from some extremely ill patients, young soldiers injured in battle, some of whom would never make it home. I saw him remove a wedding ring from a dying man and put it in his pocket. When I confronted him, he denied it, but when his bags were searched by his commanding officer, they found various rings and pocketbooks and other valuables. He blamed me. He said I had planted them and was trying to get revenge for him talking about Matthew. It was a terrible time for me.

After he left our house that day, I made enquiries about him. Some said he was a charitable man who looked after the destitute women of the city, giving them food and shelter. I called to the house and spoke to the women there. It is not a charitable foundation and never has been. It is a bordello, filled with women who are destitute, yes, but without hope, for Drake Jones keeps them prisoner. He may feed them and provide clean lodgings, but he also beats them and forces them to have intimate relations with strangers for money. Money he pockets for his own use.

There is one woman there who is willing to talk to the police. Her name is Patricia, that's if she is still alive. She was a friend of his wife. She said that they married before he went to British Natal, that he went away with nothing and came back with the deeds to the property, saying he won them in a poker game. She said they had a daughter, and after she was born, he lost interest in his wife and sold her out to strangers for money. She said that when his daughter came of age, he bedded her and gave her two children. When his daughter died in childbirth, he moved the children out and bought a home for them. He feigned respectability and pretended to be a loving grandfather looking after his orphaned grandchildren.

He arranged abortions for the women in his bordello. They had no choice in the matter. Some escaped, more didn't, and up until the day he died, they were still there, trapped. I hope his death has given them release. I pray it has, for that is the only small modicum of hope I cling to.

I never told you he tried to blackmail me. He waylaid me and demanded money. He said he would tell you and everyone I knew that I was a thief. I ignored him, but he arrived at the house some weeks later. He stood in my kitchen and demanded money. He put his hand on me and threatened me that he would have my money, or he would have me. He pushed me back against the range, and the flat iron was there, heating up, ready to iron the sheets. His face was sneering into mine, and his hands touched me, and I grabbed the iron and hit him with it. He fell to the ground, and I dropped the iron and prayed. But then he started moaning. I feared for my life. There was no one else home. The girls were gone to the shops and Tommy to collect stone, so I knew I was alone. He started to stand up, and I backed away. The rolling pin was sitting on the table, and I lifted it to protect myself. When he came at me again, I hit him again and again. I blacked out, and when I came to, he was dead, on the floor. I am sorry for what I did next, but it was as if I could not help myself, as if some other person had inhabited my body. I put him in the wheelbarrow, and I brought him over to the hole dug out at the side of the house. I tipped his body into it, covered it with jute bags, and used the soil dug out to partially cover them. When Tommy got back with the stone, I got him to fill in the hole with the rest of the soil.

I stood over him and watched, and I got him to help me install the fountain. May God forgive me, but I made Tommy help me hide my crime without telling him what he was doing. Maybe it is poetic justice that it was Tommy who made the discovery that led to that body resurfacing. It was meant to be for no one should get away with the murder of another human being. I can no longer bear to have it on my conscience. I am so sorry, Jane. I wish I had done things differently that day. But that is what happened, and I cannot change it now. I only wish I could.

Please think kindly of me when you think of me in the future. I am now and always have been your loyal friend.

Yours faithfully

Agnes

Detective O'Neill gave a huge sigh and handed the letter to Detective Smith.

"Do you believe this to be a true account of what happened that day?"

"I have no reason not to, Detective. Why else… why else would Agnes have written such… things?" She gave up on any attempt to disguise the tears that flowed freely as her words petered into sobs.

Mrs Best hung her head as the tears flowed silently. She

wiped them away with her handkerchief and slowly sank onto the chair at the opposite side of the room.

"Thank you, Mrs Best. We will need to keep this letter. We will be in touch if we need anything else, but that pretty much sums up what happened."

Mrs Best nodded. She couldn't bring herself to speak, afraid her words would choke her on their way out through the beat of her heart in her throat. Her hand found its way to the frill at her neck. An image of Agnes rolling pastry at the kitchen table danced with the image of Agnes beating Drake Jones to death with the rolling pin in the back hall.

"Everything she has said in this letter confirms information we already have. We have spoken to this Patricia; we were aware of Mr Jones's part in running that house, and there are questions about the death of his wife, amongst others."

Detective O'Neill shook his head as he folded the letter inside his notebook. The detectives took their leave unescorted. Mrs Best sat still, unable to move, unable to get the images out of her head.

Evening fell, and when Mary went into the parlour to close the drapes, she found her, still sitting there, as if in shock. In halting tones, Mrs Best told Mary about the note left by Mrs Williams. She watched Mary's facial expressions change from concern to shock, then horror.

"We cannot allow what happened to change how we felt about Mrs Williams. She was a wonderful woman. A horrible thing happened to her, and she dealt with it. That doesn't change who she was."

"Oh, Mrs Best. I could not think badly of Mrs Williams. She was like a mother to me. If she had to defend herself against that man, then so be it." Mary wiped her eyes. "Now if you will excuse me, I will tell the other staff before they hear it elsewhere. Rest assured, everyone that knew Mrs Williams will understand."

Mrs Best nodded. Mary was right. She walked out to the hall and checked her appearance in the hall mirror. Her reflection cheered her. She looked well for a woman in her sixties. Mrs Best pinched her cheeks to add some colour and stared into James's grey eyes. She fixed the lace ruffle at her neck and smoothed down her skirts. Then, head held high, she swept into the dining room where her young women boarders were assembled for their evening meal. Mrs Best presided over the table, ready to do honour to the memory of her dearest friend and lover, Agnes Williams.

THE END

Author's Notes

It is impossible to tell a story, even a fictional one, without mentioning the world that influences the characters. This book is a work of historical fiction, but I have tried to keep the underlying facts supporting the characters as accurate as possible.

The events of one hundred years continue to influence our lives to this day, not just in Ireland but worldwide. In Ireland we decided to commemorate those pivotal moments in our history over the last decade, hence www.decadeofcentenaries.com. It was a challenging task which proved controversial at times but opened up a conversation about our past which hopefully will have a beneficial effect on our future.

I hope this brief explanation of people and places that are mentioned in *Tangled Webs* will be of benefit to readers.

Michael Collins: 1890–1922

Born in Cork in 1890, Irish freedom fighter and politician, Michael Collins, was a leading figure in the early 20th century

Irish struggle for independence against. He served as Director of Intelligence during the War of Independence and led the negotiations with Britain which culminated in Anglo Irish Treaty signed on 6th December 1921. Michael Collins became Chairman of the Provisional Government of the Irish Free State and Commander in Chief of the National Army, during a bloody civil war. He was killed in an ambush by anti-Treaty forces in his native Cork in August 1922 and is buried in Glasnevin Cemetery, Dublin.

The Dundalk Educational Institute: 1739 to present day

Now known as Dundalk Grammar School, it is a fee-paying school under Protestant management. The school buildings are held in trust by the Incorporated Society for Promoting Protestant Schools in Ireland, while the day-to-day running of the school is directed by a locally based Board of Governors advised by the Board of Management. From 1739 to 1835 it was a Charter School until it was reorganised by Rev. Elias Thackeray, as the Dundalk Educational Institution. It was in abeyance during World War I and in 1921 revived by a local committee and reconstituted as Dundalk Grammar School.

Florence Nightingale: 1820–1910

Known as 'The Lady with the Lamp' Florence Nightingale was a British nurse, social reformer, statistician and the founder of modern nursing. She came to prominence in the Crimean War where she revolutionised the management of infectious diseases and sanitation. She established St. Thomas' Hospital in London and the Nightingale School of Nursing in 1860.

Home Rule: 1874–1918

In 1870 Isaac Butt, a Protestant Lawyer, called for an Irish parliament, sitting in Dublin to govern the affairs of the island of Ireland. In 1873 the Home Rule League replaced the association under Charles Stewart Parnell. From the beginning the concept of Home Rule proved controversial. The first Home Rule bill was defeated at the House of Lords in 1885, the second Home Rule Bill in 1893 was again defeated. The introduction in 1912 of a third Home Rule bill led to militant opposition. Edward Carson, a Dublin Protestant barrister, fiercely opposed it. The Ulster Volunteer Force was set up and there were fears of civil war. The third Home Rule bill became law in September 1914, but its enactment was postponed due to the outbreak of World War I. As many as 200,000 Irish men went to fight with the British believing that their participation would lead to Home Rule for Ireland. However, on their return, the Easter Rising and changing attitudes of the Irish people led to the outbreak of the War of Independence in 1919. The Government of Ireland Act 1920 introduced partition of the island, leaving the northern part of Ireland under British rule and the other twenty-six counties became a democratic republic.

Anglo-Zulu War: 1879

Natal was a British colony in south-eastern Africa and is now the KwaZulu-Natal province of South Africa. In 1879 the British under Sir Bartle Frere invaded neighbouring Zululand. On 22nd January 1879 the Zulus defeated the British forces in the Battle of Isandlwana which claimed the lives of approx. 1,300 British soldiers. Later that evening a force of 3,000 Zulus attacked a British mission station six miles away at Rorke's Drift. It was defended by 150 men and was immortalised in the film *Zulu Dawn*.

SS *Princess Alice* in the River Thames

The SS *Princess Alice* was a passenger paddle steamer owned by the London Steamboat Co which carried passengers between Swan Pier, near London Bridge downstream to Sheerness in Kent. On 3rd September 1878 *Princess Alice* was returning to London when it collided with the collier SS *Bywell Castle*, at an area in the Thames where 75 million gallons of London's raw sewage had just been released. The ship broke in three places and sank quickly. Between 600 and 700 passengers died, some drowned, others died from ingesting the polluted waters.

As a direct result of the tragedy, the release and treatment of sewerage was moved from the Thames to the sea.

Acknowledgements

Writing is a solitary occupation, but I have been fortunate to have the help and support of so many people. The first readers of my work are the members of Ink Tank Creative Writing Group. I owe them a debt of gratitude for reading, critiquing and for their unwavering support.

Of course, it's not possible to be a writer without first and foremost, being a reader. Our little book club encourages us all to read books from different genres than we normally would. Our opinions are normally split. It's a valuable education and reminds me that some people will love my writing, and some won't. Thank you, ladies, for your unanimous approval of my books.

While I appreciate the benefits of instant research capabilities on the internet, nowhere beats your local library. There is a wealth of information waiting inside those doors and friendly informative staff eager to help. A special word of thanks to my local library in Newbridge, Co Kildare.

To my publishers, Bloodhound Books, thank you for having faith in me. I enjoyed writing *Tangled Webs* but loved the process of bringing it to publication. I love the cover they designed for *Tangled Webs* and everything the Bloodhound team have done to bring my book to this stage. To my editor, Shirley Khan, thank you so much for your attention to detail and your insight.

A special word of thanks to my family. My brothers and sisters have always been supportive while keeping my feet firmly on the ground. My adult children are a constant reminder that I am mother and grandmother first and foremost. Thank you, Kevin, Paul, Eilis and Gearoid for your support every day. The last word of thanks goes to my biggest cheerleader, my husband Gerry. Thank you for everything you do.

Also by Maria McDonald

The Devil's Own

A note from the publisher

Thank you for reading this book. If you enjoyed it please do consider leaving a review on Amazon to help others find it too.

We hate typos. All of our books have been rigorously edited and proofread, but sometimes mistakes do slip through. If you have spotted a typo, please do let us know and we can get it amended within hours.

info@bloodhoundbooks.com

Printed in Great Britain
by Amazon

28685682R00182